The Girl in the Mustard Coat
Names, characters, places and inc
of the author's imagination and are
resemblance to actual persons, livi ⌣ ⸻ ⸺⸺⸺, ⸺ıocales
is entirely coincidental.

For Ange. With eternal love and gratitude…

The Girl in the Mustard Coat
By Emily Rose Chriscoli

"The floor seemed wonderfully solid. It was comforting to know I had fallen and could fall no further." – Sylvia Plath

Prologue
2005

It would be easy, comforting even, to say that 31st October 2005 felt like an odd day from the moment I woke up. It would certainly have made sense to feel this way, but it didn't. The day started out like any other day, but the sequence of events had been etched into my brain ever since.

Despite my three alarms going off, Mum ended up banging on my bedroom door with a frying pan. Annoying as it was to be woken up this way, it was also a great motivation to get up as it was clear that Mum was making a cooked breakfast. Normally, we only ever had cooked breakfasts on a Sunday but as my brother was taking part in a home exchange programme with a child from Germany, Mum was trying her best to create the image of a perfect British family. Never mind the fact that we lived in a small semi-detached house in a not so nice area with peeling wallpaper and well-worn carpets. And never mind the fact that Dad was spending longer and longer in the garage and came home reeking of beer every night that this kid was staying with us. No. It was important to Mum that eleven year old Mathias had a good, albeit false, impression of our family life.

31st October 2005 was Mathias' final day staying with our family and after breakfast, Mum was taking him and Daniel to the airport. Mum was already stressing about how late it would make her for work. Not that it really mattered. Most people's mums didn't work, but she worked on the tills in our local Sainsbury's. It was hardly the job of the millennium but she acted like it was, ironing her work t-shirt and fleece religiously every night, and talking about how she hadn't sat down all day.

I headed to the bathroom, which was predictably occupied by another inhabitant of our cramped house. As was daily practice, I began whinging about the need for a second bathroom. Brushing past me to head downstairs, my father sighed and started spouting the usual spiel about money not growing on trees. I noticed he'd missed a button on his shirt, which led to a gaping hole over his hairy protruding belly button. Smirking, I decided not to tell him and instead, banged on the bathroom door again, hopping about from foot to foot as I tried not to wet myself.

"Finally," I sighed, as my sister emerged from the

bathroom, a trail of steam following her. "You were taking a shower?"

"Yes," she said, nonchalantly, as she went straight into her bedroom without taking so much as a glance at me.

"You had a bath last night!" I exclaimed to no avail, as I slammed the bathroom door shut and was immediately engulfed in the steam.

I did all the usual stuff that a girl needs to do in the initial bathroom visit of the day, including standing in front of the slightly cracked mirror and wondering with mild curiosity what my sister had written in the steam. Was it KB? Racking my brains trying to think of Beth's classmates, I couldn't for the life of me think of a boy with the initials KB, but I was convinced it was about a boy. Beth was thirteen, and when I was thirteen, boys were a pivotal part of my universe.

Grinning, I wiped it off to get a closer look at my pock marked face. Despite forking out my measly earnings from my weekly newspaper round on face wash and allegedly miracle concealer, I still looked like I was recovering from a bad bout of chicken pox. As I was running late, I didn't have the time needed to dedicate the concentration required to covering my spots, so I lashed on a bit of foundation and hoped for the best. It wasn't as if I was even really bothered. Most girls wore makeup to school in an effort to bag a good looking boyfriend. While he may not have been Brad Pitt, my boyfriend Oliver was still alright looking. In fact, Rachel Bailey had put him as her number four in her list of top ten most kissable boys at St Alban's.

Mum had left a plate of toast, eggs, bacon and mushrooms in the microwave for me. All our food was left in hard to reach places, to keep out of Dumbledore, our greedy and considerably overweight Labrador's, way. He was lying down in front of the microwave, staring into the abyss. Grimacing at the soggy mushrooms, I swore under my breath. Almost sixteen years of living in the same house as me and my mother still couldn't remember that I hated mushrooms. I wolfed down the rest of my food, swigged a glass of fresh orange juice and grabbed my bag.

"Are you ready?" I shouted up to Beth, who still hadn't materialised downstairs.

Without answering, she stumbled down the stairs, buckling under the weight of three bags. It was a Tuesday, which meant that Beth had both PE and cooking.

"What are you making today?" I asked her as we both zipped up our coats, stroked the dog goodbye and walked out of the house.

"Bread and butter pudding."

I snorted. "Vile," was my input.

The bus was late, as usual, and predictably full to the brim of hormone pumped teenagers, all discussing last night's episode of Coronation Street. I took a seat next to Mandeep Singh, who was ignoring the prattle around her whilst she listened to her mp3 player. A glance across told me she was listening to a band I'd never heard of. My sister sloped past me and sat with two of her usual mates, all sporting identical French plaits.

The day was nothing out of the ordinary, with the exception that it was Halloween. School had made somewhat of an effort by decorating the noticeboards with cut out pictures of pumpkins and broomsticks to advertise the school Halloween party later that afternoon. No one I knew was going. School parties were always a bit crap, only ever made more exciting with a secret swig from an illicit bottle of vodka poorly disguised as mineral water.

I got home just before four o'clock, ravenous as usual, and made myself two crumpets with lashings of butter and a frothy coffee. I couldn't help but think how grown up I was and my mind instantly raced to the future, when I'd graduated from university and was living with Oliver, making crumpets everyday for our breakfast with a diamond the size of Calcutta hanging off my finger.

By four thirty, I realised all my coursework had been finished and I was enjoying having the house to myself. Mum and Dad weren't home from work, my brother was out trick or treating with one of the kids from his school and Mum was picking him up on her way home, and my sister had gone to the Halloween party.

After watching the soaps, I treated myself to a bath, making sure to use plenty of Mum's fancy bubble baths and creams while she wasn't in to shout at me. Every now and then I could hear the doorbell ringing and little knocks at the door. I ignored them. It was only trick or treaters and we didn't have anything in to give them after Dad had eaten his way through the

Sainsbury's own sweets Mum had brought home two days earlier.

Hearing the front door slam, I realised I was no longer home alone and reluctantly pulled the plug and ended my soapy relaxation. I towel dried my body and scooped a smaller towel around my sopping wet hair before padding across to my room. It was quiet downstairs, so I shouted "hello?" but didn't hear a response. I pulled on my old comfy Eeyore pyjamas and was blow drying my hair when I realised my bedroom door was wide open and Mum was saying something inaudible to me.

"What did you say?" I asked, whilst turning the hairdryer off.

"What time does this party finish?" she sighed.

"What party?"

"The Halloween party up at the school."

"Oh, I don't know. Sorry," I added, before turning back to my mirror and continuing to blast my hair dry.

It was about an hour later that Mum started to panic. Sick of her shouting things up to me from the foot of the stairs, I gave in and went into the living room where she was stood, pacing, holding the landline phone in her hand.

"It's almost nine o'clock," she said, not really to anyone in particular.

"So?"

"So, your sister hasn't come home yet," she snapped.

"Have you rang Grace's house?"

"Yes. Grace got home an hour and a half ago. She said your sister wasn't at this flipping party. She came home to get something," she murmured, running her hands through her hair. For the first time in my life, I remembered thinking that Mum looked old.

"She might be hanging out with that new girl. I can't remember her name," I admitted.

"Which new girl?"

"I've just said. I don't know her name. Or she might be sneaking off with a boy," I said, remembering the initials drawn in the mirror earlier that day.

"What? Which boy? Who?" Mum frowned.

I repeated what I'd seen on the bathroom mirror and Mum immediately dismissed it with a snort.

"I think I ought to ring the police," she said, biting her lip.

"I'm starting to worry."

"If you think it will help."

"I don't want to cause a fuss," she went on, not really speaking to me. "I might wait to see what your father thinks. Be a good girl, Sophie, and run down to the Walton Arms to fetch your father, will you?"

"It's pouring down!"

"Put your coat on."

It wasn't a request. Reluctantly, and rolling my eyes so far back I thought they would get whip lash, I put my coat on with the hood firmly tucked around my freshly washed hair. The Walton Arms was less than a five minute walk from our house, so I decided to run it. By the time I got there, I was sweaty, out of breath and my boobs were hurting as I wasn't wearing a bra. So much for them resembling fried eggs like I'd always thought.

There were just a few people in the pub, dotted around different tables. My dad wasn't one of them. I asked at the bar and gave a brief description of him but the barman didn't recognise him. Strange, I thought, considering he's in here practically every night.

I ran back to the house, slightly slower than my previous journey, and before I turned the corner to our street, I could hear sirens. Within seconds, I could see blue lights flashing on John McCabe's Land Rover across the road. My heart sank. Had something happened to Dad? As is common in these types of situations, my fifteen year old brain jumped to the very worst scenario possible, as I pictured my dad being hit in his clapped out banger whilst on his way to the Walton Arms. He was dead. I could feel it in my waters.

I made my way into the house where I found Mum sat on the sofa, a kind faced policewoman to the left of her, holding Mum's hand in hers. Out of nowhere, I burst into tears. Not the cool, subtle tears you see of sultry women in films, where a little tell-tale sign of mascara smudges ever so slightly under their eyes. No. I was weeping. Crying noisily with my mouth wide open and snot threatening to bubble out of my nose.

"Have a seat, love," a policeman I hadn't even noticed said to me, and he chivvied me into the nearest armchair. "WPC Walsh, would you mind making a pot of tea for these two?"

"We don't have a teapot," Mum said, her eyes unblinking.

"Just two cups of tea will be fine," the policeman said, glancing at Mum as if he thought perhaps she needed something stronger.

The female police officer nodded and left the room. No one said anything and we could hear the unmistakable sound of china cups bashing together. We only ever used the posh cups when Nan came to stay, but no one had the heart to tell her.

"How did it happen?" I said, bravely ignoring the lump in my throat.

My question was met with confused looks. The policeman got his notepad out and perched on the arm of the sofa.

"Do you know something, Miss Maguire?" he asked me.

"No. Something's happened to my dad. Hasn't it?"

"I – I don't know," he frowned, clearly confused. "I'm here to get as much information as possible about your sister's disappearance."

It was as if someone had shifted the world from underneath me. That was the first time anyone had ever said those words to me, but it certainly wasn't the last. I almost laughed from hysteria. I felt embarrassed that people were taking it seriously. Beth hadn't *disappeared.* She was late home from school, most likely playing tonsil tennis with the mysterious KB. She was going to be in serious trouble when she eventually showed her face, her tail between her legs. But I was mortified at having the police sitting there in our living room. Chloe Portellini lived in the next street. What would she tell people? It looked as though Mum was being arrested. And where was Dad? The whole dramatic episode was excruciatingly embarrassing.

We sat in the same positions for hours until we all began to feel a bit stiff. By midnight, I was starting to panic that I would oversleep for school and I mumbled my excuses and bade everyone goodnight. I walked past Daniel's bedroom and saw him sat at the foot of the door, clearly listening to the conversations downstairs. Wordlessly, I shrugged at him. I didn't have a clue what was going on. In unison, we both rolled our eyes. Typical Beth. Always the dramatic one.

Before I got into bed, I stuck my phone on charge and as it connected, the screen lit up. Three unread text messages. Two from Gemma and one from Lauren. Both of them had somehow gotten wind of the fact that the police had been stationed at my house and both demanded an explanation. Cringing, I sent the same text message to both of them:

My mum rang the police because Beth didn't come home from school. I think she's got a secret boyfriend and is probably at his house now. Will fill you both in tomorrow. Night x

Lying down in my room which was highlighted in a dewy blue glow from the police cars outside, I smirked to myself as I pictured how much trouble Beth was going to be in the following day.

Two days later, my sister's body was found, raped and strangled, and half buried in a nearby woods.

Chapter One

"Are you finished with the newspaper, love?"

Glancing up, I saw an old woman in a baggy nightdress smiling at me from her bed. She was hooked up to a machine very similar to my mother's. Silently, I passed the newspaper across to her and was met with a beaming toothy smile.

"Oh, you are a good girl."

Was I? I thought, as I popped another painkiller into my mouth to nurse the almighty hangover brewing behind my tired eyelids. The pill clung to my throat, forcing me to cough and spray my own arm in saliva.

"You're not eating enough veg," my mother sniffed, one eye open and squinting at me.

"Says the one who eats via a tube," I retorted and I took a much needed mouthful of coffee. It tasted like piss – not that I'd ever tried drinking my own piss, or anyone else's for that matter. But it was caffeine and I needed it.

"Heavy night, was it?"

I shrugged. "Not particularly."

"A bit of broccoli never went amiss in my day," the old lady from the bed opposite called out. "You look anaemic to me."

I certainly wasn't anaemic. I needed a decent meal with no alcohol and a good night's sleep.

"How are you feeling?" I asked Mum.

"Oh, don't you start."

"What?"

"All the namby pamby wishy washy nonsense about how I'm feeling. I feel like shit. There. Are you happy now?" she sighed.

"Ecstatic."

Mum laughed and immediately winced as the drip in her hand pulled.

"I can't wait to get out of here. I never thought I'd see the day where I have to show the contents of the toilet to a stranger every day," she went on. "They're acting like I'm dying."

"You had a heart attack, Mum. You're not even sixty yet. It's a big deal."

"Sophie, do stop going on about it, dear. If you want to make yourself useful, you can get me something tasty from the shop downstairs. Some crisps or a cake. They had some lovely iced buns in there on Tuesday."

"And you wonder why you had a heart attack, Mum? No. You can forget it. I'm not bringing anything like that to you," I insisted, whipping my phone out and checking for messages. Nothing from Calvin. I tried to ignore the sharp twinge to my own heart and the sinking feeling in my stomach. "Anyway, I need to get going."

"Tell me you're joking. You only just bloody got here."

"I'm sorry. I've got things to do."

"Oh, really? Like what? Like drowning your sorrows in the bottom of a bottle of wine by any chance?" Mum sniffed, raising an eyebrow.

"I'm twenty eight and if I want to brush my teeth with vodka, I will do," I grinned, leaning forwards and planting a kiss on Mum's pale cheek.

"Sophie, tell me you're joking. You'll end up with a pair of false teeth by the age of thirty and then you'll never get yourself a boyfriend."

I told myself it was a coincidence that the lady in the bed opposite my mother laughed at this precise moment.

"I'll be back tomorrow," I promised her, giving her hand a quick squeeze.

"Bring your brother with you next time," Mum called out as I shrugged my coat onto my shoulders and walked out of the ward.

I navigated my way out of the ward easily enough and found myself coming out of a lift next to the pharmacy. I could see them, all boxed up and glistening, calling out to me. Ignoring the little voice in my mind which told me I was crazy, I picked up another one and handed over the ridiculously large amount of money the cashier was asking me for.

Before paying for parking, I dashed into the ladies and unwrapped the box, pulling out the little stick of doom. Trying not to pee all over my hand, I held it there for five seconds longer than I needed to, before pulling it out and whipping the lid back on. It was one of those fancy digital ones where it actually says the words you need to see instead of just a line or two. A moment later and up it flashed: NOT PREGNANT.

I tried not to let my heart sink as I binned the test and all its unnecessary wrappings, including the box, before heading out of the cubicle to wash my hands. I couldn't understand it. I'd downloaded an app on my phone two months ago, which tracked my period and the time when I was most fertile. I'd made sure we'd done it six times during my peak ovulation days, which he wasn't complaining about. I tried not to let myself be too disappointed when my period arrived that first month. He couldn't understand why I was moping about the place. I worked even harder the month later and yet here we were, still not pregnant. How long would it take?

I got home and immediately headed to the fridge, where I found I was all out of wine. I tried to ignore the nagging feeling of guilt (which formed in my mother's voice) as I opened a bottle of beer. It tasted disgusting but it took the edge off my crappy day. My hands worked their way around my phone before my mind knew what it was doing and I realised I'd ordered myself a Chinese takeaway. Trying not to think of my mother hooked up to various machines with wires and tubes coming out of her, I tucked into my sweet and sour chicken with egg fried rice, washed down with my third bottle of beer.

When there was hardly any food left in the plastic containers, I left them scattered on the living room floor. It felt like far too much effort to get up and clean up after myself, particularly when the cleaning up entailed traipsing outside to my recycling bin. Clive, my slightly overweight ginger and white cat, approached the discarded packaging a little tentatively. Slowly, he reached out one almighty ginger paw and plunged it into some leftover rice and sticky pink sauce. He wasn't impressed as he bolted across the room.

Eventually, my phone rang. CALVIN flashed up on the screen.

"Hello, you," I smiled, swallowing a mouthful of beer. "Finally. You're a difficult man to get hold of, Mr Jones."

"Yeah, so sorry about today. I've been crazy busy at work."

Was it me or did he sound a little distracted?

"Oh, that's okay. I know work has to come first."

"Look, Soph, I don't really know what to say."

"About what?"

"About this. Us. I don't really know if it's going... in the right direction," he said, awkwardly.

"What are you talking about?"

"I'm talking about you with your drinking and the arguments and the smoking weed…"

"I do not smoke weed," I said, cheeks flamed.

"Soph, don't. We both know you do. Please spare me the bullshit. Look, it's been great. Most of the time. It's been a really fun four months. But I think I want it to stay that way. You know. Being fun," he stuttered.

"So do I."

"I don't think you do. You've said a few things over the last couple of weeks which have just reiterated to me that we want different things. I'm so sorry."

My stomach gurgled. I felt sick. I could feel the beer bubbling around the chicken and rice.

"I didn't want it to end this way," he added, after a minute of neither of us speaking. "For what it's worth, you're a really lovely girl. A really lovely girl."

"So lovely you feel obliged to say it twice?" I snapped, suddenly seeing red. How dare he do this to me? I thought, furious.

"Soph?"

"Don't worry about it, Cal. I didn't know how to tell you this but I've met someone else," I sniffed, desperately fighting back tears.

"No, you've not." I could hear the smirk in his voice.

"I have," I lied. "I met him when I was out with Liv last month. That's where I was two weeks ago. I wasn't on a hen do at all. I spent the entire weekend in bed with a gorgeous black man."

"Well, that's – that's great. Terrific. I'm really pleased for you both. I hope you can make a go of things," he said, sounding genuinely relieved. The bastard.

I downed the last of my beer, despite my stomach lurching. How dare he do this to me? I thought, hot tears threatening to spill down my cheeks. I was twenty eight. I didn't have time to waste anymore.

"Soph? Are you still there?" he asked after a moment.

"Um-hm."

"Okay. I'm going to go now. Once again, I'm really sorry. Take care, Sophie. Bye."

As soon as the call had ended, I threw my phone at the wall. It bounced, the screen cracking spectacularly, before ending in the fish bowl. I desperately retrieved it, and checked that Mr Darcy, my faithful aquatic companion, was okay. He was fine, although a little pissed off that his nightly routine of bobbing about had been disturbed.

The same couldn't be said for my phone.

*

I was woken from the same dream I always had, where I'm running and running through a dark forest with my hands tied behind my back. It was a dream I had most nights, which admittedly seemed to be triggered more by alcohol. I'd been woken by a loud noise, like a banging noise. I immediately jumped up from where I'd fallen asleep on the sofa, empty crisp wrappers and discarded beer bottles around me. The TV was still on, but instead of the celebrity gossip show I'd fallen asleep to, it was playing a live jewellery auction. The banging happened again and with my body awake, I realised it was coming from my front door.

Tentatively, I approached the door, wishing I'd thought to put a bra on.

"Soph?"

It was my brother.

"Dan? What time is it?" I asked, bleary eyed, as I unlocked the front door. Neither of us commented on how many locks I had in place.

"I don't know. Maybe four o'clock ish. I've just had a call from the hospital," he said, urgently.

"Why were they ringing you? Mum put me as her next of kin."

"I don't know," he repeated. "They said they tried to call you but they couldn't get through. I don't know why."

I was already pulling on an old pair of Ugg boots and a crumpled hoodie, desperately scrambling around the living room for my car keys. My bloody phone, I thought to myself, as a hazy memory of me catapulting my phone into its watery demise filtered into my brain.

"It's fine. I've got a taxi waiting outside," he said, and I caught his eyes glancing around the room at various different Sophie-isms that I accepted as normal but most people wouldn't.

These included the messy room, the various different empty alcohol bottles and the leaning pile of laundry on the armchair – some of which had been there for weeks. I'd always been untidy but I knew how bad it looked. My brother looked at me with concern on his face.

"I've found them," I cheered, as I scooped my car keys out of yesterday's jeans pocket, silently praying that my younger brother hadn't caught a glimpse of the thong contained inside the jeans.

"Soph, it's fine. There's a taxi waiting outside," he repeated.

"Save your money. I'll drive us," I insisted.

"Soph," he murmured, gesturing towards the empty beer bottles scattered around where I'd clearly been asleep not two minutes earlier.

Cheeks flamed, I nodded. He was right. I was probably still over the limit. I'd fallen asleep after losing count of how many beers I'd had, but when the beers had ran out, I'd started drinking gin. I'd polished off at least half a bottle of the gin I got from my friends at work for my birthday. Whilst locking the front door, I was ashamed at the smell of food on my clothes and alcohol on my breath. What would they think of me at the hospital?

It was only as we pulled up outside the main entrance that it occurred to me to ask Danny what he knew.

"They think she's had another heart attack."

Neither of us spoke another word as we foisted a fistful of coins into the taxi driver's hands and practically sprinted through to Ward C20. It was weird seeing the ward at night. I began to feel my stomach stirring again and it was only then that I remembered my conversation with Calvin. Up until that point, I'd put my uneasy feeling down to the unknown situation with my mother.

"Excuse me, Sister," my brother called out to a passing nurse, who immediately shushed him. "My name's Daniel Maguire. I've just had a phone call about my mother. Susan Maguire."

"Sue," I corrected him, not that it mattered.

The nurse ushered us into a waiting room just outside of the ward. It was sparse, except for two squashy sofas containing some rather dubious looking stains and a children's playmat with an ancient toy abacus. It took a moment before it sank in. They hadn't taken us to see the doctor. They hadn't offered an explanation for the urgent phone call. And they hadn't taken us to see our mum.

They'd brought us to a waiting room.

I'd only ever been in one room like that before. It was thirteen years earlier and I was sat waiting for news about my sister. My mother and father were pacing the floor, asking each other the same questions over and over again: "Surely they must know something, otherwise why would they bring us in here?" "Do you think they've found her?" "If they haven't found her, they've found something of hers. Otherwise we wouldn't be here." "Do you think they've found her?"

"Soph?" came my brother's voice, dragging me from my thoughts. I shook my head to rid myself of the memory. "Did you get that?"

"Sorry," I shook my head.

The doctor nodded, sympathetically, silently cursing me for having to deliver the bombshell for a second time. Before he said anything, I knew what he was going to say. Just like in the only other waiting room of this type that I'd been in before, I knew what was coming. People don't get put in waiting rooms simply to be told good news.

"I'm afraid your mother suffered another heart attack earlier this morning. I'm so sorry to have to tell you that she's passed away," he said, slowly.

Danny was already silently sobbing as he lowered his body onto the sofa. I didn't cry. I didn't say or do anything.

"Would you like me to get someone to bring you a cup of tea?" the doctor asked, kindly.

Flashbacks of 31st October 2005. Cups of tea from kind strangers end with your family members never coming back. I shook my head over and over again until I vomited on his neatly polished shoes.

Chapter Two

"I just want something to help me sleep."

"And why is that, Sophie? Hmm?"

"I'm not sleeping. My mother died a couple of weeks ago. It was her funeral yesterday. I'm exhausted. I have no energy to work because I'm so tired."

"I think we might need to look at the outside factors here before we make any rash decisions."

Doctor Rowena Helsby was younger than me. Not only was she younger than me but she was prettier too. Admittedly, I had seen better days. I'd always been relatively pale skinned but my face had taken on a new grey tinge at times, and I'd recently discovered that I had a waist. Having been a larger than average woman all my adult life, it was an uncomfortably pleasant turn of events to discover that I had lost almost a stone since the day my mother died. I was bereft. That was the word my line manager used when he signed me off for six weeks compassionate leave following my mother's untimely death.

At the time, six weeks seemed like a lifetime. The first week had flown by in a blur of phone calls, hushed tones and hastily made casseroles being foisted on me. It was three days before I realised I hadn't showered or brushed my teeth, and I immediately cringed at what people had thought when they'd hugged me. It was an odd sensation to be hugged again after such a long period of cutting myself off from people emotionally and physically. Up until Calvin, of course.

He was the first person I'd slept with in almost a year. I decided that it would be best to let him know about my mother's death after I'd sank almost two bottles of wine. When he didn't pick up the phone, I decided to leave a voicemail. He sent a text message the following day, offering his condolences in an unfamiliar, icily polite manner. He'd even dared to put "If there's anything I can do, just let me know" at the end of his message, followed by two kisses. It was remarkable. I provided the man with regular sex for four months and only ever got one kiss at the end of a message, if he was feeling particularly generous.

I hadn't taken him up on his offer of help. It was probably an empty promise anyway, just like the hundreds of Facebook friends who'd all rushed to speak to me when I announced my mother's passing on a needy status. Friends from university who I hadn't spoken to in years were suddenly offering me their homes to "get away from it all". I even had an old boyfriend from sixth form send me a private message, asking if I wanted to go out for a drink and a catch up. At first, I hadn't responded, having no idea how to formulate the response I felt his message deserved. Predictably, once I'd had a drink, it felt easy to scrawl a message back to him, telling him that I still hadn't forgiven him for breaking up with me over my "mood swings" at age eighteen. He'd called them mood swings. I called it post traumatic stress disorder.

He wasn't the only one to come crawling out of the woodwork. The day before my mother's funeral, I'd noticed a woman who had barely known her tagging her Facebook account in a soppy status about things happening for a reason and never leaving catching up with your friends for too long. Awash with emotion, I'd called my brother and sobbed down the phone to him.

"Why are people pretending to know her and love her?" I'd wept, a snot bubble forming in my left nostril. "She doesn't even know this Tricia woman. They met at Weight Watchers years ago."

Then there were the people who sent long, drawn out text messages or left choked up voicemails for me, telling me how brave I was to carry on "after everything that's happened". Like I had a choice. They always finalised their communication with the promise of a catch up or a drink or a cup of tea. It was crazy. My mother died and I became instantly more popular.

I'd made the decision to approach the doctor for some help sleeping after my fourth consecutive poor night's sleep. I'd never been a great sleeper but the weeks following my mum's death were particularly horrific. Night sweats, sleep paralysis and just plain insomnia were making my life a misery. When I eventually managed to drop off, I found myself trapped in the same persistent nightmare where I was running and running through a forest as though I was being chased. I always woke with a start, my heart hammering and my head aching with tiredness, but somehow I was then unable to get back to sleep.

My newly grey looking skin had broken out in spots, leaving me looking sickened, and my once vibrant chestnut coloured hair had become lank and greasy, no matter how many times I washed it. Giving in to defeat, I tied it back with one of my mum's old scrunchies on the morning of my appointment. It still smelled like her. The thought was enough to make me choke up in the doctor's office.

"Here," Doctor Helsby said whilst handing me a Kleenex. "It's good to get it all out. I'm so sorry to hear about your mum's passing. Have you considered counselling?"

Wiping my nose and knowing what I needed most of all was to blow it in the privacy of a toilet cubicle, I shook my head. I'd been offered counselling when my sister died and I found it awkward and embarrassing as I stared resolutely at the same spot on the busy floral rug on the floor of the room. I'd actually created a fictitious bedwetting problem, just to give the counsellor something to talk about.

"Maybe we should have a think about prescribing you some antidepressants?" she suggested, her head on one side. The classic look of sympathy and concern. It was somehow more debilitating to receive it from a medical professional. "How about a low dose of Sertraline? It may help you with the feelings you're currently experiencing."

"Will they help me to sleep?" I persisted.

"They might do. However, I think you could improve your chances of a good night's sleep by making some lifestyle changes, Sophie," she said, hesitating. Here it comes, I thought. "How many units of alcohol would you say you're drinking per week?"

Last night I drank a full bottle of wine, three glasses of gin and tonic and the last of a bottle of Baileys, Doctor Helsby, I thought silently.

"Um, I'm not sure," I lied, feeling my cheeks redden. "I've probably drank a bit too often lately. People keep coming round to see me and bringing bottles of wine."

It was a lie. A total lie. People had been round to see me but none of them brought wine. They brought cake and biscuits and they put the kettle on and fed Clive and Mr Darcy and tidied up around the kitchen in what they thought was a tactful manner. I saved the wine for when they'd left. One night, I realised I was out of wine and drank a bottle of champagne in the bath. I hadn't thought it was odd until I caught a glimpse of myself in the bathroom mirror, swigging straight out of the bottle like a washed up celebrity staggering out of a nightclub. I'd felt sick. My mother had died and there I was, quaffing champagne like I had something to celebrate.

"I understand," she nodded. "Maybe once the dust has settled, you can limit your intake of alcohol and perhaps keep a closer eye on your BMI."

I cringed. Mum was barely cold in the ground and this woman was criticising my weight. I felt a lump forming in my throat. I knew it had been a bad idea to see a doctor. They'd never once helped me.

"I'm sorry for wasting your time," I muttered, reaching out to grab my bag from the floor. Doctor Helsby reached out and touched my arm, gently. It was too personal, too much, too close. The tears that had threatened to spill out fulfilled their promise. I found myself sinking back into the chair, my head in my hands. "I'm sorry," I said again. "I'm just so tired."

"Take a few deep breaths, Sophie. You're doing really well," she soothed, as she whipped back around to face her computer screen, tapping away with her immaculate nails. "I've prescribed you a course of antidepressants and a course of sleeping tablets. I'd also like to take a blood sample if that's okay."

"Why?"

"Unusually long periods of tiredness and exhaustion can indicate anaemia," she explained, as she fiddled around with the syringe. "Of course, another possible trigger for tiredness is pregnancy. Is there any chance you might be pregnant?"

Her words were like a dagger to my heart.

"No," I muttered. "There's no chance."

"Would you mind doing a quick urine sample for me, just to be on the safe side? There's a toilet right next door."

Utterly humiliated, I scurried out of the room and filled a tiny plastic cup, cringing only slightly as I had to carry it back into the room whilst trying not to slop the contents onto my own hand. She took it off me and set to work as I checked my phone for a message from Calvin. Nothing. Not that I expected him to send me a message, especially when I hadn't replied to his condolences. It was stupid to think that something as small and insignificant as my mother dying would have any effect on his desire to want to make me happy.

"Would you look at that?" Doctor Helsby's voice said, pulling me away from my thoughts. "It's positive. You're pregnant. Congratulations."

"No. I can't be. I did a test a few weeks ago. It said I wasn't pregnant," I muttered, my mind flitting from one potential scenario to another. "I haven't had sex since then."

"There are a lot of reasons for why a pregnancy test might give a false negative. You might've been a bit too early on for the test to pick up the HCG hormone or your urine might've been too diluted to carry a strong enough reading or you might've bought a cheap test," Doctor Helsby explained as she threw the test and my sample in the bin and began washing her hands. She was smiling. "Congratulations," she said again.

I didn't move. I couldn't think of what to say, what to do. All the planning that had gone into falling pregnant and it had gone tits up before I could fulfil the plan to its potential. I'd planned on falling pregnant "accidentally" and announcing it to Calvin, who would think it was soon but who would ultimately be pleased. In my silly little head, I'd pictured the most romantic of scenes as we clasped hands whilst I had the cool jelly squirted onto my abdomen, our eyes feasting hungrily on the tiny little person wriggling around on the screen in front of us. I'd pictured a hastily planned "baby moon" a few months later where he whisked me off somewhere which was still warm in the usual bitter February climate. I'd had my heart set on a surprise proposal, well documented later on social media. And as I was fast approaching the waddling stage, I'd pictured my mother throwing me a not-so-secret surprise baby shower, donned with sickeningly pink or blue balloons.

Except Calvin and I had split up. It had all gone wrong. I was pregnant, on my own and without the support of my mum.

"This is happy news?" Doctor Helsby asked, uncertainly.

Frightened that the wrong answer might result in me having my baby taken off me, I nodded a little too enthusiastically.

"Yes. It's just – it's a surprise is all."

"Lovely. You'll get a letter in the next few days arranging an ultrasound and your first midwife appointment. You can continue on the course of antidepressants but try to avoid the sleeping pills for now. You can buy some herbal remedies in your local chemist, but of course, a natural sleep aid is a warm milky drink before bed."

My mind whirring into action, I calculated I was about seven weeks pregnant. Maybe even eight. Good grief, I thought as I drove away from the surgery. How hadn't I realised I was pregnant? But, a little voice in my head reminded me, the symptoms of early pregnancy were painstakingly similar to the symptoms of grief.

I was at home, sat on the sofa with a cat sprawled across my lap and a mug of tea in my hands, staring at my (newly purchased) phone and wondering what on earth I could tell Calvin when my phone jolted into life. Startled, I almost dropped it, but managed to clasp it between my clammy hands. It was a phone number I didn't recognise.

"Hello?"

"Good morning. Is that Sophie Maguire?" came an unfamiliar voice.

"Yes. Who's this?"

"My name's Luke Garcia. I'm a third year student at the University of Liverpool, studying Criminology. I was hoping to talk to you about your sister Beth and the events surrounding how she died?"

My heart physically stopped beating. In the nanosecond between it stopping beating and me taking a breath, my only thought was that I was going to die from a heart attack like my mother had. The thought was enough to make me inhale.

"Hello? Are you still there?" the voice said again.

"How did you get this number?" I demanded.

"I messaged a couple of your Facebook friends," he admitted, seemingly bashful.

"You do realise that that is a total invasion of my privacy," I snapped. "Not to mention that you're contacting me at a very difficult time. My mother died three weeks ago."

"I'm so sorry to hear that," he said, predictably. "Look, I don't want to disturb you at such a bad time, but when you're feeling up to it, would you be happy to meet me to talk about Beth?"

"No. I wouldn't. I'm not interested. Leave me alone. Don't contact me again," I spat, and terminated the call.

Not for the first time that day, my mind flitted to my

younger sister. In another world in another life, I'd have imagined a first time pregnancy to be a happy occasion, filled with excited hugs and squeals from my loved ones. As I lay there on the couch, my hands clasped around my abdomen, I was filled with dread.

I had no mother, no sister, no partner and another sleepless night ahead of me.

Chapter Three

"Wow. A baby. Blimey," Danny said, an unmistakeable grin emerging on his face.

"You think this is good news?" I asked him.

"Course it is! It's great news. I'm so happy for you, sis," he said, leaning in and engulfing me in a huge bear hug. My newly found hormones were raging through my body and I had to bite my lip to stop myself from crying. "I hope you don't mind me asking but whose is it?"

"That's just it. I was seeing someone for a while. Only for about four months. His name's Calvin. I haven't told him yet. I needed a bit of time to get my own head around it. I don't think he'll be very happy. It wasn't exactly planned," I lied, suddenly feeling ashamed.

"I'll tell him for you if you like."

"No, Dan, you don't need to do that. But you could come with me?"

"Are you scared of this bloke? Do you think he's likely to hit you?"

"What? No, no, not at all," I insisted, the absurd thought of it making me smile. "I just don't know what to say to him."

"This is the best news I've heard all year," he smiled, leaning back into the armchair. "It's just a shame that Mum…"

His voice trailed off. I knew where he was going with it. Our mother had been an old battle axe at the best of times but she was desperate to be a granny. It was a very cruel world we lived in that allowed her to be a granny, even for a fleeting moment, but then took her away from it.

"Have you told Dad?" he said, suddenly.

"Dan, I don't think I've spoken to Dad once this year."

"Oh right."

"Why? Have you?"

"He rang me and left a message the day before the funeral. Offering his condolences and so on and so forth."

"Yet it didn't occur to him to actually show up," I sniffed, dismissively.

Actually, I'd been glad that he didn't. In the years that followed my sister's death, my father had turned into an alcoholic. We'd always suspected he had an overly friendly relationship with alcohol but he was one step away from day drinking out of a brown paper bag. For years, I'd maintained an exhausting effort to keep our relationship going, but I grew tired. Tired of making excuses for him. Tired of waiting around in restaurants and bars for plans which he'd forgotten about, or watching a meal I'd prepared in my kitchen go stone cold because he'd chosen the pub over visiting his own daughter. I'd grown tired of picking him up from the police station when he'd been screaming at shoppers in the local retail park. On one particularly excruciating occasion, I'd had a phone call from a kind passer by who'd found my dad unconscious in the park. She'd sat with him, called an ambulance and then managed to work his phone to call me. He'd wet himself.

Worst of all, I'd seen a side to my father which reminded me scarily of myself.

"Soph," Danny said, gently. "He'd want to know."

I had no relationship with my father. I didn't know if he still lived at the same address. I'd had two new phone contracts since the last time I called him and I no longer had his phone number. Perhaps it was that I grew closer to my mother as I got older. Perhaps it was that I never really forgave him for his affair.

On the night my sister went missing, Dad was nowhere to be found. He returned in the early hours of the morning, drunk as a skunk, despite driving himself home. According to Mum, he reeked of alcohol and cheap perfume. The police turned a blind eye. It didn't seem right to arrest someone for drink driving when their child was missing.

It wasn't the welcome home party he'd expected. He'd planned to tell my mother that night that he was leaving her for another woman. Someone from work. Cassie someone. I suppose your thirteen year old daughter going missing puts certain plans on hold, and my father held his tongue – and his affair – for a few months.

I'd read enough books and seen enough films about people's fathers walking out on them to build a certain expectation of the event. I thought it would have been a tearful day, with my mother pleading with him not to go as me and my brother looked out of our windows at him backing out of the drive with longing faces. I pictured him toying with the idea of going but then doing a U turn in the road and coming back to us, enveloping us in his smell of washing powder and cigarette smoke. In my silliest daydreams, I pictured us all breaking into song and dance like in a cheesy musical, with Beth suddenly turning up at the door. Like the whole thing had been a nightmare. That the heavy ache I carried around with me would be lifted, and I'd be free to smile and laugh and love again.

The reality was that no one cared. Or maybe no one even noticed. When Beth died, it was like our family shut itself off. From everyone, including each other. People were kind at first. I'd lost count of the amount of cakes and lasagnes and hot pots that had been left on our doorstep with a post it note stuck on the top of the Tupperware tub. But as time moved on, so did everyone around us. There were less lasagnes, less flowers, less phone calls. People still gave us *the look* if we were caught buying milk from the corner shop or half-heartedly pushing a trolley around the supermarket. The look of pity, of sympathy, of "Yes, it's all very sad, but I'm so glad it was them and not us". People were still kind but they'd moved on, remembering my sister but not dwelling over her. Whereas we stayed locked in our grey area. No Man's Land. A time warp of gloom.

At times, No Man's Land felt stifling, like I couldn't breathe. Sometimes it felt desperately lonely. We were a family but we weren't complete. We couldn't move on. We couldn't move past what had happened, no matter how much time passed. There were reminders every day. Sometimes, it was the smaller things – like the lack of singing coming from the bathroom or the bedroom door that stayed permanently shut – which were suffocating. Sometimes it was as simple as her missing name. I cried myself to sleep the night of my seventeenth birthday. The words: "Love from Mum and Daniel" just didn't feel right, like when a teacher mispronounces your name or like wearing someone else's shoes.

It was the feeling of too much, but with a gaping hole.

It was about six months after Beth died that Dad told us he'd lost his job. He'd been a car mechanic all his life, working for Jack Connolly's garage in the heart of the village. Everyone knew Jack Connolly. He'd had his hands in the cars of ninety percent of the village, if not more. There were only three of them working at the garage at the time – Jack, Dad and another mechanic called Robbie – along with an ever-changing receptionist, who was almost always a temp supplied by a nearby recruitment agency. That was how Dad had met Cassie.

Jack had been kind to Dad at first, allowing him some time off to grieve. He'd always been kind to my father, having worked with my grandad for many years before him. But then the world turned on my father, seemingly overnight, accusing him of being behind Beth's death. Despite the obvious ridiculousness of the accusations, my father's name and photograph were repeatedly on the front page of every newspaper stocked in the newsagents. People would shout things at him as he was crossing the road. He never told us what they said, but I had a good idea. Slowly, the people of the village started using another garage, sometimes driving for up to twenty minutes to use a mechanic in Hawleybrook, the next town down. It was clear that people thought Dad was guilty. No one wants to have a murderer fixing their faulty brake pads.

Eventually, Jack Connolly told my father to stop working for him and sent him on his way with a fistful of cash and a sorrowful expression.

Growing up in Arlington Heath had been wonderfully idyllic for the most part of my childhood. It was a small, tight knit village where everybody knew everybody else. There was one primary school and no high schools. Kids were loaded onto the school bus in a morning and taken on a twenty minute journey to Hawleybrook High School. There was one church, one post office, one doctors surgery and one dentist. If anyone was particularly ill or injured, they were taken to Hawleybrook Hospital. If anyone wanted to buy anything that wasn't a staple part of a household's fridge or freezer, they had to hop on the number seven bus to Hawleybrook.

Arlington Heath was a safe village. A safe place, full of safe people. It was the sort of place where you could forget to lock your front door when going on holiday, but it didn't matter because your neighbours would keep an eye on things while you were gone.

Mum always used to say, "People don't move in or out of Arlington Heath. It's the sort of place you grow into and stay in."

Following Beth's death, it all changed. Arlington Heath was no longer the quiet, picturesque village on the outskirts of a busy town. It was the place where a child was murdered. Instead of mums pushing babies in prams along the pavements, journalists and photographers stood, snapping picture after picture of whoever they could find. On the day that Beth was taken, the total population of Arlington Heath was four hundred and sixty five. Statistically, her murderer was one of the four hundred and sixty four people which were left. It was a fact which thrilled the British public and fuelled the fire the media juggled with for so long.

After a while, people began to move. Parents were frightened, permanently watching over their shoulder and worrying about their children. Businesses were suffering as people began to trust each other less and less, preferring the twenty minute bus ride into Hawleybrook to pick up bread and milk just to avoid being questioned by the press outside the village shops. Children were tired of being lectured about stranger danger and not accepting sweets from men in cars. The two schools were tired of extinguishing rumours about what happened to Beth. Within a year of her being killed, the village was unrecognisable. People had moved away for a fresh start, but no one wanted to move into their empty houses. The village was like a ghost town. No one stopped you in the street to chat anymore, unless it was to complete an interview for the six o'clock news.

Arlington Heath became a bad omen. As soon as I was in a position to afford my own house, I moved closer to the city, happy and relieved to be leaving Arlington Heath in the past. It was a good half an hour drive away. Plenty of space. Room to breathe. Danny followed in my footsteps, living in a flat not too far from my house. Dad hadn't moved. He said he couldn't. He felt attached to the village. I assumed it was because Beth was buried there.

I don't think Dad and Cassie had lasted particularly long. I suppose, as always, the novelty of the affair had worn off and reality set in for poor Cassie, having to cope with an unemployed alcoholic who was grieving for his child. There was the additional unexpected bonus of Cassie being subjected to numerous interviews with the police about her relationship with Dad. Needless to say, it eventually fizzled out. I don't think either of them were particularly upset.

There was a string of other women popping in and out of his life once he was no longer with Cassie, but none of them stayed long. The more years that passed, the drunker Dad got.

And more aggressive. He'd punched our Uncle Tony at Nan's funeral, and narrowly avoided getting arrested.

We didn't speak about Beth for years. Trigger dates were hard to face, such as her birthday, her anniversary, Christmas. So we just didn't face them. We buried our heads in the sand and pretended it wasn't happening. Days would pass without anyone even speaking in our house. The dog got walked and fed and cared for but even Dumbledore wasn't quite right. We all missed my sister but it was bigger than that. We missed the hole in the jigsaw her life had created to fill. Her death signalled the end of our lives. We merely existed after that fateful day.

When I turned eighteen, I went off to university with mediocre A Level results and a stinking attitude. I took a pointless course and was awarded with a pointless degree. I moved back home three years later but found it tiresome having to explain to my mother what I was eating, why I was drinking so much, where I was going, what time I would be back. My sister's death had taken a toll on her mental health. I wondered briefly whether it was to blame for her heart attacks too.

My brother's recent words echoing in my mind, I nervously rang the doorbell to my father's house later that day. There was no answer. I knew it was a pointless visit, one I'd carried out more so that I could say that I'd tried than anything else.

As I turned to walk back down the garden path, noticing the absence of the overly grown weeds poking out of every bush, a voice startled me. It was not my father's.

"It's Sophie, isn't it?"

"Do I know you?" I asked the man stood in front of me. He towered above me but I felt strangely not intimidated by him. Perhaps it was the lingering smell of washing powder I detected from his clothes. A man who takes such pride in his laundry cannot be frightening, I reasoned.

"We spoke on the phone last week. My name is Luke Garcia," he said, offering me his hand. I shook it, trying to place his name, his face, anything. I couldn't.

The last five days had been a blur. While I had tried to steer clear of any alcohol for the baby (which I had affectionately named Pickle), it had been harder than I thought and a few times I found myself taking medicinal sips of wine. For some reason, I thought if I mixed mouthfuls of wine with slices of cheese, it made the whole affair classier.

"I'm a student at the University of Liverpool, studying criminology?"

Suddenly it clicked. My blood boiled at the thought of this stranger barging his way into my dad's house. My vulnerable dad. My poor, vulnerable, drunken, grieving dad.

"What the hell do you think you're playing at?" I shouted. My voice was so loud that it even took me by surprise. "Get out of my dad's house. Now."

"Soph."

At last, a voice I recognised as my father's. Except this time it wasn't stuttering or slurring. He sounded remarkably sober.

"Come in, won't you? I don't want the neighbours gawking at you. We're not in a pantomime."

It was an old phrase of my mum's. As children, our mum would smile and nod and pretend everything was okay if we misbehaved whilst out in public but the moment we were inside, our backsides would be red.

I realised it had been over two years since I last stepped foot inside my dad's house. The last time I was there, it had been messy and dishevelled and smelled of unwashed clothes and rotting food. As soon as I'd left, I remember sniffing my clothes and thinking that I stank like an old forgotten shoe. Rather like my father himself, who would go days without eating or washing or even changing his underpants at times. Cringing, I realised that the apple didn't fall too far from the tree.

As I walked through an undeniably clean house, I was surprised. My father's personal appearance had drastically improved since the last time I saw him. He'd easily lost at least two stone and he'd bought new clothes, instead of donning the same worn out gear he'd kept hold of for years.

"Is everything okay?" he asked me, as I hovered awkwardly in the living room doorway. Luke had taken a seat on the smaller sofa and my dad was sat in his spot on the larger one. "Has something happened?"

"No. Nothing's happened. I just…"

My voice trailed off. I couldn't tell my father that I was pregnant with a stranger in the room.

"I think I'll leave it there for today, Mr Maguire," Luke said, taking the hint and packing away a stack of papers into a briefcase. "Same time on Friday?"

Dad saw him out of the house and returned, the same shocked look on his face that I knew I bore on my own.

"What's happened?" he asked again, his voice a little tender.

"Why was he here?"

"Luke?" he asked, the familiar use of his first name sparking a little rage inside me. "He's – well – it's a long story."

"He rang me. A few days ago now. He wanted to speak about... He wanted to ask some questions about her. About Beth," I choked out.

"Aye," my father said, sitting back in his chair. He held a mug to his mouth. From what I could see, the contents looked surprisingly like tea. "He's not a journalist."

"I should hope not. You know better than that by now."

"He's a student up at one of the universities in Liverpool. He's studying criminology. He wants to do his dissertation on Beth's death. I saw no harm in him asking a few questions."

"Ha," I spat out, rolling my hands into fists.

"Wouldn't you rather he asked one of us about it instead of just using whatever he can find on the internet or asking people who weren't involved?" he said, quietly.

"Why does he have to write about her? Why can't he write about another crime? There's bloody millions of crimes he could choose from, so why Beth?" I spat.

"Why not?" Dad asked simply. He wasn't being unkind.

"I don't like strangers asking questions. Poking their noses in. We're not a freak show."

There was a moment of silence, except for the blood rushing around my body and the slow, steady ticking of Dad's watch.

"She was my daughter."

"I'm your daughter too."

He looked at me with the slightest flash of concern across his face. It was one thing for a medical professional to have concerns about the weeping woman begging for sleeping tablets. It was another thing altogether for my alcoholic father to have concerns about me. Swallowing, I could feel a lump forming in my throat.

"I'm pregnant," I said, finally.

"Gosh," Dad said.

"Is that all you have to say?"

"I didn't know you were seeing anyone."

"I'm not."

"Ah, right. I see. Are you keeping it?"

I nodded, through gritted teeth. I knew there and then that there was nothing further to discuss with my father, so I picked up my handbag, clutching my car keys in my hand, and turned on my heel. The lump in my throat had grown. I was dangerously close to tears.

"Wait. Soph. Please don't go. Not just yet. I haven't seen you for so long."

"I wonder why that is."

"I haven't touched a drop in seven months."

"Well done," I sniffed.

"I know it doesn't seem like much but it's been a mountain to climb for me. Every bloody day."

"No. I meant it. Well done," I whispered, my eyes pricking with tears. Damn hormones. "I'm sorry, Dad. I've got to go now. But I'll come back soon, I promise."

With that, I headed to the front door, tearing it open with gusto as I stood, breathing in the cool air. It felt good on my skin as I realised how clammy I felt. Just before I closed the door, I came face to face with my father again.

"Sophie," he said, awkwardly, clearing his throat. "I was sorry to hear about your mum. She was a good woman."

"Yes, she was."

Chapter Four

It hadn't seemed strange to me that I'd never been to Calvin's house during the brief spell we were an item. I had my own house and while it wasn't Buckingham Palace, it did the job. I lived nearer to the city centre, so it was the most logical place to meet or drunkenly stagger back to after a night in the pub. It was only when I went to put his address into the sat nav that Danny picked up on how odd it was.

"You know what they say about blokes who don't invite you back to their houses, don't you?"

"What? They still live with their mum?"

"Nope. Their wife."

We pulled up outside a very nice modern looking house, a definite new build development in a posh area of the city. Neither of us spoke a word as we parked up, locked the car and walked up to the white front door. The garden was well tended with nice potted plants in each corner. It didn't go unnoticed by Danny, who raised his eyebrows as I knocked on the door.

If it wasn't such a serious situation, I would've burst out laughing at the look on Calvin's face when he realised it was me knocking on the door. His eyebrows practically disappearing into his hairline, his eyes went from me to Danny to me again.

"Sophie," he hissed, half closing the front door behind him and standing on the front step despite his bare feet. He was wearing pyjamas. He'd never worn pyjamas when he'd stayed at my house. "What are you – what are you doing here?"

"Can we come in?" I asked, politely.

"Now isn't actually a very good time for me," he muttered, with a quick glance over his shoulder into the house. "Can I meet you somewhere? Maybe the Wetherspoons on Town Road?"

That hadn't been part of the plan. On our drive over, Danny and I had recited what felt like a script as I informed Calvin that something was growing inside my uterus which was half mine, half his. I'd pictured saying it sat on his sofa, not in a public place. What if I start to cry? I thought, worriedly.

"That's fine. You've got ten minutes," I found myself saying and without another word, I turned on my heel and retreated back to the car. Silently, we drove the five minute journey to the pub and waited in the car park.

"Do you think he'll be a no show?" Danny asked as I drummed my fingers against the steering wheel.

"I think he's curious enough to turn up but I don't think he knows what I'm going to say."

Within a minute, I saw his white BMW pull into the car park and reverse into the space next to my little Ford Fiesta. Was it me or did Calvin look as though he was about to throw up?

From an outsider's perspective, we looked like three friends meeting for a pint after work, except there were no frivolities, no laughter and no conversation as we silently headed into the pub and found a small table in a deserted area. Thankfully, the pub was quiet enough that I felt we wouldn't be disturbed but not so quiet that I would be announcing my secret to the staff themselves as they wiped down the tables whilst eavesdropping.

"Can I – do you want – what do you want?" Calvin asked, his forehead creased with confusion.

"Right now, I want a small orange juice and a packet of salt and vinegar crisps. Dan?" I turned to my brother.

"I quite fancy the same myself. Can I get you a drink?" he asked Calvin, his good manners seeming almost inappropriate.

"No," Calvin said, still confused. "No thanks."

Danny got up and headed to the bar. Although it hadn't been part of the official plan to come to a pub, it felt okay. Natural. I felt in control of the situation. Danny had obviously pushed off to give us a bit of privacy, but it was good to know he was close by in case I had a wobble.

"What's all this about?" Calvin asked, eyeing me suspiciously. "Do you want money?"

"Money for what?"

"You're trying to blackmail me, aren't you?"

The thought was so ludicrous that the hysteria building up inside me forced its way out into a loud laugh. It was so loud that a family four tables down from us turned round to stare. Shit, I thought. An audience wasn't part of the agenda.

"No, Calvin," I said, still chortling. "I'm not trying to blackmail you."

"Well, what do you want then? You turn up at my house uninvited with your latest squeeze on your arm and for what? Are you trying to flaunt him in my face? Is that it?" he hissed, his voice barely audible. "When will you get it, Sophie? I'm not interested in you."

"First of all, Danny's my brother. Not my boyfriend. And second of all, I'm pregnant."

There. I sat back in my seat, enjoying the moment that the reality hit him and watched his cheeks turn from a slightly tinged pink to the colour of corned beef.

"Don't be ridiculous," he sniffed.

"I'm not being anything of the sort. I'm pregnant. About eight weeks by now."

"Is it mine?" he asked, little beads of sweat starting to form on his upper lip.

It was a fair enough question. The last phone call we'd had involved me bragging about a wholly fictitious character who I'd been allegedly bonking for weeks.

"Yes."

"How can you be so sure?"

"Because I've only slept with you in the last year."

"What about this other fella? The one you were secretly shagging? There's got to be a chance that it's his, surely," he said, diplomatically, his eyebrows burrowed in confusion.

Cheeks reddening from shame, I shook my head. I couldn't quite meet his eyes.

"Ah," said Calvin. "The penny drops. There was no mysterious man. You made him up."

"Yes," I whispered.

The moment was disturbed by Danny bringing my drink over. He hovered, awkwardly, standing slightly in front of me, rather like a lioness protecting its cubs.

"It's okay, Dan," I reassured him. "Calvin isn't going to go mad at me, are you?"

He shook his head and let out an almighty sigh. Taking this as confirmation, Danny wandered back to the bar where I watched him hitch himself up on the bar stool and began nibbling at the little bowl of peanuts on offer. I tried to block out the mental image of the different germs festering on those peanuts.

"I don't get how this happened," Calvin said after a while.

"What are you after, a drawing?" I snapped.

"You know what I mean," he hissed, nervously glancing around the pub in fear of anyone overhearing my outburst. He was no longer corn beef coloured. He was positively puce. "I thought you were on the pill or something."

"Or something."

"You mean you weren't?"

"You didn't bother to ask so I didn't bother to tell you. It's a two way street, pal," I sniffed.

"You – how could you – you are bang out of order!" he exclaimed. "You've done this on purpose. You've set me up."

"Set you up how exactly? As far as I knew, we were going to be together forever and ever. Yes, okay, perhaps I should have been more transparent with you, but I don't remember you reaching for the Durex either. Besides, I didn't plan for you to give up at the first hurdle."

"It wasn't so much a hurdle, Sophie, as it was a crossroads. We wanted completely different things out of our…relationship. When we first met, I liked your tenacity and your spirit. You had this energy about you. A fun energy. You made me laugh. I liked sleeping with you. I liked you cooking for me and I enjoyed going to bars and the theatre with you. But then it was as if something changed within a month or two. You kept talking about the future and where we would be in twelve months' time and whether or not I thought we should move in together. It was insane. I'm sorry, Sophie, but I think this is a really terrible idea," he said, speaking so quickly that it was almost a rant. It was only when he stopped speaking that we both realised he was breathless.

"I'm not exactly jumping for joy about this myself but it's here, it's happened and I'm dealing with it as best I can," I said, tears pricking my eyes. Damn hormones. I'd gone three days without shedding so much as one tear and then found myself sobbing because Tesco was all out of organic tomatoes. My boobs were aching, my lower back was aching, I had an almost permanent headache and the worst taste in my mouth that made everything I consumed taste like metal.

"I really don't know what you expected me to say. Did you think I'd be pleased?"

Sipping my orange juice nonchalantly, I couldn't bring myself to reply. The truth was yes, I did think he would be. Even as he drove into the car park, I'd been secretly praying for a reunion.

"Do you want to keep it?" he asked, suddenly.

"Yes," I answered, defiantly.

He nodded, slowly. "And there's no changing your mind over that?"

"No. I'm sorry. If you don't want anything to do with the baby, that's your choice but I have no intention of terminating this pregnancy."

"Even if I told you I was engaged?"

His words came to me like a foghorn in a storm; slow but deafening. My heart thudded painfully as I gasped for breath. For the second time in my life, my thoughts turned to my mother's death and I wondered briefly, dramatically, if I was going the same way. I couldn't speak. I tried but all that came out was a brief croak. Without any indication, I burped noisily and quickly clapped my hand against my mouth in case I vomited. Calvin's cringe was so visible that I couldn't ignore it.

I felt a lump in my throat. It wasn't vomit. It was tears. Tears threatening to spill out, loudly and pumped up with hormones.

"I'm sorry," he murmured, his eyes on the table and his fingernail tracing the edge of the beer mat in front of him. "I know I should've been honest with you from the start. But like I said, I just really liked you. You're a nice girl."

I'd only ever been called a nice girl once before. It was a few months after my sister died. A month before Dad left. I was walking home from school when I saw a cat lying at the side of the road. It had been hit by a car and it was clearly dead, although I couldn't see any blood. I took my coat off and peeled off a layer of clothing, wrapping the cat inside my school blazer and picking it up. The cat was wearing a collar with a phone number printed on it, so I carried the cat the two minute walk back to my house and lay it on the floor in front of the stairs as I rang the number. A man answered it and I explained what had happened. He was shocked and a little upset, but offered to come round to collect the cat's body.

Alarm bells had started to ring and I explained that I was home alone and wanted to wait for my parents to return before he came round. When he turned up a few hours later, he commended my attitude towards stranger danger. It was an odd comment to make considering I was sixteen years old and legally able to marry, have a family and join the army (if I'd wanted to).

Rubbing my shoulder ever so gently, Mum explained to the man that my sister had recently gone missing and been found dead. His facial expression changed significantly and he adopted an even kinder smile as he tucked his now lifeless pet under his arm, still wrapped in my school blazer.

"You're a nice girl, Miss Maguire," he'd said, nodding at my parents and leaving the house.

We hadn't given him our second name. My sister was the only child to go missing within twenty miles of our postcode. He knew who we were.

"Sophie?" Calvin's voice came out, pulling me from my thoughts.

"My sister was abducted in 2005," I said, suddenly. "She was taken from school by a stranger, raped and strangled. Her body was found two days later in Griffin Woods."

"Jesus," breathed Calvin. He didn't know how to process the information. It was a crude awakening moment for me. We might have had sex with each other but we hadn't been intimate. Intimacy was more than just being naked and touching each other and making each other orgasm. Intimacy was about opening up to one another, swapping secrets, talking about the things you didn't talk about to anyone else. How had I thought he was so important to me when he didn't even know about my sister?

"I don't know why I'm telling you this."

He shrugged. "You can tell me anything."

I raised an eyebrow in disbelief. "Yet you couldn't remember to tell me that you're marrying someone else?"

"It isn't really that sort of engagement. We've been together since university. I proposed three years ago. We aren't actually planning to get married."

"Your lack of commitment is really reassuring," I rolled my eyes.

He grinned. "Look, if you want to keep this baby, then we need to do this properly. I'll need to speak to Lorna. Tell her about you. And…" his voice trailed off as he gestured towards my stomach.

"Our child?" I prompted him.

"She'll kick me out, obviously. I'll have to move into your place."

"What?"

"I haven't got anywhere else to go. I can't turn up at my parents' house. They adore Lorna. She's a part of our family. They'll be devastated."

"We don't need to live together to have a baby together. We can quite successfully co-parent from entirely separate locations, you know. And besides, this little Pickle of ours is about the size of a kidney bean right now. You don't need to make any life changing decisions just yet. I've not even had my first scan yet."

"When's that?"

"On Thursday. It's at half twelve at the hospital."

"Is there something wrong with the baby?" he frowned.

"It's just routine. I've been having pains down my left hand side, so they need to rule out an ectopic pregnancy. And I've got to hang around afterwards and have some tests done."

"Tests for what?" he frowned. I could tell what I was saying was like a different language to Calvin.

"I'm not really sure. I think they're just checking that everything's going okay."

We'd found the natural close of our conversation and we stood, me finishing the last of my juice, whilst pulling our coats back on. Danny came over within seconds, still standing slightly in front of me.

"Calvin, this is my brother, Danny. Danny, this is Calvin. You might as well get to know each other. You're practically family now," I pointed out and they nodded, shaking hands a little warily.

As we walked back outside into the car park, Danny's phone began to ring and he dashed off to answer it while me and Calvin stood, somewhat awkwardly, waiting for his return. We stood in silence, the pair of us buried deep inside our respective coats, clinging onto the warmth.

"You can get going," I nodded towards his car.

"I'll wait for your brother to come back," he insisted, although I couldn't really see a point. I presumed he was attempting to act chivalrous. "Can I ask you something? About your sister?"

I nodded.

"Was she called Bethany?"

"Beth," I automatically corrected him.

"Beth. Sorry. Yeah, I remember the hype at the time. I know I lived miles away back then but it was still a really big deal, this kid going missing. It was awful. Did they ever find the bloke who did it?" he asked, his head on one side. Ah, the classic sympathetic angle.

Watching my brother come back to the car, I simply turned my face to the father of my child and said, "No. No, they didn't."

Chapter Five

"So, you've trapped him then?"

I'd known Erica Barnes for the best part of three years. We'd started on the same day at work and been thrown in the deep end as we both realised we were completely out of our depths. The end of that daunting first week had culminated in the pair of us being blind drunk at the White Hart pub, which we'd happily discovered was just a two minute walk from the office. After six months, we were inseparable as we went for (far too frequent) post-work drinks and spent the first half an hour of every shift hovering around the tiny kitchenette talking in hushed tones about everything from men and their inability to communicate to what to buy for the office bitch, Brenda, for her birthday.

"I wouldn't say that exactly," I rolled my eyes as I spooned coffee into a chipped mug. It dawned on me that all of my mugs were chipped. I couldn't remember the last time I'd bought anything remotely homely. All that was soon to change, I thought, as I pictured Calvin painting the nursery and adding a designated breastfeeding rocking chair as a final touch. I shook my head to rid myself of the thought. It was as though my newly produced hormones were adding fuel to the fire when it came to my wishful daydreams.

"You slept with a bloke who thought you were on the pill but you weren't on the pill and instead, you were actively sleeping with him during peak ovulation? Sounds like trapping to me."

Erica was six years older than me and had been with the same man since school. Neither of them seemed particularly keen to commit. These were people in their thirties who had proper houses with mortgages in nice, homely areas as opposed to extortionately priced rented box houses in horrible areas where people relieved themselves in the bus stop across the road. There was nothing remotely pleasant about witnessing that through my living room window.

Erica and Will had never so much as mentioned having children or getting married. In fact, Erica had never even discussed it with me. It dawned on me that in the three years that I'd known and loved Erica, and poured my heart and soul out to the girl, I didn't even know if my friend wanted children or if she knew that I did.

"It wasn't quite like that," I said, giving the milk bottle a precarious sniff. "It just sort of happened. Haven't you ever done anything crazy and impulsive before?"

"Crazy and impulsive, yes. Recklessly life changing? No."

We sat in silence for a moment as I nursed my chipped Lisa Simpson mug and tried not to gag over the smell of coffee coming from Erica's. Pregnancy had forced me to switch from my beloved (and sometimes needed) coffee to decaf tea bags. As if it wasn't bad enough that I couldn't drown my sorrows into a bottle of wine or a rare piece of steak.

"How do you feel about it?" Erica asked, softly. I could feel her eyeing me up. "I mean… you're pregnant. *Pregnant*," she repeated, as if I was suddenly blissfully unaware of the kidney bean growing inside me which was half mine, half Calvin's.

"I've not given it much thought to be honest. I'm not sure it's really sunk in yet."

"You don't have to go through with it, you know."

Her words came from nowhere. I blinked and I was transported back to my first Christmas at university. I was sat in the communal kitchen that I shared with five other people in my halls, unenthusiastically toying with my second Pot Noodle of the day, when my flatmate Kimmy walked in. Her face, usually so deftly made up with fierce eyebrows and piercing outlined eyes, was blotchy. Her hair was unkempt and shoved back in a scruffy ponytail. The bags under her eyes were only slightly smaller than the frown imprinted on her forehead. She thrust a little white stick at me, which I clutched for just a moment too long. I'd never had to use one before but I knew instantly what it was and what the two blue lines, shining like a beacon, meant.

Kimmy hadn't gone through with it and I'd gone with her to all three appointments. I was surprised by how quick and easy it was to access this sort of procedure. One appointment with the on-site university doctor, two appointments in a clinic in the city centre a fortnight later and we were home; Kimmy lay under her duvet with a hot water bottle tucked in her pyjama pants. She'd cried for days, weeks, but she was adamant from the start that it was the right decision for her, even when the university doctor was cold and dismissive as she gave Kimmy a scathing look and a bag of condoms "for the future, so this doesn't happen again".

Kimmy didn't graduate with us two years later. She didn't even make it to the end of the first year. I still had her as a friend on Facebook and occasionally looked at her photos on Instagram. She seemed happy, at least.

"It's not for everyone," Erica said, her voice piercing into my memories. "I'm just saying. A positive pregnancy test doesn't have to mean parenthood. You've got a lot going on right now. That bastard Calvin isn't being much help either. God, I could just swing for him. He'll leave you high and dry, I'm telling you. Maybe this just isn't the right time, Soph. You're not in a relationship with the baby's dad. The baby's dad is engaged to somebody else. And you've just lost your lovely mum."

I'd met Erica's mum, Wendy, just once during our three year friendship. When Erica turned thirty three, Will had arranged a surprise gathering at Erica's favourite Indian restaurant. He'd invited all of her friends, her brother and his wife, and her mum. Wendy was probably around the same age as my own mother but whereas my mother was kitted out in Marks and Spencer's finest clothes, she was dressed provocatively, in a low cut silver dress which showed a lot of leg. She drank three bottles of red wine as easily as if it was soda water and then vomited in the toilets. Mortified, Erica asked me to put her mum in a taxi but every taxi that pulled up took one look at a vomit spattered sixty year old and drove away again.

I'd ended up ringing my own mother, who turned up within ten minutes and bundled Wendy into the passenger seat of her Ford Focus, calmly wrapping a blanket around her bare shoulders as Wendy sobbed, mascara pouring down her heavily made up cheeks. My mum chatted away to Wendy as she drove, as if it was perfectly normal to have a sick covered stranger in your car on a Saturday evening. I had a lump in my throat as I watched my mum link arms with Wendy and walk her to her front door, let them both in and make her a cup of tea. I sat in the car outside Wendy's house fighting back tears as I realised both my brother and I had distanced ourselves from our mother as we grew older.

All my mum had wanted to do was to mother us. Protect us. Look after us. All the things she couldn't do for Beth.

I let Erica's words circle my brain one last time.

"Maybe that's all the more reason to keep it."

Chapter Six

I'd always expected pregnancy to be a beautiful time. Somehow, I must have missed the memo about throwing your guts up at any given point during the day, I thought to myself as I swilled my mouth out with an extra-long mouthful from my bottle of water.

"Are you okay?" Calvin asked, trying his best to look concerned and not too grossed out. "You've got a bit of – there's something in your hair."

Cringing, I dashed back into the toilet cubicle to scrub my hair with a crinkled up piece of toilet roll. Hardly the most glamorous of looks I'd ever rocked before, but I didn't care. Hospital toilets might have been rather basic but they were always clean.

"I thought pregnant women were only sick in the morning?" Calvin said as I re-emerged from the toilet cubicle, trying not to think about my unwashed hair. "Maybe you've got a bug."

Incredulous, I said, "I don't have a bug, Calvin, I have a baby. I feel sick and I'm exhausted and my boobs are hurting beyond belief and I haven't been able to force out a shit for three days now, so my stomach is full of baby and full of crap and I feel uncomfortable and heavy and gross."

Mortified, Calvin tried to ignore the nurse and the old man she was pushing in a wheelchair, who were both eyeballing us. We'd been to the scan and seen the baby moving around inside of me. Even though I'd been upfront with Calvin regarding the conception, I was frightened that there would be some sort of giveaway on the screen or that someone would ask me "So, was this pregnancy planned or unplanned?" and I'd have to launch into an explanation that would make everyone feel uncomfortable.

As it was, I couldn't have been further from the truth. There were two women in the room with us. One was the sonographer and the other was tapping away at the computer keyboard. Both were very nice and on the large side, which, for some inexplicable reason, comforted me.

"I'm struggling to see anything clearly at the moment. I don't think your bladder's full enough, duck," said the sonographer, glancing to and from the screen.

It felt full enough. In the letter I'd received a week earlier inviting me to the scan, I'd been forewarned about drinking enough water to give a clear reading on the screen, cue me waiting in the hospital car park for Calvin whilst downing a large bottle of fizzy fruity water. This had earned me a sceptical look from the father of my child. To be fair, it wasn't quite nine o'clock in the morning. He should consider himself lucky, I'd thought, wondering what he'd have said if I was drinking what I'd wanted to drink – a crisp glass of pinot grigio.

"Would you mind popping your undergarments off and we can try an internal scan? It won't hurt you or the baby. It's just this," the other lady suggested, as she held up what looked like a white wand. I'd tried to ignore Calvin's uncomfortable squirms as I lay on the bed and let a complete stranger probe me in an intimate area. It hadn't been that long since he'd put his own wand inside me. Smirking, I realised it was his wand which had led to the scan.

"You're a little bit further along than your dates would suggest," the sonographer said, squinting at the screen and stopping every few moments to take some still shots. "Based on the size of the sac and the foetus itself, I'd say you were almost ten weeks. Nine weeks and five days to be precise."

Whilst I lay there trying desperately hard to keep my face plain of any emotion, I was baffled. The app I'd spent two pounds downloading, installing and using to memorise my monthly cycle with was clearly a load of crap. I'd expected the shape on the screen to resemble a blob, maybe even a little bean, but it was very clearly and unmistakeably baby-like. I risked a glance at Calvin, expecting to see his face looking bored or dismissive or perhaps even just disappointed. I got a jolt in my stomach when I saw he had tears in his eyes.

As we walked out of the ultrasound ward, I could see him checking his watch and itching to get himself to work. He was a financial advisor. Although he'd explained his career choice to me multiple times before, I wasn't quite sure what it was that he actually did.

"You go on ahead," I insisted. "I've just remembered I had a phone call from the hospital a fortnight ago, reminding me to collect some of my mum's things from the ward."

"Are you sure you don't want me to come with you?" he

asked.

I wanted to be alone. The more time we spent together, the more he realised that I liked my own company. I didn't get *lonely* like other people did. Solitude and independence was what comforted me.

The feeling I got as I approached the ward my mother had died in was a strange one. I couldn't put my finger on it. It wasn't as though I was nervous, but apprehensive perhaps. The last time I stepped foot inside the ward, my mother had been alive. It was ridiculous, I knew, but I half expected to see her lay in bed, ordering me around and criticising my diet and my love life.

"Can I help you?" asked a hard faced nurse as she was taking someone's blood pressure from the bed next to where my mother lay. Her bed had been occupied by a new patient: a tiny little old Indian lady, still wearing some fabulous jewellery over her nightie.

"I'm Sophie Maguire. I had a phone call a few weeks back asking me to pop in and collect my mum's belongings," I explained.

"What was your mum's name?"

"Sue Maguire. Susan."

"Give me a minute and I'll dig them out for you."

I was debating dashing down to buy a coffee from the vending machine outside but I hesitated, not wanting anything to fuel the fire that was my morning sickness. I'd read that eating ginger biscuits was supposed to help but I'd bought a gingerbread man from the bakery near my house and it had barely touched the sides before coming straight back up again. There was something rather perverse about seeing a regurgitated smiling man.

"Hello, stranger."

I looked up to be greeted with the wide toothy grin of the old lady who'd been in the bed opposite my mother. She looked definitively perkier, as though she had a little spring in her step. Without realising, I found myself smiling. I was pleased to see her. This lady knew my mother, even if only briefly.

The problem with having a relatively small family was that when the ones you're close to die, you have no one you can talk to about them. I'd even found myself ringing my dad and on one unheard of occasion, I'd invited him round for some food. He was seemingly thrilled by the idea, but the affair turned rather sour and uncomfortable because I'd forgotten that I'd also arranged to meet Calvin for a pub tea. As a result, it ended up being the three of us foisted together in my tiny little kitchen. I only had two kitchen chairs so Calvin ended up eating curry crouched over the worktop. He'd moaned that he had indigestion all night.

"I was sorry to hear about your lovely mum," she went on. "It's Sophie, isn't it?"

"Yes. Sorry, what was your name again?"

"Patsy," she grinned. "Are you picking up your mum's cardigan? I was hoping you'd forgotten about it, to be honest. I quite fancied it myself. It's from Marks and Spencer, I could just tell."

"You can have it if you want," I offered her, which she immediately dismissed with a wave of her hand.

"What would I do with a lovely cardigan like that, eh? Stick it on over my nightie?" Patsy clucked.

"No chance of you getting out of here soon then?" I asked.

"I doubt it," she replied, sadly. "But I can't say I'm too fussed. What have I got waiting for me at home? A few microwave meals and a visit once a day from a carer."

"Why don't you get a cat?" I suggested.

Laughing, Patsy shook her head. "Can't stand the little buggers. No, I'll be fine. I'll stay in here as long as I can. At least this way I can get some decent conversation. So, tell me about you. How have you been since your mum passed on?"

"I'm alright. Actually, I'm – well, I'm pregnant. I've just been for a scan," I beamed, handing across the little black and white photo of my bean. Patsy accepted it, oohing and aahing over it. A little wobble crossed my bottom lip as I realised this was what I was craving - a mother figure to coo over the exciting milestones.

"How far gone are you?" Patsy asked, smiling, as she handed back my scan picture.

"According to this, I'm exactly nine weeks and five days."

"Oh, I remember being at that stage with both of mine. Had terrible morning sickness when I was expecting our Rebecca," she smiled. "Have you had much sickness, Sophie, love?"

"I've not been too bad, actually. It's more that I'm struggling to find anything which takes my appetite. Last night, I fancied spaghetti bolognese but as soon as I put the mince in the frying pan, I…"

My voice trailed off as I realised I was looking at a photograph of my own face staring back at me. The little Indian lady was half hidden behind a newspaper. A newspaper which had a photograph of my entire family plastered on the front of it.

"Is something the matter?" Patsy asked, confused, as I stamped across the ward to the Indian lady. I didn't even need to say anything before she held the newspaper out to me. It felt as though I was under water, kicking for the surface but sinking further back down. The background noise around me paled into one and the only clear sound I could hear was my pulse radiating through my pores. Legs wobbling, I sat on the plastic chair next to Patsy's hospital bed. "Are you alright, chick?"

I couldn't respond. I couldn't even read the article. The only part I could take in was the headline: EXCLUSIVE - THE GIRL IN THE MUSTARD COAT – HER FATHER'S STORY. How had this happened? I thought, my heart hammering painfully in my chest.

"Ah. I see. Is that girl your sister, Sophie?" Patsy asked me.

I nodded.

"I remember when she went missing. Such a dreadful thing to happen, it was. Nasty business. I remember it as clear as day. I could've sworn she'd gone off with someone from school. You know what teenagers are like. They'll go with whoever takes their fancy. I take it you never found out who did it then?"

The eyes of every person in the ward were boring into the back of my head as I scooped the newspaper up, rolled it up and tucked it underneath my arm. I walked out of the ward, ignoring the pleas of both Patsy and what I presumed to be the nurse bringing my mother's belongings. Heart hammering, chest tightening and throat thickening, I sped out of the ward and into the lift, my hands shaking as I pressed the ground floor button.

Before I'd even got to the car, I was already on the phone to Danny.

"I know," he answered, before I'd even spoken a word. "I've already seen it, Soph."

"How did they – who's spoken to them? What are they playing at?" I cried, gulping down air. Fumbling with my car keys, I could feel people looking at me. A smartly dressed man in a suit went to approach me, then looked as if he'd thought better of it.

"It's Dad, isn't it?" Danny said, calmly. "The bloke he's been speaking to. He wasn't a student. He was a reporter. A journalist. He played right into their hands, didn't he?"

"How could he be so stupid?" I gasped, pummelling my chest in a bid to breathe easier. "I can't believe this. Why won't they just let it go? How are we meant to live our…"

I couldn't finish my sentence out of guilt. I had a life to live. Poor Beth had hers taken away from her. We didn't know which bastard was responsible. It was a fact I'd learned to accept a long time ago. The alternative was to live my life like my mother had, drowning in a world of despair and uncertainty. She'd never come to terms with Beth's death. She'd said it was because it was unnatural for a mother to have to bury her child. But it was more than that. It ate away at her, bit by bit, year after year of the unsolved case passing us by.

For years, my mother spoke to Beth as if she was still alive. "Come on now, Bethany, let's get these curtains open". "Time for a cup of tea, I think, Beth". "Happy birthday, Bethany Rose." It was stifling. I couldn't stand it. Danny had more patience than I did but even he couldn't tolerate it after a while, driving him to move out when he was still at sixth form.

We didn't talk about my sister because there was nothing to talk about. It wasn't that we didn't want to remember *her*. We just didn't want to remember.

"Soph, where are you? Do you want me to come and meet you? I'm at work but I could have an early dart."

"No, no, it's fine. I'm just coming out of the hospital now. I'm sat in the car. I'm going straight round to that dozy prick's house and giving him a mouthful. So much for staying sober. I don't believe this is happening," I cried. "What if it all gets trudged up again? What if people start staring at us when we're in the supermarket or shouting things out to us when we're in the street again? I can't – I don't – I don't think I can stomach going through it all again."

"You need to take a deep breath, Soph. None of that will happen because there's no new evidence, is there? It's just Dad chirping away to some brain dead reporter, desperate for a scoop.

I've read the article online. It's crap. Boring, even. There's nothing in that article that people haven't known for the last decade. It'll be tomorrow's chip paper."

That didn't stop me tear arsing round to father's house, driving in fifth gear the entire way there. He was expecting me, I could tell, as he was stood at the living room window, peering through the net curtains when I stomped up the garden path. The door opened without me needing to knock and he stepped to one side to let me in.

"Tea, love?" he asked me, quietly.

"I'm not going to sit here and exchange pleasantries with you, Dad. You can stuff your tea. We made a deal years ago. A pact. We agreed that we weren't going to talk about Beth to the press."

"And as far as I knew, I wasn't. How was I to know he was from the media?"

"You mean you didn't even ask to see any ID?" I screeched. "This bloke could have been anyone, Dad. You've got to be more careful. He was a journalist. A leech. You remember what the papers said about you twelve years ago, don't you? Do you really want to go back to that again? Or what if they start dragging out some made up shit about Mum? Is that what you want?" I roared, dimly aware that I had accidentally spat on his face as I shouted.

"No."

"The person who killed Beth is still out there, Dad. He's out there somewhere, going about his business, not a care in the world. He's probably gone on to hurt dozens of other people. He's a rapist. He's *scum*. That sick bastard will know who we are and what our names are and what we look like thanks to the press printing our life stories donkey's years ago. He could be watching us. It could've been the bloke you gave all that information to."

I was breathless; apoplectic with rage.

"Sophie, you're getting yourself far too worked up. You need to think about the baby. Please calm down. I'm sorry. It was an accident. A mistake. I should've been more careful but I wasn't. And it won't have been Luke – if that was his real name – because he was far too young. Barely out of short trousers."

My heart was racing so fast that I felt I'd have been able to see it moving my t-shirt up and down. Ultimately, I was angry with a number of things. Only one of them was that my dad had spoken to a journalist. The rest – me being pregnant outside of wedlock, my mother dying, my sister dying, the patronising letter I'd had from my boss, inviting me into work for a catch up – were all things outside of his control. He was my scapegoat and he knew it, taking my anger and criticism in exchange for spending time with me. It was sad, really.

Before I knew what was happening, my father had pulled me into a hug as I wept, soaking his shoulder with my tears and most probably my snot too. I cried and cried until I had nothing left inside of me to give.

"You should know one more thing though, Soph," he said into my ear as I sniffled. "I had a phone call from Frank Perry just before you got here. He's retired now. Got a bad leg too, apparently. Anyway, he's read the article himself and he wants to meet me."

"Why?"

"To discuss the case. It won't be anything official. Like I say, he's not in the force anymore. But he still wants to talk to me. He said he can die happily when he knows that bastard is locked up for what he did to her."

"Why are you doing this?" I whispered, pulling myself away from him. "Why can't you just let it go? Some things are never meant to be found out. I've accepted that. Why can't you?"

"Because she's my daughter, Sophie," he croaked, his voice catching. "And I let her down. You might not understand that now, but come to me when your baby's born and you'll know. You'll just know."

Chapter Seven

"This is ridiculous," I muttered, as we climbed into a mottled grey lift which had the intangible scent of piss in the air. There was a young girl leant against the wall of the lift, no older than sixteen, with a toddler lay in a well-worn pushchair, kicking her chubby little legs. The mother had a definite bump protruding over her tracksuit bottoms. Mentally, I calculated how much further along she was than me and shivered when I thought she was the type of person most people pictured when they heard the words *single mother*. Except I wasn't a single mother, I reminded myself. I was a single woman. I had a "baby daddy". He was just engaged to somebody else.

I wasn't sure which was worse.

Swallowing hard, I tried to ignore the puddle to the left of me, convinced I'd located the source of the smell. The lift doors closed, engulfing the four of us in darkness as the light above us crackled and occasionally sparked. The toddler started whinging and her mother leaned down to her, handing her a bottle. The bottle was see through and the liquid was a dark brown. I cringed as I realised she was giving her two year old Coca Cola. That wasn't the worst part. As the lift stopped at the sixth floor and she heaved the pushchair out, I saw definite marks on her scrawny arms. Track marks.

I'd never been to the Mercer Estate before in my life. I'd expected it to be rough but I hadn't pictured it quite as bad as it was, as I tilted my head to one side to read the hastily scrawled graffiti on the lift wall (*"Megan <3 Tommy 2k17"*). Growing up, we'd had next to no money but we were always clean, with our mother supervising our nightly baths and stuffing our pudgy arms down clean shirt sleeves every morning.

The lift stopped on the thirteenth floor and we got out, immediately facing a group of teenage boys. It was a Tuesday afternoon. I couldn't fathom why they weren't in school. Eyeballing us as we walked past, they called something out to me. Whilst it was intended to be complimentary, I felt my cheeks flush and my pace quickened.

"Here it is," Dad murmured, as we approached a khaki coloured door with the number 64 written on it. One lone hanging basket dangled precariously next to the door. Whatever had been inside it was long gone, leaving just soil and remains behind. I shook my head to rid myself of the thought of my sister's body in Griffin Woods.

"Are you sure you're alright?" Dad asked, frowning at me again. He'd quizzed me on the journey over, lecturing me about my breakfast choice that morning (Coco Pops and a packet of Quavers). I didn't have chance to answer as the door opened, creaking noisily.

Frank Perry had always been a large man in all senses of the word. He was well over six feet tall and easily twenty stone when he was investigating my sister's disappearance. Whilst he'd noticeably withered with age, his stomach had bulged significantly. His belly button pressed against his too tight T-shirt as he wobbled, putting his weight on his walking stick.

"A fondness of Chinese takeaways," he admitted with a rueful grin when he caught me looking. "And a bottle of red wine a night."

It was like looking into the future.

"Tea? Coffee?" he said, turning on his heel and leading us through the hall and into the living room. One tiny television stood resolute on a stand with just one sad armchair plonked in front of it. Despite the beaming faces coming from the numerous frames dotted around the room, I got the distinct impression that Frank Perry rarely had any visitors. The thought pulled at my chest as I realised my father often went weeks, sometimes months, without seeing people. I remembered picking him up from the supermarket once when he'd been asked to leave as he was so intoxicated. "I only wanted to chat," he'd said, hiccupping. It embarrassed me at the time as I stuffed him into the back of my car with an empty carrier bag for the inevitable vomit. It sickened me as I stood in Frank Perry's bare and lifeless flat.

"Do me a favour, doll, and pull out the spare fold up chairs from the kitchen. It's not often I have such a gathering," he smiled.

The two chairs weren't really heavy so I pulled them through and propped them up before turning on my heel to fill the kettle.

"Don't worry about that, love. I can be Mother," he called out.

"It's fine. How do you take your tea?"

"Milky, with lots of sugar," he grinned. His face was the colour of badly mixed blackcurrant ice cream. His clothes were outdated. His flat was tidy but sparse. This was a man in need of attention, I thought to myself, and immediately cursed his children for neglecting their father.

I busied myself making the tea, taking my time because I didn't particularly want to start a conversation surrounding my dead sister. There wasn't enough milk to make tea for all three of us, so I had mine black. I felt guilty putting the empty milk carton in the recycling bin, knowing it would be difficult for Frank to get to the shop to pick up some more.

"There's some custard creams in the biscuit tin. Cupboard near the kettle," Frank's voice instructed me from the next room.

It didn't surprise me that the biscuit tin was well stocked, and I selected a handful and placed them on a little side plate which I took back into the living room on a tray with the tea. We were silent as I passed the mugs around. No one reached for the biscuits.

"I must say, I was surprised when you agreed to see me," Frank said, finally, squinting behind his glasses at my father. "The last time we met, you called me a sanctimonious little shit."

"I'm sorry," my father said, gruffly, clearing his throat. "I was…" His voice trailed off and he looked down at his tea.

"You were grieving the loss of your child who had been taken from you in the worst possible way," smiled Frank. "You're forgiven."

"What made you think it was me?" Dad asked, quietly.

Frank thought about his answer before he spoke, reaching out for a biscuit and nibbling the ends, absentmindedly.

"Over eighty percent of child murders are at the hands of a parent."

"There must have been more to it than that."

"Aye. There was."

The atmosphere changed. Dad shifted uncomfortably in his seat.

"Such as?"

"A few things. On the night that your daughter went missing, no one could account for your movements. There was a period of around ninety minutes where you disappeared off the radar. You turned up hours later than your wife expected. You were sozzled. Uniform stated that you were perturbed in some way."

Nodding, Dad sipped his tea, even though it was much too hot. He didn't even seem to notice.

"I understand now that you were having sex in Cassandra Blenkinsop's house. You had an alibi. Your car was captured by ANPR cameras crossing the bridge near her house just before and after that ninety minute period. Your story checked out. My apologies if I hurt your feelings," said Frank, smiling, "but it was my job to find the man responsible for your daughter's death. I had to explore all avenues."

Sixty seconds of total silence passed, only slightly spoiled by Frank's stomach gurgling. He didn't seem to notice as he dunked another biscuit in his tea.

"I've lived a half life since 2005," Dad said, quietly, his eyes staring firmly down at his mug of tea. "I stopped living the day Beth died. I've tried my best to move on. I know it's boring for people to have to listen to. Subjected to. That's what my brother said to me once when I spoke about Beth. He said he felt he was being subjected to by having to listen to me talk about her. Deep down, I think people grow tired of listening. They nod, they smile, they make all the right noises and say all the right words but really... they're tired. I've been in a dark place for a long time. I've drank myself into a stupor more times than I care to admit, just in an attempt to forget about this black hole, this never-ending pain in my chest. I won't be able to rest until I know that the bastard – the slimy, shitty excuse of a man – who killed my child is punished. This will be the death of me, I know it. I need answers, Frank. Now more than ever."

His words echoed around the tiny room, bouncing off the framed photographs and into the abyss.

"Why now?" Frank asked, softly.

"Sophie's having a baby. I'll be a grandfather soon. Her mother passed away recently. Aside from our Daniel, I'm all she has," he said, simply. Quietly. His words touched me, bringing a solid lump to my throat.

"Congratulations," Frank beamed at me. "Wonderful news. I'm sorry to hear about your mother, though. Sue was a lovely lady. Such a tragic set of circumstances."

"I've always hated it when people – often total strangers –

would describe my sister's death as being tragic. The word *tragic* implies a catastrophe. An accident. A devastating event. A child drowning in a swimming pool is a tragedy. A child being knocked down by a bus is a tragedy. A child being abducted from their school, taken to a nearby woods, raped and murdered by a stranger is not tragic. It was *horrific*. It was unfair. It was evil, calculated and criminal. But to liken that set of circumstances to a tragedy sets my teeth on edge. The Titanic sinking was a tragedy. Something unexpected and awful that nobody could prevent. My sister's murder was intentional."

I hadn't realised I'd spoken aloud. Frank looked uncomfortable as he shifted in his seat. My dad didn't seem to notice I'd spoken. He was still eyeballing his tea.

"I'm sorry, pet," Frank murmured and I immediately felt sick.

"No. It's fine. You've got nothing to apologise for. It was tragic in a sense. My mother died without knowing who killed her daughter. That's tragic," I muttered, wiping away unexpected tears from my cheeks.

"There's tissues in the kitchen."

I could feel my stomach starting to stir. I made my excuses for fresh air, blaming some ill-timed morning sickness, and left them to it as I burst onto the corridor. It was stiflingly hot in Frank's flat, the thick air clogging my lungs. Before I had chance to process it, I was stood in the lift and making my way back out the way I'd come. The fresh air was welcome and I gulped it down gratefully before heading to the little convenience store situated further down the street. I filled my basket with essentials – bread, butter, milk, tea bags, washing up liquid, toilet roll and cereal – before foisting a fistful of cash at the young Asian man on the till and walking the two minute walk back to the block of flats.

Letting myself in, I saw that the living room was empty except for the two additional chairs and the three mugs, seeming like intruders. What was my dad thinking, barging into this old man's house? I thought, as I put the shopping away in what I hoped were the right cupboards.

"Ah, there you are," Dad said, walking out of a room next to the living room. "Frank's just been digging out copies of the reports from Beth's case."

"I had someone round here a couple of years back," Frank said, his breathing heavy as he lowered his vast body into his chair. He took a handkerchief out of his trouser pocket and dabbed at his brow. "Someone working on cold cases. Must have been about two, three years back now. Nice girl, she was. Pregnant. Little bit ditsy. And I got the impression they'd palmed her off with something to do until she went off on maternity leave. She made copies of everything for me. Think she felt a bit sorry for me, actually. She never found him though. No one ever did."

"So, where do we start?" Dad asked.

Frank laughed, wheezing. "Wherever you like, son. I've got copies of virtually everything here, except for copies of the phone calls and text messages and what have you. You'll only get your hands on those if you go to the police and the case is opened again for investigation."

"Is that likely to happen?"

Shrugging, Frank said, "Possibly. The murder of a child is so horrific that it's terrible when it goes unsolved. But they might not see a point. It'll cost them to re-open the case and it's already been looked at so many times that it's likely to be dismissed."

"Who would I need to speak to in order to get it re-opened?" Dad asked.

"The detective chief inspector of cold cases. A Robert Muir. He's a nice enough chap, but he's about twelve. His father's Dickie Muir so you take a wild guess at how he climbed the greasy pole."

"Would you speak to him for me? I could come with you," Dad offered, his eyes glittering. "I want to look at everything. Start right from the beginning. A fresh pair of eyes."

"It's worth a try," Frank nodded. "Meanwhile, you take those boxes back with you and do with them what you will."

We stood up and made our way back to the front door, our undrunk teas standing out like beacons. Dad hesitated, clearing his throat gruffly. "Thanks, Frank. For everything. I know how much you tried. I appreciate it."

"Thirty eight years I worked on the force," Frank said, not really to anyone in particular. "And I've never forgotten Beth Maguire. I always thought I'd get him. But he was the one who got away. Bastard."

Chapter Eight

"When do you think you'll be back then, Sophie? Hmm?"

Chris Sheridan was the sort of man who meant well but never quite understood how to communicate with actual human beings. His flaming red hair didn't help. It always gave the impression that he was angry. He knew this and he tried desperately to tame the ginger by adding copious amounts of gel to it. I always wondered what his wife did when she was kissing him. She couldn't run her hands through his hair, I thought. It was far too gloopy.

"Sophie?" he said again, nervously clearing his throat. It was clear that Chris hadn't wanted to host this meeting and had probably tried to pass the buck to some poor sod in HR. However, as my direct line manager, it fell under his responsibilities. Awkwardly, he shifted the knot of his tie and cleared his throat again. "Do you think you'll be back on Monday once your compassionate leave has come to an end?"

"Do I have much choice?"

"Well, if you don't think you're ready," he began and cleared his throat again. It was beginning to annoy me. "The thing is, we've got a meeting booked in next week to talk about – to talk about the possibility of redundancy."

My stomach dropped.

"What?"

"Nothing definite," he croaked, looking increasingly uncomfortable. "It's just a consultation. An opportunity to ask any burning questions."

"I don't have any burning questions because I didn't have a clue this was happening."

"You haven't been in work for almost six weeks," Chris pointed out.

"Oh, I'm so sorry for my mother dying," I fired back.

Chris shifted in his seat, weighing up his options. Before he could say another word, I dropped my bombshell.

"I'm ten weeks pregnant."

"Really? God. I mean, that's terrific. Wonderful news. Congratulations. This must be such a happy time for you," he stammered, wiping his desk as though there was something on there he needed to get rid of. Me, I thought coldly.

"Considering that my mum's just dropped dead and I've just been told that I could be about to lose my job, I'd say it was far from a happy time, Chris, but thanks all the same."

I knew I was being a bitch but I couldn't help it. I was like a lion, sensing weak prey. Chris wasn't prepared for this curveball and he visibly shrank back in his seat.

"Perhaps I ought to consult with HR about this," he suggested weakly and picked up the phone next to his computer.

"Perhaps you should," I agreed. "Meanwhile, I'll get going if it's alright with you. And in answer to your earlier question, no. I'm not ready to come back to work next week. If you can't grant me longer compassionate leave, I'll get a sick note from my doctor. Bye, Chris."

I was getting out of the lift and heading towards the main doors in the foyer when Erica caught up with me, her laptop tucked under her arm and her glasses propping her hair back.

"Did you know?" I asked, unexpectedly annoyed with her.

Perplexed, Erica frowned. "Know what?"

"We're being made redundant," I choked. Why oh why was I filling up with tears? I thought, breathing deeply in an effort to stop them.

Biting her lip, Erica glanced around. No one was in ear shot. "Can you give me five minutes? I'll take an early lunch. I'll meet you in the White Hart."

It was only when I was settled in our usual spot near the bar that I realised it wasn't quite eleven o'clock. I stifled a giggle as I imagined Erica explaining to Brenda the Bitch that she was popping out for her lunch.

Ten minutes later, Erica walked in and without glancing around, instantly slotted into the chair next to me. I'd ordered us both a coffee, even though mine was making my heart race. I hadn't had a proper coffee in weeks. Wordlessly, she sipped hers and smacked her lips in appreciation, a tiny foam moustache barely visible. For reasons unbeknownst to me, I chose not to tell her.

"Right. Spill," I ordered.

"First of all, it's not definite," she began.

"That's exactly what Chris said to me this morning," I rolled my eyes. "Clearly you've swallowed the office policy hook, line and sinker."

"It's true," she insisted, swallowing another mouthful of coffee. "Redundancy is always a last resort. You know that. When I worked at the bank, they talked about it all the time but nothing ever happened. It was mentioned about a month ago in a meeting with the shareholders. I didn't mention it to you at the time because you've had so much going on. I didn't want to add to your already overflowing plate."

"Hang on. What were you doing at a meeting with the shareholders?" I frowned.

Both Erica and I were clerical assistants. The money was okay, but not enough for me to have organic tomatoes from Tesco all the time. We spent our days typing, filing and inputting data with the occasional awkward phone call to deal with. It was mind numbingly boring but the hours were flexible enough for me to have a proper weekend social life. With a jolt, I realised that that was a thing of the past.

Awkwardly, Erica sipped her coffee again, taking her time. "I was offered a six month secondment."

"When was this? What's the secondment for? Why didn't you tell me?" I blurted out. When Erica's face creased in confusion, I realised I'd spoken so quickly that my words were unidentifiable. I repeated my questions.

"I'm Chris's new personal assistant," she said, not quite meeting my eyes. "I was offered the job about six weeks ago and I accepted it. I started a week later."

"Why didn't you tell me?" I repeated. "I take it you're not at risk of redundancy then?"

"No, I'm not," she admitted.

"Is that why Chris offered you the job? To save you from being made redundant?"

"No. He offered me the job before I knew anything about the possibility of redundancies."

"But I bet *he* knew!"

"Maybe he did. I don't know. He doesn't talk to me about anything like that. You know what he's like. Corporate blood through and through, that man. I was kind of hoping he'd start flirting with me. Anything to spice my day up a bit but no such luck," she sighed.

At this, I burst out laughing. "You want Chris Sheridan to flirt with you?"

"Not particularly, but it might make the day go a bit faster. Besides, you know what Brenda the Bitch always says. It's not what you know or who you know, it's who you blow."

"Erica," I scolded good naturedly as I chortled into my coffee. "I can't believe you didn't tell me about your new job. Or the redundancies!"

"Like I said, you've had a lot on your plate. Your mum died, then you had the funeral, then you found out you were pregnant and then you found out that the father of your child is marrying someone else. I didn't feel I should burden you with the news of my meagre pay rise. Anyway, let's move on to more important things. How are things going with your sister's investigation?"

Rolling my eyes, I began to describe the events of the previous evening.

Sprawled out on my living room floor, Dad was rifling through boxes upon boxes of files and paperwork. Utterly defiant and believing that no good would come from trudging everything up again, I had refused to help and instead I watched an over the top trashy reality TV show which I knew Dad despised. Not that he seemed particularly bothered by the show or in my lack of interest. He was fixated on the case files in front of him. He had used Sellotape to stick several A4 pieces of paper together, which he then used blue tack to stick to my wall. He'd started writing a timeline of events on the paper, starting with Beth and me leaving the house on the morning of 31st October 2005.

"The only problem is, we don't really have a good account of her movements that day," I explained to Erica, warming my hands on my now half empty mug. "We know she got on the school bus at one minute past eight. We know she walked through the school gates at twenty five past eight."

"Which is when the photograph was taken?" Erica interjected.

Nodding, I said, "Yes. The infamous photo."

My dead sister had been dubbed the girl in the mustard coat after a photograph of her emerged the day after she went missing. Taken by her school friend on a pink digital camera, Beth was walking into the school grounds, grinning and laughing. Her mustard yellow coat was hauntingly noticeable. It was that which we clung to in those early days. It was easily distinguishable from the sea of navy, black and grey coats which the other kids wore. You could have seen Beth coming a mile off.

Chillingly, Beth's coat was never found. Her body was found in Griffin Woods. She was dressed in her school uniform but with no coat. Every time I pictured her lying there, I had to swallow hard to rid myself of the lump in my throat. I always wondered if she'd been cold.

It was because of her mustard coat that we knew she'd been taken from school by someone in a car. The school's CCTV had been poor but it had captured her coming into the school, like a mustard beacon in a flood of darkness. It didn't capture her coming out. The school were nauseatingly apologetic at the time. Not all of the cameras actually worked. They were deterrents, set up to look menacing and official, but they weren't all working. Only three of them worked and it was the one on the side of the school's entrance which had captured Beth coming in. There was only one plausible explanation for the cameras failing to detect her exit. Beth had left the school via the back gate near to the car park and was taken by someone waiting in a car.

"We know she was in all of her classes all day," I went on. "We know she didn't leave school with any friends because she was meant to be staying for the Halloween party but then told a friend that she was going to nip home to pick something up. We always assumed someone pulled her into their car after waiting in the school car park or just outside it. CCTV was bloody useless, with half the cameras not even working. The police contacted the nearby residents for information about any of the cars which had driven past at any point that day, but no one seemed to know anything. Most people were at work but the ones who weren't hadn't seen anything. I don't know what the police were expecting to be honest. It would be terribly coincidental if a stay at home mum or a couple of old dears enjoying their retirement were able to say that they'd seen a man acting suspiciously in a car and that they'd jotted down his number plate."

"It might be worth knocking on their doors again though," Erica said, thoughtfully.

"You really think people will remember something now, thirteen years later?"

"Possibly. You know what people are like. They don't like to make a fuss, do they? It's like when Reg Bartram was being investigated for sexual harassment at work," she began. "HR asked me if there was anything I'd noticed or seen. I said no. It was only a few weeks later that I remembered he'd made a weird comment to me about one of the interns when we were in the lift. I mean, by that point he'd already been turfed out – and rightly so, the dirty bastard. But do you see what I'm saying? People don't know that they know anything. And the ones that *do* know something might have been too frightened to say anything at the time. It was a big story."

"You're telling me," I scoffed.

"It might be a good place to start. And have you thought about semen?"

"About what?"

"Semen," she continued, finishing her coffee. "The traces of semen that were found…inside her."

"Funnily enough, no, I've not been sat here thinking about the semen which was found inside my dead sister's body," I hissed, nervously glancing around in case anyone was in earshot.

"And I totally get that," Erica soothed. "But isn't it worth getting a sample of that – I don't know - sent off to a lab or something? Surely there's got to be more they can do nowadays, what with technology having advanced by the bucket load."

"It doesn't really work like that. We don't have access to this guy's semen sample. The police will have that."

"Oh." Erica looked disappointed.

"We do have a list of people who presented themselves for a voluntary elimination screening," I pointed out.

Pouting her lips in a brooding manner, Erica said, "Does that mean what I think it means? The police got a load of men from the village to…provide a sample of their semen?"

Chortling, I said, "No. They put out a notice asking men over the age of eighteen to provide a voluntary sample of DNA. A saliva swab, if I remember rightly. Dad had to give one." It didn't stop the press from hounding him and calling him a murderer though.

"Well, if you can work out who's missing off the list, then you could start asking them questions," Erica pointed out.

"Such as?"

"Such as why the hell wouldn't you provide a DNA sample if it meant clearing you for child murder? Or, even better, where were you on the night Beth Maguire went missing?"

"I don't know," I murmured, picturing burly middle aged men slamming the door in my face – or worse.

"He's out there, Soph," she said, quietly. "And he will get caught. You can only hide something this big for so long. His time's running out. I just know it."

We shrugged on our coats and scarves and left a handful of change in the dish on our table as we headed out into the bitter cold. Gulping down the fresh air felt good but I wondered dimly if I was going to throw up my much appreciated proper coffee.

"The night she went missing," Erica said, suddenly. "Didn't you say you could hear the front door slamming when you were in the bath that night?"

I nodded.

"It was trick or treaters. I must have misheard the noise. It wasn't the door opening and closing. It was just little terrors knocking on it over and over again."

"What if it wasn't? I know you've always said she was abducted from school. But what if the noise you heard was Beth letting herself into the house and then leaving again?" Erica said, finally.

As much as I wanted to, I couldn't dismiss the thought all day. I said my goodbyes to Erica – finally admitting that she had a slightly foamy upper lip – and booked an emergency doctors appointment. I was surprised to hear that I was able to be squeezed in for later that afternoon. The perks of being pregnant, I thought.

This time, it seemed relatively easy to speak to Doctor Rowena Helsby, who greeted me with a huge toothy smile and batted her preposterously long thick eyelashes. I made sure I said all the right things about me feeling stressed which was affecting my sleep and therefore making me feel drained during what was already a very tiresome time. Smirking, I walked out of the appointment clutching a sick note which stated I wasn't fit for work for at least four weeks.

"Won't you get into some sort of trouble?" Calvin asked that evening, as I served up a huge serving of spaghetti bolognese.

"Why on earth would I get into trouble for being ill?"

"Because you're not ill."

"I'm pregnant," I sniffed. "I'm pregnant and I'm grieving

and I'm possibly about to lose my job."

"You don't know that," he soothed, sprinkling a generous helping of parmesan onto his food. "Anyway, I don't think employers are allowed to fire pregnant women. I'm sure there's some sort of law in place."

"You better hope there is, otherwise you'll be paying for this baby alone."

"Actually, Soph, while we're on this subject, there's something I need to talk to you about."

Calvin shifted uncomfortably in his seat, toying with his pasta but not eating it. I could smell a rat.

"What?"

"I don't think I'll be able to contribute anything financially yet."

"What?" I repeated, dropping my fork and letting it clatter on my plate.

"I'm not saying I won't be buying things for the baby in the future. I'm just saying that right now… I think Lorna would notice. She's being really careful with finances at the minute. She wants to go to Mexico in the new year," he added.

"Please tell me you're joking?"

"No, honestly. I believe it's still rather warm there in winter."

"Sorry, Calvin. I don't think I made myself particularly clear. I wasn't asking if you were joking about the holiday recommendation. I wanted to know if you were joking about you being the sort of father who won't provide for his child. I wanted to know if you were joking about Lorna wanting you to whisk her away on some holiday."

He hesitated.

"Well, I said we could go."

"Why did you say that? You're meant to be telling her about me, Calvin. About the baby. *Our* baby. Or are we just to stay as your dirty little secret, is that it? Don't worry about me. I'm potentially facing redundancy and might not be able to feed myself or our baby, but you get yourself to Mexico and have a lovely time. Bring me back a souvenir, you prick. I can't believe you could be so selfish," I spat, my meal lying forgotten.

"Me being selfish?" he hissed. "Can you hear yourself? You tricked me into getting pregnant. You lied to me."

"I didn't lie to you."

"You weren't honest with me. That's tantamount to lying in my book!" Calvin exclaimed, getting up from his seat at the kitchen table and gesticulating wildly and unnecessarily with his hands.

"Says the man who pretended he didn't have a fiancée for four months," I snapped.

"Is this a bad time?" came a voice, causing the pair of us to stop in our tracks and turn to face the kitchen door. My father had let himself into the house with the key I'd given him just one day earlier, and was stood bashfully witnessing his eldest child having the mother of all rows with the man who had spawned him an illegitimate grandchild.

"No, Mike. I was just leaving," Calvin said pointedly, tugging on his coat and heading into the hall with me at his heels.

"Calvin," I said, as he opened the front door and headed onto my doorstep.

"I'll tell her. I'll tell her on Saturday. She's away with work until then," he muttered, his eyes unblinking. He turned on his heel and began walking down the path from the garden to the street, before stopping and turning back. "You can think whatever you like about me, Sophie. You can think I'm a liar for not telling you about Lorna. And you'd be right. I was wrong to not tell you about her. You can call me a prick for trying to have my cake and eat it. You can slag me off to your mates, your brother, your dad, whoever you want. But don't ever tell me that I'm not the sort of father who will provide for his child. I'm dropping everything for this child. I'm going to go home and plan what to say to someone I've loved for years. Someone I thought I'd marry and have children with one day. I've got to tell her that I've got another woman pregnant and that I'm standing by her. And she'll want nothing more to do with me. I will provide you with money, food, clothes, company, anything you need to make sure that I'm doing the right thing by this baby. Because I'm a decent guy. Please don't ever tell me that I'm being selfish."

And with that, he was gone.

Chapter Nine

"I don't think you realise how big a task that is," Frank Perry said, rubbing his head with his hands.

We were sat in my living room, which had turned into an investigation suite, seemingly overnight. My furniture was hidden under boxes and my laminate flooring had disappeared under empty plates, some with leftover Chinese food congealing. On the walls lay a timeline of events. It started out definitively and ended almost comically empty and vague. It was almost midnight and we'd been sat in the same positions for hours. My back was aching and I stood up and paced around the living room to relieve it.

"It's doable though, isn't it?" Dad persisted, papers clutched in his hands. "Sophie's right. If we've got the list of names of people who willingly gave a DNA sample, that means we have a list of the names of people who didn't. We just don't know their names yet. If we can work out who's missing, we've got a list of men who didn't want to help the police with their investigation. You've got to ask yourself why. Why wouldn't you? What would you have to lose? A child was dead. If finding the person behind her death brought her family just a shred of comfort, you'd march yourself down to that police station and spit in a bloody cup if that's what it took. I did. So did practically everyone I know. Nobody batted an eyelid. As far as most people were concerned, it was just something that needed to be done."

"Why was the screening only open for men over the age of eighteen?" asked Danny, looking at Frank.

"We couldn't ask children to come forward and provide a sample."

"But seeing as how Beth was only thirteen, there's got to be a possibility that her murderer was of a similar age?" Danny frowned. "And seeing as how she was taken from school, there's a good chance the killer was a schoolboy, surely?"

"Possibly," Frank nodded. "But statistically speaking, the murder of a child is usually committed by an adult."

"Why wasn't this done earlier?" I asked. "The police have had the list of men who willingly gave a DNA sample. They've had the list since January 2006 when the samples were given. Why didn't anything get done then?"

Slowly, Frank said, "It didn't seem like a good plan at the time. I agree that we have a list of men who are not responsible for Beth's murder. But we don't know that the man we're looking for is from Arlington Heath. We don't know that he's over the age of eighteen, like Danny says. We couldn't extend the search and ask any male of any age from any area within a fifteen mile radius to provide a sample. It was suggested by one of my investigating officers at the time. But it felt like a needle in a haystack."

"Let's start racking our brains. We need to think of all the men who are missing from that list. Then we'll split into teams of two and visit them and interview them."

"You're talking about a lot of men who probably don't live in Arlington Heath anymore. Some of these men are probably dead by now," Frank pointed out.

"It's a starting point, surely?" Dad continued. Frank sighed. Dad grinned, knowing he'd defeated him. Fumbling with sheets of paper, he handed three pieces to me. "Those are the names. How many are there?"

Eyes whirring down the pages, I totted up the amount. "One hundred and ninety eight."

"How many men were living in the village when Beth was murdered?" Dad asked Frank, but it was Danny that answered after holding up a sheet of paper in his hands. "Two hundred and thirty one."

"Which means there were thirty three men who didn't come forward with a DNA sample," Dad calculated. He whipped the lid off a black marker pen and stuck another piece of paper to the wall with blue tac. "Right, let's think. Which men were living in the village at the time? We'll match them against the list and whoever's missing goes on the new list."

It was easier than we thought. Living in Arlington Heath was like being in a gated community. Between us, we knew every house on our street and the streets on either side, and reeled off the names of the men who had lived there. Every single name already appeared in the list of people who'd provided a sample. We moved onto the next street. Then the street after that. Then the street after that. In some cases, the names meant nothing to me or Danny but Dad was confident in his choices.

After half an hour of running names past one another, we had a list of twenty nine men who hadn't given a sample. My father's face had turned the colour of gone off meat as he paced back and forth, desperately trying to think of the missing four names.

"Instead of thinking of houses, why don't we think of occupations?" suggested Frank.

"Yes!" Dad agreed. "Let's take a mental walk through the village as it was in 2005. We've got the barbers on the left, the butchers next door, the doctors opposite…"

"Is Doctor O'Hara on there?" Danny asked me. Consulting the list, I confirmed he was, while my father scolded my brother – "We've already checked him, Daniel!" "I'm sorry. I'm shattered!"

But it was as if the thought of the rosy cheeked Doctor O'Hara had sparked something inside my brain. I blurted out, "What was the name of the new doctor? The bald one? Didn't he start round about the same time Beth went missing?"

"Doctor Keeling?" Dad asked, shaking his head. "That was years later, love."

"How can you be so sure?"

"The week he moved to the village was the week the reconstruction of Beth's disappearance was shown on Crimewatch. Doctor Keeling was in the pub that night and I remember him introducing himself to me. He asked me about the reconstruction. I remember it vividly. No one else spoke to me all night," Dad said, quietly.

"This is so hard," Danny murmured.

"You know who'd be really good at this?" I asked the room at large.

"Your mother," said both Dad and Frank at the same time. I smiled, catching a glazed look in Dad's eyes.

It was true. Before the untimely death of her daughter, our mother had been a definite curtain twitcher. Working in a supermarket in Hawleybrook meant she came home every night with mindless gossip that nobody really cared about but listened to because it was important to Mum. When we'd been small, she was a stay at home parent, never missing a school play or assembly. After dropping us at the school gates, Mum would often invite the other mothers back to our house for tea and coffee. Everybody knew Sue Maguire. And Sue Maguire knew everybody.

It was another hour before we'd worked out three of the

four missing men. We'd had to talk Dad out of putting a plea on social media for help with the last missing name.

"Just think of the press buzzing round," I whined. "They'd know what we were doing and they'd come knocking on my door. We don't need that sort of attention, not now."

It was almost one o'clock in the morning. We were all stifling yawns and the living room had begun to smell like unwashed bodies and, of course, food.

"Perhaps that's enough for tonight," Frank suggested, and he struggled to bend down to pick up his empty plate. There was no chance that Frank would have left any sweet and sour pork to congeal on his plate.

"Let me do that," I insisted, taking the plate from him and collecting the others. I took them through to the kitchen, filling the washing up bowl with scorching hot water and bubbles. A couple of trips to and from the living room with cups, mugs and glasses meant I took up the post of chief washer upper and I took solace in the work, mindlessly scrubbing at the plates until they gleamed. It was therapeutic and I became lost in the rhythm of it until I felt a hand touch the small of my back. Turning, I saw my brother by my side, his forehead creased with worry.

"What is it?" I asked, drying my hands on a tea towel.

"I've just worked out who's missing off that list. It's so obvious. I can't believe we didn't realise he was missing," Danny murmured in a low voice.

"Who is it?"

Danny, clouded with worry and something else I couldn't quite work out, appeared to visibly shrink in front of me.

"It's Uncle Tony."

Chapter Ten

Tony Maguire was the sort of man you'd describe as being rough. He was five years younger than his brother, our dad. He'd lived with our Nan until he was in his thirties. Neither me nor my siblings had ever known our grandad, who'd died when we were little, so Nan's house was always known as "Nan and Uncle Tony's house".

Tony was a painter and decorator by trade, but it was clear to anyone who knew him that he also liked to dabble in anything a bit untoward. When I was in primary school, he'd been selling meat door to door. God knows where he'd got his hands on thirty beef joints, but he sold them all and used the money to pay for a new tattoo, some beer and a packet of Benson and Hedges. He was the only person I knew who smoked during my childhood. Even when he finally moved out from living with Nan and got himself a flat in Hawleybrook, his clothes and his furniture always stank of stale smoke. My nose wrinkled with the thought.

When Beth and I were in high school, he would offer us alcohol. Not a sip of wine or a swig of beer like Mum or Dad did. Uncle Tony was happy to buy us alcohol from the shop, providing that he took payment in the form of one can.

As I got older, it became clear to him that I thought very little of him. It wasn't particularly his lifestyle, as I led a very similar one during my university years. I simply had nothing to say to him. Our family spent the years from 2005 to 2010 in a fog. Every day was like wading through treacle, the most simple of tasks seemingly insurmountable. Even when I moved away for university, I had to remind myself to complete basic human functions such as showering daily, brushing my teeth, taking my clothes out of the washing machine and hanging them on the clothes horse.

The only person seemingly unaffected by Beth's death was her uncle. He went to her funeral and he cried and he helped to carry her coffin and he handed round plates of sandwiches and sausage rolls at our house at her wake. He got drunk. So did everyone else. He was found by my mum, pissed as a fart, crying in our back garden. He'd been too drunk to walk home and had slept it off on the sofa, keeping us all awake with his snoring. After that, we didn't see him for weeks. Christmas came and went. Then the annual New Year's Eve party he always hosted at Nan's house didn't materialise. He stopped returning Dad's calls. He didn't pop round like he'd used to.

He gradually faded out of the picture, sporadically bobbing up here and there at important functions, like Nan's funeral in 2007, where he'd ended up scrapping with Dad. Uncle Tony had come off worse, with a broken nose and a black eye. The police had been called by someone who worked at the church, but Dad didn't get arrested as Uncle Tony had refused to press charges. My father had never told me what they were fighting about, but as he was very often drunk, I'd assumed he was to blame.

Tony married a Polish woman he'd met on holiday when I was about twenty five. The woman's name was Magda, and she had three children from a previous marriage. Tony remained childless. They'd married abroad eight months after meeting, telling nobody their plans, and moved into a house in the city. "The Arlington Heath curse," Mum had said at the time. I had only ever met Tony's wife Magda once before when I'd bumped into her and Tony as me and Mum were out Christmas shopping one year. Tony had seemed awkward, uncomfortable almost, and was quick to turn down our offer of a Christmas drink. He'd told us he had too much on. I was surprised at the time to realise I'd felt relieved when he said that.

It was the morning after Danny's discovery that our uncle was missing off the list of people who'd presented themselves for a voluntary DNA sample when we drove round to Uncle Tony's house.

"Have you been before, Dad?" I asked, glancing at the sat nav and indicating left.

"Yes," he replied. "Twice."

"Does it smell of smoke?"

"No, actually, it was incredibly clean. Magda seems very house proud."

As if to substantiate Dad's comment, Magda came to the door wearing an apron, with a little sprinkling of flour on her arm. She looked from Dad to Frank to me again with confusion. I realised from an outsider's perspective, we looked like we were impersonating the Hardy boys with our sullen expressions and enormous energy.

"Mike!" she exclaimed, smiling warmly.

"Hello, Magda. Can we come in?"

"Of course, of course," she murmured, stepping back and holding the door open for us. The house was lovely – all oak furniture, laminate flooring and shaggy rugs. The radio was on in the kitchen and classical music was playing.

"I've just been doing some baking with Liam," she said, apologetically, gesturing to her apron and flour sprinkling. "Can you take over from here? We've got visitors," she said to an unknown person hidden within the depths of the kitchen. "Would anyone like a cup of tea or coffee?" she added, politely.

We all said no. It felt uncomfortable accepting cups of tea and exchanging pleasantries with someone whose husband we were about to grill for information about the death of a child.

"Is Tony in?" Dad asked. Straight to the point. I knew he wouldn't want to waste any time. When we'd told him that the missing person on our list was his brother, his face had dropped. Then it turned red very quickly, as Dad was stuffing his arms into his coat sleeves and rifling around in his jeans pockets for his car keys. We'd managed to talk him out of storming round to Uncle Tony's house. It was almost two o'clock in the morning. With the promise of visiting him the next day, he'd backed down. As it had been so late, I gave Frank a lift home and offered my father the spare room in my house. He'd accepted it but I could hear him up pacing the room all night.

"He's just nipped out," Magda said, her eyes darting from Dad to me, then to Frank. "Do you want me to call him?"

"Yes, I think you should," Dad said, sharply.

"Has something happened?" she asked, looking alarmed.

Dad couldn't answer. Instead, he stood up and walked to the other side of the room, rubbing his head with his hands. He was agitated, nervous, angry. I hadn't seen him like that since the early days of Beth's death.

It was Frank who took the position of the messenger. "My name's Frank Perry. I'm retired now but in my heyday, I was Detective Chief Inspector Frank Perry. I was the lead investigating officer in the disappearance and murder of Beth Maguire."

"Who?" Magda frowned.

"My daughter," Dad said, not able to look at her. "My daughter. Sophie and Daniel's sister. Tony's niece. She died in

2005. Has Tony never talked about her?"

Magda shook her head, wordlessly glancing at us all again. She was nervous. Her leg kept tapping up and down but she was seemingly unaware.

"Mike's daughter – Tony's niece – was thirteen when she was abducted from school, raped and murdered. Her body was found in Griffin Woods two days after she disappeared," Frank calmly explained. Magda's eyes were as wide as saucers. "We're here to ask Tony some questions."

"Questions about what?" Magda asked, her forehead wrinkled in confusion.

"When Beth's body was found, there were traces of semen inside her. We were unable to get a match on the police database, so we asked all men living in Arlington Heath at the time to come forward to provide a voluntary DNA sample. A cheek swab," Frank explained, gesturing to the side of his face. "We now realise that Tony didn't come forward to give a sample."

"So, you're here to ask him for a sample?" Magda asked, uncertainly.

"Yes," said Dad, quickly.

"If Tony's willing to give us a cheek swab today, that would be wonderful," Frank smiled, the skin around his eyes crinkling. "But right now, we'd be satisfied with him answering a few of our questions. So perhaps that phone call isn't such a bad idea, love."

Magda didn't get to make the phone call. She didn't need to. The front door opened and closed less than ten seconds later, and I heard my uncle whistling and carrying a plastic bag. He walked into the living room to find his brother stood staring at him, his niece sat solemnly in an armchair and a perfect stranger sat on his couch next to his wife. The whistling ceased. The carrier bag stopped jauntily swinging through the air. Tony looked worried.

"What's going on? What's happened?" he asked, echoing his wife's words.

Dad opened his mouth to begin speaking but one look from Frank told him it wasn't a good idea.

"My name's Frank Perry," he said, calmly. "I don't know if you remember me. I'm retired now but I was the lead investigating officer on the investigation of Beth Maguire's murder."

If silence had a sound, it would be the crackle of electricity. In the nanosecond it took for Frank's words to reach Tony's brain, his body drained of blood, leaving him pale and thinner looking than he had just one moment earlier. Dad watched him, a sneer affixed to his mouth.

"Right. Yeah. I think I remember."

"Do you, Tony? Because I don't actually remember you having much to do with the investigation into my daughter's murder. Your niece's murder," Dad added.

"Sorry, what's this about?" Tony asked, his eyes flickering towards Dad every few seconds.

"We've been looking into the case files of the investigation and we've noticed something which we're hoping you can provide some clarity on," Frank went on. "In January 2006, the police asked for all adult men living in Arlington Heath to provide a DNA sample in order for them to be eliminated from our enquiries. Quite a few people came forward. In fact, almost two hundred men came forward to give us a DNA sample. However, you didn't. We were hoping you could explain why."

Tony shifted his weight from one foot to the other, the blue plastic bag still dangling from his hands. "I don't know."

"You don't know what?" Frank asked.

"I don't know why I didn't give a sample."

"Were you aware of the opportunity to provide a sample?"

"Of course I was aware of it," sniffed Tony. "There were posters stuck up all through the village. It was all over the news. I couldn't not be aware of it."

"So why didn't you go?"

"I've just told you. I don't know," he muttered, his gaze dropping from Frank to his feet.

"You see, this is what I don't understand," Dad said, his voice barely louder than a whisper. He spoke with his teeth bared, like he was a panther, ready to attack. "I remember talking to Mum about it. She specifically told me that you'd got time off work to go and give your sample. And I remember thinking, that's good of O'Brien to give you the time off but why wouldn't he because after all, it was your niece that was dead. Why would our mother make that up?"

"I don't..."

Tony's muffled response was interrupted by Dad, who roared: "Don't start with the 'I don't know' bollocks, Tony. You do know. You're an adult. Stop messing around and tell the bloody truth."

"I *am* telling the truth," Tony snapped. "I don't know what you lot are getting at. I hope to God you're not about to accuse me of anything. You'll live to regret that if you are."

"Is that a threat?" snapped Dad, his top lip still sneering. "I've not forgotten what an angry man you used to be, Tony. All those fights you got into as a kid. You've got a temper, that's for sure."

Magda shifted uncomfortably on the couch.

"Everyone has a scrap when they're a teenager. It doesn't make me a bad person. And it certainly doesn't make me a murderer, Mike."

"Go on then. If you're innocent – if you have nothing to hide – you'll give us a sample today. It'll take ten seconds to get a cheek swab," said Dad.

The room plunged into an empty silence.

"If this was you – if this was your child, your daughter, one of Magda's three – I wouldn't think twice about eliminating myself from the enquiry," Dad said. "It's just something you do because it needs to be done. No one wants to be known as the nonce who refused to give a sample. People will start to talk. They'll start to ask questions. Like why would the uncle of the girl who was raped and murdered not want to help the police and rule himself out in the process? Did you know that the vast majority of murdered children are killed by someone they know? More often than not, it's a parent but what if it was another family member? An uncle, for example."

"I didn't want to, alright?" Uncle Tony roared. "I'd been involved in some stuff in the past. Bad stuff. I didn't want it catching up with me. I knew if I gave a sample, there was a chance I could get done for something else."

"Bull shit," Dad sneered.

"Bad stuff? What bad stuff?" Magda whispered, horrified.

"God, nothing like that," Tony said, gasping for breath. "Jesus Christ. I'm no angel but I'm no murderer either. And my own niece? For God's sake."

"I don't understand you," I said, everyone turning to look

at me. Up until that moment, I'd not spoken a word. "Your niece had been killed in the most horrific way. She was thirteen. A child. And she'd been raped and strangled and left in the woods for days for someone to find while he was out walking his dog. It tore us apart. Her death tore us to shreds. We've not been the same since. If that was my niece, I'd do anything – *anything* – to help find the person responsible. If that meant I might get my comeuppance for previous misdemeanours, so be it. You're unbelievable."

"I don't know what you want me to say," Tony said, slowly.

"What I find weird is that you haven't even told your own wife about Beth," Dad said, not really talking to anyone in particular, but staring fixatedly at the rug. "When you meet someone and you start a relationship, it's normal to talk about your family. Why wouldn't you say anything to Magda about your niece being murdered? After what – three years? – you're telling me it hasn't occurred to you to at least mention her?"

"I didn't see any reason in bringing it all up. It was a long time ago, Mike."

"Maybe to you."

"What do you want me to say?" Tony cried. "Do you want me to say that I'm a shit house? That I'm a coward? That I put my own needs before the needs of my family? I couldn't give a sample. I'm not the same person now that I was twenty five years ago. I've turned a corner. I couldn't give a sample at the time because it was as good as handing myself into the police as far as I was concerned."

"Did you kill my daughter?" Dad spat.

The electric silence descended upon us once more. Magda sat open mouthed, terrified of what was unfolding in front of her.

"You don't understand. I had nothing to do with Beth dying. How could you even think that?" he whispered.

"We don't think that," Frank soothed. "We're just asking some questions. That's all."

"You're not even a police officer anymore! You've said yourself you're retired so why do I have to stand here in my own home and be questioned about something so ludicrously untrue?"

"If you wanted to provide a cheek swab to eliminate yourself, you'd be –"

"Get out. All of you. Get out now!" he shouted.

For a second, I thought my father was about to punch his brother. Instead, breathing heavily, he stormed out of the house, with me and Frank in quick succession. Wasting no time, we bundled into the car. My hand was shaking as I turned on the ignition and put the car into gear, driving away with my legs shaking on the pedals. I drove to the end of the street, turned left and pulled up next to a park, my heart hammering in my chest. I turned the key in the ignition, switching the car off and plummeting us into silence.

No one said anything for a long while. Until –

"It's him," Dad said, quietly. "I can just feel it. He killed her."

Chapter Eleven

"That's it. She knows. I've told her."

It was the following Tuesday evening and I was stood with my front door open, staring at Calvin who was holding an enormous duffel bag in his arms.

"Right," I said, sighing. "You'd better come in then."

Calvin followed me through the hall and into the living room where I'd been lay on the couch with a fleecy blanket wrapped round me watching The Muppets Christmas Carol. To the side of the couch were the cardboard boxes, full to the brim of the case notes from the investigation. We'd given ourselves the night off. It felt as though we'd done nothing but work on the investigation for weeks. To reward myself, I'd ordered a Chinese takeaway and allowed myself a small glass of white wine. It didn't go unnoticed by Calvin, who immediately eyed the wine on the coffee table and looked at me, shaking his head.

"It's one glass," I said, defensively. "I've had a really hard few days. I needed it."

"Well, I've had a barrel of laughs myself," he said, sighing, dumping the duffel bag on the floor and swinging himself onto the armchair.

"Go on then," I instructed, lying back into my previous position and lowering the volume on the TV. "Spill."

"Not much to tell. She came back from her work trip late on Sunday evening. She was due back the day before. I'd sort of talked myself into telling her on the Saturday so the change in plan really threw me. She knew something was up straight away. I must've been nervous because I kept dropping things, forgetting what I'd walked into a room for, burning food when I was cooking. That sort of thing. Then yesterday, I got in from work and she was sat in the kitchen. Crying. She'd found a bright pink hair bobble in my trouser pocket. Your bright pink hair bobble," he added, raising an eyebrow.

"Don't look at me. I didn't plant it there to be found."

"I know. I put it there after you were being sick in the hospital. It still had sick stains on it," he grimaced. "She thought I was having an affair. I knew I couldn't lie to her so I told her the truth. I said I'm not having an affair but I was previously, and that you're pregnant and I'm standing by you. And the baby."

Drawing a sharp intake of breath, I asked, "How did she take it?"

"I'm sat in your living room with a bag full of clothes. What do you think?"

"I'm sorry, Cal," I said, quietly, my cheeks red with shame. "This is all my fault."

Nodding, he said, "Yes. But you didn't know I was engaged. It's my fault too."

"Did you tell her who I was?" I asked.

"She wanted to know your name, where you live, how we met, how long it had been going on for, how far gone you are. The list was endless. In the end, I told her your name and that you're twelve weeks pregnant. I told her there was nothing romantic between us anymore and that we're just two friends having a baby. She asked me to leave. I said I'd book myself into a hotel for a couple of nights to give her some space. She laughed and asked me to move out."

"At least the house is only rented. Makes it all much easier," I pointed out, but Calvin stared at me like I was mad. "Sorry. I know that probably isn't helping."

We were interrupted by a knock on my front door, so I scooped up the ten pound note resting on the coffee table and went to retrieve my Chinese feast.

"There's plenty of food if you're hungry?" I said, dishing up some sweet and sour pork onto a plate.

It was surprisingly comfortable, the two of us sprawled out on the couch with plates of food and containers of more food on the coffee table. He helped himself to a large glass of wine which he drank like medicine, knocking his head back and glugging it down as though it would make him feel better. Perhaps it was the warm glow of the wine, but we found ourselves laughing. I realised sadly that it was the first time I'd laughed in ages.

When I was at school, I was always being told off for laughing and giggling in class. Marie Doran was the worst one for giggling with me. Mrs Daniels, our slightly eccentric form tutor and English teacher, was forever shouting at us and saying: "Oh, I'm sorry, girls. Is my lesson getting in the way of your conversation?" Once I was sixteen and Beth was gone, I stopped laughing. I even stopped smiling, walking round in a bubble of worry and doubt. Frighteningly, it was alcohol that helped me to find the giggly girl inside me, which is perhaps how I ended up hospitalised and having my stomach pumped during my university days.

Of all the things to have happened as a result of my sister dying, not laughing was the one which hurt the most.

"What is it?" Calvin asked me, his eyes searching my face.

"What's what?"

"You've just – I dunno - clammed up or something. Like you've just remembered something you need to do," he described, scraping his plate with his fork, eating the last scraps of rice and balancing the empty plate on the coffee table.

"Oh, it's nothing," I smiled. "I was just thinking about my sister."

He nodded but didn't say anything.

"Sorry. You must be sick of hearing about her by now."

"Not at all. I think it's healthy for you to talk about her. I still can't believe I didn't work out she was your sister. Everyone has heard of Beth Maguire," he said.

"Not everyone. My uncle's wife had never heard of her," I said, and I found myself telling Calvin about the visit to my uncle's house. He listened to the entire story, his eyes wide and unblinking.

"Shit. Do you really think it was your uncle who did it?" he asked.

"I don't know. It's definitely odd, but whether he's the one who killed her... I'm not sure. My dad's never been more convinced of anything in his life though."

"What does the retired copper think?"

"He said it's a possibility but he doesn't think we have enough to go to the police with. They wouldn't re-open the official investigation over it. We'd have to have something more, something bigger."

We sat for a moment in silence, both of us thinking. Until –

"Did your sister have a boyfriend?" Calvin asked.

"No. She was only thirteen."

"That doesn't mean much though, does it? I had my first girlfriend when I was about twelve."

"Alright, Casanova. No need to brag," I smirked and Calvin grinned at me, flashing a glimpse of his straight white teeth. "She didn't have a boyfriend as far as we know but I suppose it's possible. She definitely had a crush. On the morning she went missing, she'd written some initials in the condensation on the bathroom mirror. The letters K and B, or so it looked like. I had to include the story about the initials in my witness statement."

"Can't you get hold of a list of the boys she went to school with and speak to any of them with those initials?" he suggested.

"Frank told us that they did all that years ago when she first died. There was just one child in the school with the initials KB and it was a little Year Seven lad called Kieran Butler who lived in Hawleybrook. The police spoke to him but Frank said it was clear Beth hadn't been having a secret relationship with him. He looked about eight for a start but he was actually in hospital having his tonsils out on the day Beth went missing."

"Maybe KB wasn't a student. Maybe it was a teacher."

Dismissing his suggestion with nothing more than a snort, I rolled my eyes. Hawleybrook High School didn't have any young, good looking teachers like the ones that featured in Australian soap operas. They were old and dowdy and crumbling. There was a youngish PE teacher who came for a term to cover another teacher while he was off sick. But even then, he wasn't particularly attractive.

"I think it's more likely that KB is a popstar or a celebrity," I said, finally. I'd tried Googling the initials to see which famous people existed in Beth's lifetime with might fit the bill but I'd had no luck. I couldn't explain why but it somehow felt important to me to solve the riddle. Whoever KB was had obviously been important enough to Beth for her to have captured their initials on our bathroom mirror, knowing that KB would never see it. It wasn't as though it was a love note. It felt like more of a declaration. An announcement to the world.

Suddenly, I sat bolt up right on the couch, sending my pink cushion flying.

"What? What is it?" Calvin asked.

"All this time, we've assumed that KB was a secret boyfriend or a boy who Beth had a crush on. What if KB was more than just a crush for Beth? What if KB was a sense of identity, a realisation that she wasn't like everyone else? And that finally Beth felt proud and confident enough to declare her feelings for KB to the world?"

"You mean you think KB was a girl?"

"Yes!" I exclaimed. Calvin squinted at me, immediately identifying an error. "I know. Beth was raped. There was definitely a man involved somewhere. But what if I'm right? All this time we've been looking for a man or a boy with the initials K and B, in case he has access to some secret information about Beth, or in case Beth was planning to run away with him."

Then it hit me, in a way I'd only ever experienced when falling asleep and something had jolted me awake.

"What if it wasn't a B? What if it was a number eight?"

"K Eight?" Calvin asked, uncertainly.

"It's like text talk, isn't it? In 2005, it was perfectly acceptable to text someone saying r u ok. Everything was abbreviated. K8. *Kate.*"

Calvin shrugged, but said nothing, evidently frightened of dismissing my suggestion.

"Don't you see?" I persisted.

"I guess it's possible. But wouldn't you know if your little sister had been a lesbian?"

"Not necessarily," I retorted, my mind flitting from one potential scenario to another. "She was thirteen. She was still learning things about herself. Discovering things every day. She might not have known she was a lesbian. Maybe she thought it was just a crush."

"On a girl called Kate?"

"Yes. Exactly."

"Did Beth know someone called Kate?"

"Actually, yes. There was a girl who'd joined our school in the September. She was in Beth's form. She was quite pally with Beth. Her name was Kate...something," I said, wracking my brains to think of her surname.

"And you think she had something to do with your sister's murder?"

"I don't know, but I think it's worth tracking her down. Don't you?"

Chapter Twelve

December arrived, bringing with it an icy wind which we could hear whistling in the trees and a frost which we could feel crunching underfoot in the early hours. Every step taken outside was bitter, with the weather forcing its victims to hide amongst layers of clothing. My ever expanding body had caused me to ditch the contents of my wardrobe, and I found myself begging Erica to accompany me on a Saturday morning shopping trip to find something both comfy and practical to wear.

"It's not even just my stomach," I called out from behind the curtains of the changing room in Next. "It's everything. My boobs could suddenly rival Pamela Anderson's in her Baywatch years and my arse is the size of Calcutta."

"Yeah, I know what you mean," soothed Erica from outside the changing room.

"Cheeky cow," I laughed, throwing open the curtains and standing in front of her, turning to the left, then the right whilst I examined my abdomen. I was wearing dungarees.

"That doesn't look too bad," she commented.

Rolling my eyes, I laughed. "Compliments are terrible when you're pregnant. You're constantly told how big you look and when you try on a new outfit, you're told it doesn't look too bad. Whatever happened to a simple 'you look nice', eh?"

"You know what I mean," she chortled. "Maternity clothes will never win any awards for fashion, will they? But you look kind of cute in stripes."

"Like a sailor?"

"A sailor with a football up its shirt," she grinned. "How many weeks are you now?"

"Fourteen. My baby is the size of a lemon," I informed her, stomping back into the changing room to get dressed. At the age of twenty eight, I didn't imagine I would ever be wearing stripy t-shirts and dungarees again. As far as I was concerned, dungarees were something only the under fives and Blue Peter presenters wore. Yet where maternity garments were concerned, designers obviously thought that they were the height of fashion.

"It's so you can get your boob out easily and discreetly when the baby's here," Erica said when I'd voiced my thoughts to her. We were walking through the shopping centre, arms linked.

"It's not just to wear while you're pregnant. It's for when you've spawned the little runt as well."

"Are you calling my child a runt?"

"Yes, I am. Don't get me wrong. I love the little runt's mother. But the father? His nickname rhymes with the word 'runt'," she laughed.

"He's not been too bad recently," I insisted, as we took a turn into a coffee shop and threw ourselves onto the comfy squashy armchairs. "In fact, we get along like a house on fire. He's surprisingly easy to live with. He cooks, he cleans, he's as neat as a pin. Never leaves the toilet seat up or pisses on it. It's just a shame that there's nothing going on romantically."

"A shame? I'd have thought that was a good thing," she said, one eyebrow raised as she examined the menu in front of her. "You don't want to blur any lines, do you?"

"God forbid a man and a woman who are expecting a baby develop feelings for one another," I sighed.

"You don't think it's a good idea though, surely? Calvin is a liar. You know that more than anyone," she went on. "Do you really want to muddle through the scary, early days of motherhood with the whole 'will he, won't he' debacle hanging over your head? You two get on well. So make sure you keep things like they are. A happy mum is a happy baby. Isn't that what Brenda the Bitch is always saying to Fiona?"

I was still thinking about Erica's words when she went up to the counter to place our order. I realised that she was right. Calvin and I were friends, which was more than I could have hoped for on the day I dropped the pregnancy bombshell on him at the pub. My thoughts were interrupted by my phone buzzing. It was an unknown number. Fully expecting it to be Chris Sheridan from work, I toyed with the idea of ignoring his call. I only had one week left of my sick note and I didn't particularly want to spoil my girly shopping trip with Erica by thinking about returning to work, despite knowing that I had to at some point.

"Hello?" I said quietly into my phone, half hoping Chris had hung up by that point.

"Hi. Is that Sophie Maguire?"

It wasn't Chris Sheridan. It was a young woman's voice. A midwife perhaps? I thought.

"Yes," I said, tentatively. "Who's this?"

"It's Kate Marshall," replied the voice. At first, I was unable to place the voice and the name together. Then it hit me. It was KB.

Following my revelation with Calvin, I'd called my father and my brother separately and told them my thoughts. They were easier to persuade than Calvin, but perhaps it was because they were desperate to try any avenue. I'd told them both that I wanted to contact the girl who I suspected was the mysterious KB to arrange a meeting. Both had been supportive.

It hadn't been too difficult. Using the powers of social media, I'd scoured through all the Kates in a ten mile radius of Arlington Heath. When that proved too difficult – with every Kate, Katy and Katie popping up as a suggestion – I changed my tactics and requested to join a private Facebook group for alumni of Hawleybrook High School. My request was approved within a day and I set to work scrolling through the images of the group members. There were two Kates and a Katie, but they were all too old to be KB, with two of them being a couple of school years above me.

Refusing to be defeated, I changed tactics again, posting a comment in the group itself asking the members if any of them remembered a Kate from my sister's year group. Four people replied tagging a person called Joanne Kate in their response. I'd sent Joanne Kate a friend request and a message, briefly introducing myself and explaining that I needed to talk to her about my sister Beth. I'd left my phone number. A few hours later, I'd seen that she'd read my message but she didn't respond, nor did she accept or reject my friend request. Days had passed with no response. I'd followed up my message with another message, which had, too, been ignored.

"Kate," I said, searching for the right words. "Thank you for calling me."

"It's fine," she said, simply. "What's all this about?"

"My dad and brother and me have been going through the case files from my sister's investigation. We've been trying to piece things together. We're working with the lead investigating officer from the case. He's retired now," I explained. Erica returned to the table, carefully carrying a tray containing two enormous mugs of hot chocolate and two plates of shortbread.

"Okay," Kate said into my ear, her voice sounding

uncertain. "So, what has that got to do with me?"

"I was – it's a – I'm not really sure where to start," I admitted, laughing bitterly. "I'm all flustered. You've caught me unawares. I'm sat in that new coffee shop that's just opened in Riverside Shopping Centre."

"Should I call you back later?" she suggested.

"No, no, it's fine. I'm just so grateful for you calling. It's just tricky finding the right words."

"Would it help if we met up? I could be at the coffee shop in about an hour?" she suggested.

It felt more acceptable and appropriate to discuss my dead sister's sexuality face to face than it did over the phone with a perfect stranger. As soon as we'd agreed to meet, I quickly briefed Erica on the topic, before sending separate messages to my father, my brother and Frank Perry. My father was the first to arrive on the scene, a little red faced and sweaty, and worrying about whether he'd paid enough for parking. Erica decided to leave us to it – "I don't think this poor girl will want us all gawking at her" – and she quickly departed after planting an air kiss towards my cheek with the promise of a phone call in the next few days. Her absence was quickly followed by the arrival of my brother and Frank, who had travelled down together.

"I hope you know what you're doing," Danny said, drumming his fingers on the side of the armchair he was squashed into, nervously tugging at the checked scarf wrapped around his neck.

"I don't know what I'm doing," I admitted. "I might be about to have a completely pointless and irrelevant conversation with a person who is totally uninvolved with this case. But if we can rule her out of everything, then it's worth it. Isn't it?"

They didn't look convinced.

Within five minutes of the three of them ordering coffees – with me ordering a pot of tea – a short, thin blonde girl arrived, a whirlwind of colour and windswept hair.

"Sophie?" she asked, looking around the coffee shop and squinting at me with uncertainty.

"Kate," I said, warmly, gesturing for her to join us. She looked at the three men sat around the small table with alarm. "Oh, Kate, this is my dad, Mike, my brother, Danny, and Detective Chief Inspector Frank Perry."

She nodded and smiled at everyone, but remained rooted to the spot. Again, I gestured to the chair nearest to the wall and thankfully, she took a seat. Before any of us could say another word, the barista shouted Danny's name and he retreated to the other side of the room where he collected a tray with four mugs and a teapot balanced on it. He set the tray down on the table in silence.

"Thank you for coming," I began, smiling at Kate. She looked too worried and confused to return the smile. "You're probably wondering what all of this is about."

"Yes."

"Dad?" I prompted. "Do you want to take it from here?"

Swirling a spoon around his frothy coffee, Dad carefully chose his words. "I'm Sophie, Beth and Danny's father. I recently had a conversation with a journalist. I wasn't aware he was a journalist. He published a story in a national newspaper about Beth's death, which led to Frank contacting me. He was the lead investigating officer of Beth's murder when it first happened. The case hasn't been officially reopened. We're just working together – the four of us – to try to piece together bits from 2005, in the hope that we can find enough information to persuade the police to reopen the case. In the hope that we can find the man responsible for my daughter's death," he said, slowly.

Kate nodded. "How do you think I could be of help?"

The table fell silent. All eyes bore into mine.

"On the morning of the day that Beth went missing, we were getting ready for school. Beth came out of the bathroom. I went in straight after her. She'd had a shower, so the bathroom was really misty. The mirror was all steamed up. I saw that Beth had written some initials in the condensation on the mirror. It was the letters K and B. For years, I thought that KB was a mysterious boyfriend of hers that no one knew about. The police thought exactly the same," I said, my hand gesturing towards Frank. "We assumed that Beth was in a secret relationship with KB, and that she'd been preparing to run away with him, or that he'd been abusing her and that she was going to tell someone about him, so he had to stop her. This entire time, we thought that KB was pivotal to the investigation."

"Okay," Kate said, her forehead creased with confusion. It was clear that she had no idea where this was going.

"It was only a week or so ago that I realised perhaps it wasn't the letters K and B that I saw on the mirror. I realised that perhaps it was the letter K and the number eight. Kay-eight. *Kate*," I said, finally.

Kate's porcelain white face was tinged with pink. She'd maintained her gaze the entire time, her blue eyes wide and unblinking, but at the sound of her own name, her eyes dropped to the crumbs scattered on the table in front of us.

"I don't know what you want me to say," she replied, her voice barely louder than a whisper. It was hardly audible with the swish and hiss from the coffee machines in close proximity to her. "I didn't tell Beth to write anything on that mirror. I wasn't even aware that she *had.*"

"Do you think it's possible that Beth had developed feelings for you, Kate?" Frank persisted.

She stared at him, her tiny chest heaving up and down as she caught her breath.

"You're not in any trouble," Frank reminded her, kindly. "You're just helping us to piece a few bits together. Anything you tell us might be really helpful."

"She liked me," Kate said, finally. She'd dropped her hands to her lap, where she was absentmindedly picking at a hangnail. "I hardly knew her, really. I'd been living in Manchester until the summer of 2005. My dad had been promoted at work and it meant uprooting us all. None of us were particularly happy about it, but we didn't exactly get a choice. I started at Hawleybrook High School in September 2005. Beth was in my form and a couple of my classes. She was kind to me. I knew no one, no one at all. I think she felt a bit sorry for me. I lived in Hawleybrook so I didn't get the school bus like most of the others. I usually walked home. One night, I was coming out of netball practice and I saw Beth waiting at the bus stop. She'd been asked to stay behind after class and she'd missed the bus. Because it was so late, my mum was picking me up. She was waiting for me in the car at the end of the street. We gave Beth a lift home. That night, she added me on MSN Messenger. You remember MSN Messenger?"

Danny and I nodded. The two dinosaurs looked utterly perplexed.

"It was a bit like instant messenger," Danny explained to

them. "I guess the nearest thing to it these days is Skype. It was pretty big back in the day. I suppose it was a bit like social media at the time."

"We spoke quite a bit after that. She started playing netball on a Tuesday night. She tried, but she was rubbish," Kate smiled. She stopped, hesitating for a moment. She swallowed. "Maybe I knew deep down that she…liked me, but I was just so grateful for a friend," she whispered, her big eyes full and glistening. "She was funny. She made me laugh. And she was bright. She helped me with my German homework twice in the time I knew her. She was a good mate to have. It was a shame I didn't get to know her any better."

"How could you be so sure she liked you?" Danny asked, his head cocked to one side.

Shrugging, she said, "I can't really explain it. How can you ever tell when someone has developed feelings for you? You just get…the vibe, don't you? The feeling? I'd catch her looking at me sometimes. She'd playfully push me. She tickled me once."

"Did anything ever happen between you?" I asked.

"No, no, nothing like that," Kate insisted, shaking her head. "I was really shocked to hear what had happened to Beth. It upset me a lot. She was such a nice girl. But we weren't – we didn't – we weren't in a relationship. I'm straight," she added.

"But *she* was a lesbian?" I persisted.

Shrugging, Kate said, "I don't know. I know she liked me. I could tell. Whether that was a confused teenage crush or whether it was more…deep rooted than that, I have no idea. Like I said, I met her in the September and by the October…"

"She was dead," I finished.

"Did Beth ever talk to you about anything personal? Boyfriends, girlfriends, any arguments?" Frank asked.

She shrugged again.

"I'm really sorry. It was so long ago."

"Anything," Dad croaked. "Anything you can remember. Did she ever say anything to you about her uncle?"

Frank's eyes met mine. I knew what he was thinking. Dad was leading her. Goading her into a conversation she knew nothing about.

"No. Sorry," Kate replied, simply.

"Did she say anything to you about the Halloween party?

Was she planning to meet someone there or later that day?" Dad pushed.

Wordlessly, Kate shook her head.

"Did she ever talk to you about her family?"

"Not really," Kate shrugged.

"What do you mean? Either she did or she didn't."

"Dad," I hissed. "Stop it. Thank you, Kate. You've been really helpful."

Kate looked at me, gratefully. She was uncomfortable, shifting from side to side in her seat.

"If you think of anything else..." my voice trailed off.

"I've got your number. I'll call you," she promised, smiling a quick, reassured smile. She stood up, pulling her coat tighter around her with a nervous glance at us all. "Oh. There is just one thing."

"Yes?" Dad said.

"On the news, they always referred to her as the girl in the mustard coat. I know the coat they're on about. I remember her wearing it over her blazer to and from school. But I was with her after school on Halloween. We were killing time between our last class and the start of the Halloween party. She wasn't wearing a coat," she said.

"She wouldn't be wearing it inside, would she?" Frank reasoned.

"Oh no. This was outside. We were in the courtyard at the rear of the school. We were hanging around to see if any of the older kids had any alcohol. Eventually, we gave up and Beth said she was going to nip home to see if she could get her hands on any," she admitted, rather bashfully. "She was shivering. It was freezing. But she didn't have her coat."

"Are you saying she'd lost it?" Frank persisted.

Kate shrugged. "I don't know. Possibly. She had it in the morning, she had it at lunchtime but she wasn't wearing it before the party."

"Did you tell the police this?" Dad whispered.

"No. I never gave it much thought. I was only ever questioned once, like everyone at school was, the day after she went missing. I was asked the usual questions – whether she had a boyfriend, whether she was happy at home, whether she got on with her family. No one asked about her coat, so I assumed it wasn't a big deal," she explained.

And with that, Kate left, promising to call if she thought of anything else. We plummeted into an empty silence, our drinks lying in front of us, untouched.

"What does this – what does this mean?" Danny breathed.

"It means all this time, we've searched for images on CCTV of Beth leaving school in her coat. And all this time, she wasn't wearing her bloody coat," Frank said, huskily, shaking his head.

"So, where is her coat?" Danny persisted. "It has to be somewhere. It was never found."

"God knows," Frank sighed, suddenly looking very tired.

"If the investigation was focused on finding images of Beth leaving Hawleybrook High School in the mustard coloured coat, and we've discovered that Beth left school without it... does this mean that the investigation will be re-opened by the police?" Dad said, turning to face Frank.

"I think we've got a very good chance of the case being re-opened now."

Chapter Thirteen

As Christmas was fast approaching, I returned to work. I was inexplicably nervous when I walked through the glass doors to the office on the morning in question, my stomach writhing; an audible bubble of anxiety and contempt. Erica greeted me outside the lifts with two Starbucks coffee cups in her hands and a laptop tucked under her armpit. We walked into the empty lift together, silently, my sweaty palms paling in comparison to the overpowering scent of expensive perfume coming from Erica's neck.

"It's Chanel," she explained, grinning a wide toothy grin out of her perfectly applied red lips. It was strange seeing her wearing makeup to work. We'd both previously agreed that the only sort of women who wore a full face of makeup to work were either desperate or shagging their boss. As the lift doors opened to reveal Chris Sheridan, his hair carefully slicked back over his slimy forehead, I prayed it was not the latter.

"How are you feeling, Sophie?" Chris asked me five minutes later as he closed the door to his office and nervously adjusted the knot of his tie.

Calvin had prepped me the night before, feeding me with carefully prepared answers to my inevitable back to work questions.

"I'm much better. Thanks for asking," I smiled.

Chris, visibly relaxing, sank back in his leather seat. It was clear that he'd anticipated another meeting like our previous one, where I'd allowed my newly discovered hormones to commandeer the conversation. An emotional, grieving pregnant woman was to be avoided at all costs as far as Chris Sheridan was concerned.

"Should I get us both a coffee?" he suggested, his eyes already fixated on the red and white Christmas edition cup in my hands. "Ah. You're already sorted. Excellent. Just one for me then."

He made quite a meal out of using the intercom to buzz through to his heavily moustached assistant, Janet, who arrived a few moments later with a cappuccino on a saucer for him. He took it from her without saying thanks. I smiled at Janet, guiltily, as if to apologise for his lack of manners. As she left the room, she held the door open for a smiling woman in her thirties with impossibly shiny brown hair, who took a seat next to me.

"Right. Now then. I've asked Claire from Human Resources to join us in our meeting this morning if you don't mind, Sophie?" he asked.

"It's a bit late if I do mind, considering that she's sat here with us right this second," I pointed out.

Terrified that the conversation was going to go down an all too familiar route, Chris looked at Claire in sheer panic. The words deer and headlight sprang to mind.

"I'm only here to support you, Sophie. You've just had a long absence from work. I want to make sure that you're fully supported in your return to work," Claire explained, still smiling. "If you'd prefer, I can arrange a separate meeting with just the two of us for later on this morning."

"It's fine," I murmured. My heart race quickened. Was I about to be told I'd been made redundant? "I just want to get settled back in."

"Absolutely. Terrific," was Chris's wholly inadequate input.

"In line with our absence management policy, you're entitled to apply for a phased return to work. If you choose to do this, you'll be on reduced, set hours per shift. For example, this week, you would be working from nine o'clock until one o'clock," Claire explained. "You'd be paid in full, as though you were completing your usual shift pattern."

And so it was agreed. For my first four weeks back, I would be working reduced hours. The purpose of the reduced hours was to take the pressure off the transition between being at home all day, every day and working full time again. It felt like a happy balance between showing my face at work and concentrating my energy on Beth's investigation, which had seemingly dominated my every waking thought.

A few days before I'd returned to work, Frank had told us with some trepidation that the police were not prepared to reopen the investigation officially. It had been a blow for us all, but especially Dad. He hadn't said anything, but he sat in the armchair in my living room and wept.

"I just cannot understand this," Danny had repeated, stomping back and forth so much that I felt a breeze. "How can they possibly think this isn't new information? They were working off the wrong description of her! This is ridiculous. Do you think we should make some sort of formal complaint?"

"They said they didn't think it was a big enough development to justify re-opening it. They spent a lot of money on re-opening the case a couple of years ago when it was passed to cold cases. It never went anywhere," Frank explained, calmly.

"Because they were looking at it all wrong!" Danny roared. "They were looking for a girl in a yellow coloured coat which isn't right. How do they decide which cases are worthy of spending money on? I bet if Beth had been younger or if she..." his voice trailed off, angry tears welling in his eyes. "Who did you speak to?"

"Robert Muir."

"I'm going down there tomorrow morning and asking to speak to this Robert Muir then. I want to know what the criteria is for a case to be re-opened," Danny spat. "I bet if this was *his* sister, if she was Beth Muir, the case would be re-opened in a heartbeat. Or if Beth was a toddler snatched out of her bed, the case would never have been closed. But because Beth was a teenager, no one gives a shit. They think she ran away with an older... It's disgusting."

"Dan, calm down," I muttered, unable to take my eyes off my weeping father.

"I can't calm down. This is ridiculous. I cannot understand it," Danny began, the pacing continuing. "We'll have to speak to the school to see if we can get our hands on the CCTV footage ourselves. I'll speak to James at work. He's an IT whizz. He'll be able to blow up the images or something. Make them a bit bigger. A bit clearer. We'll be able to pick her out of a crowd leaving the school, surely?"

"I don't know," I murmured. "That's a lot of kids leaving the school wearing the same sort of clothes, and the images themselves won't be great either. It was a long time ago."

"But Beth didn't leave the school at the same time as everyone else, did she? If what Kate said is true, she'd have left a bit later than most of the other kids. Kate said she hung around in the courtyard for a bit between the end of the school day and the start of the Halloween party. School used to finish at what – three fifteen?" he asked no one in particular. "What time did the party start?"

"Four o'clock," Frank replied.

"And she hung around the courtyard for a while. So we've got about a half hour window, from say three thirty to four o'clock. That should narrow the search down a little?" Danny insisted.

"I guess so," I admitted. "Don't forget not all of the cameras were working, so she still might not have been captured leaving, Dan."

"We won't need to speak to the school to get copies of the CCTV footage. They probably wouldn't have it anymore anyway. You can ask the police for a copy of the footage on a disc," Frank said to Dad. He looked up, his eyes wide and teary. "As Beth's parent, her next of kin, you could request a copy. It's not guaranteed that you'd get it but it's worth a try."

"We're going down there first thing tomorrow, Dad," Danny persisted, his arms folded. "Sod work. I'll have to tell them I've got a doctors appointment or something."

Their visit hadn't gone as well as they'd hoped, with Robert Muir being out of the office. However, they'd requested a phone call from him, which they'd been assured would be returned within five working days. After I'd been back at work for two days, I made the stomach sinking decision which I'd been putting off for weeks. I sent Danny a text message, suggesting that we met at our mother's house to go through her things in anticipation of the house being sold.

I'd expected a difficult few evenings, rifling through our mother's possessions – constant reminders of the life she'd once had, eaten away by grief and despair. Danny hadn't been able to make the first evening I'd proposed, but I decided to go by myself. Something was niggling in the back of my mind. I'd put it off for long enough and knew that the more pregnant I got, the more difficult it would be to sort things into boxes and rifle through cupboards and drawers. There was nothing good on television and I didn't have the concentration required to watch anything on Netflix with a half decent plot, so it seemed as good a night as any to begin the work at the house.

As I was grabbing my car keys to head out to my mother's house, Calvin stopped me.

"I'm not sure it's such a good idea for you to go there. Not on your own. Not tonight. Why don't you wait until your brother's free so you can do it together?" he suggested.

"I'll be fine," I insisted, buttoning up my coat. I tried to pretend it wasn't straining across my ever expanding chest. "It needs doing. I can't keep putting it off any longer. It's not fair to Mum."

"Okay. I'll come with you."

"You don't need to do that."

"I know I don't. I want to," he smiled, and picked his own car keys up out of the bowl next to the front door. We drove to my mother's house making comfortable conversation, both half listening to the nauseatingly happy Christmas music playing on the radio. I hadn't celebrated a Christmas properly since 2004. I switched the radio off, sending the car into an unexpected silence. Calvin didn't push it but I caught him making worried glances at me as we pulled up outside my childhood home.

Since Beth had died, I hadn't liked walking into our old family house. It was an aching reminder, a sad nostalgia filled with what if's and maybe's. I had always been unable to fathom how and why my mother had chosen to remain living in the house which her youngest daughter had never returned to, but as I put the key in the lock and pushed open the front door, I was greeted with the biggest wave of longing and wistfulness emanating through my body.

It was clear why Mum had decided to stay there. It was where her family was made. There were bucket loads of happy memories – the three of us rushing down the stairs on Christmas morning, our eyes glistening with delight at the sight of three stuffed stockings and wrapped presents strewn all over the living room, blowing out the candles on our birthday cakes, taking our first steps, proudly showing off our too big uniforms on our first days at school.

As I walked through to the kitchen, breathing in an unfamiliar musty smell, my mind flitted back to one of my earliest memories. I was five and a half, and I was sat in the bath with a tiny little Beth. Nan was sat on the floor, reaching over us with a plastic cup to wash our hair. Beth had cried, hating having suds in her eyes. The front door clicked open and then closed. A moment passed. Nan looked up. Mum and Dad walked in to the bathroom, clutching a tiny bundle in their arms, their faces lit up at the sight of their family meeting each other for the first time.

I sat at the kitchen table, a lump burning in my throat as I finally understood why Mum had stayed rooted to the same house. Her children had grown up there.

All but one.

"I've put all the post in a pile on the cabinet by the front door," Calvin called out, walking into the kitchen to find me with tears streaming down my cheeks. "I know this must be really hard, Soph. You don't have to do this, you know."

"I do," I insisted, wiping my sodden cheeks with the sleeve of my coat. "Right. Let's get cracking. Should we open a window for a bit? I know it's cold but it's a bit musty, isn't it?"

Calvin opened the kitchen window and immediately retreated back from the sink, where he discovered what had previously been a cup with coffee dregs in it. It was green and growing and very much alive. He started filling the washing up bowl with hot water, which took a while to heat up.

"You might be best putting the heating on for a bit," Calvin called out to me as I walked back into the hall. "The pipes might freeze over soon. You don't want a leak. And check your mum's post. She might have some overdue bills. You'll need to ring her utility companies in the morning to let them know. They'll want a copy of her death certificate."

Following Calvin's advice, I switched the dial for the gas central heating and, to my relief, heard the familiar whooshing sound from the radiator behind me. Spying an enormous pile of letters, I sat at the bottom of the stairs, rifling through each one. Nearly all of them were bills. With a pang, I realised that some of them were Christmas cards, sent by people who still believed my mother was alive. Then –

"Calvin?" I called out, clutching the brown jiffy bag in my hands. "Come here! Quickly!"

He appeared at the foot of the stairs, his hands wet and suddy. He wiped them on his jeans as I passed the padded envelope to him, his brows furrowed in confusion as he pulled out a piece of paper, which contained a handwritten note, hastily scrawled in smudgy black biro.

"What the hell is this?" he asked, holding the note up to the light and examining the contents. "*I didn't know your address. This house was all I could find online. I'm sorry it's taken me so long,*" Calvin read out. "*I couldn't get it from him easily. I hope*

you can bring me some answers. I am a scared mother. Magda."
Calvin squinted at the note, turning it over in a bid to see any further information. "Who's Magda?"

"My uncle's wife."

"*I couldn't get it from him easily.* What is she talking about?" he asked.

"This," I said, simply, holding up a small plastic tub. "There are some of my uncle's hairs in this tub. We have a DNA sample."

Chapter Fourteen

Christmas Day was normally a time I shied away from, buried under a blanket, nursing a stonking hangover and wishing the entire time would disappear. Christmas as a twenty six year old had been spent asleep on the couch in the living room, disturbed only by next door's TV blaring out the EastEnders theme tune in the evening. Bleary eyed, I'd checked my phone to find sixteen unanswered phone calls and twelve unread text messages, all off my mother and brother, demanding to know why I hadn't bothered to turn up at the annual festivities.

I didn't know why they bothered year after year. I had almost entirely forgotten how it felt to celebrate Christmas. Winter in general was a dismal time for me; the gloomy weather a direct reflection of my mental state. However, in the days after I'd returned to work, I found myself stopping at the supermarket on my drive home to pick up a Christmas tree and some decorations. I found myself enjoying listening to Christmas music as I decorated the tree with tinsel and twinkly lights. I found myself whistling the tune to The Fairy Tale of New York as I washed the dishes. And on Christmas Eve, as Calvin, my dad, my brother and I settled down in front of the television with a banquet of food in front of us, I felt undeniably Christmassy.

Christmas Day was being held at my mother's house. It had seemed the only logical solution as there were suddenly so many of us celebrating together and my dining table was just about big enough for four people. Danny had never possessed a dining table, having always preferred to eat off a cushion on his lap in front of the TV. Dad had been spending less and less time in his own house. Part of me wondered if he felt lonely there. The other part of me didn't mind because I was enjoying his company and finding his input towards the investigation helpful. Calvin was accompanying us somewhat quietly. His parents had been mightily unimpressed with the news of his affair and the breakdown of his relationship, and had decided to take the opportunity to spend Christmas in Australia visiting his sister and her two children.

We'd also invited Frank along to join us. It was clear that his seemingly estranged children weren't going to invite him to their houses for the festive period, and neither me nor the others could stomach the thought of him cooped up on his own on Christmas Day. Somehow, the five of us together felt more than the usual gang. It began to look and feel like a party.

"Are you sure she wouldn't mind?" I whispered to Danny, as we piled out of the two cars and into the house, all of us clutching bags of food and Christmas crackers.

"Nah. Would she heck," Danny retorted. "She'd probably be made up that we're actually all together today."

I realised he was right. Mum had always loved Christmas. In the years following Beth's death, she found solace in religion. The church had always comforted her in times of distress but following October 2005, Mum had become almost superstitious about praying with her rosary beads.

Typically, she spent most of Christmas Day on her knees praying at church. It didn't stop her preparing a full Christmas dinner, which she made to feed approximately twelve people, despite there only being the three of us – and at times when I simply couldn't face it, just her and Danny.

"You can have a small glass, you know," Calvin's voice said from next to me. I was mashing carrot and swede together, little beads of sweat forming on the back of my neck.

"I'm not bothered about having a drink," I lied. There was nothing I fancied more than sitting on the couch and enjoying a large glass of ice cold chardonnay waiting for the queen's speech. "I just feel a bit sick around all this food."

"Go outside. Get some fresh air. I'll take over," he instructed and he took the masher off me, our hands touching briefly. A moment passed where we both registered what had happened. We couldn't pretend there hadn't been a bolt of electricity charge between us when we'd touched. Without another word, I pushed open the kitchen door which led into the back garden and I found myself sitting on one of the black plastic garden chairs, dimly aware of the seat being damp. I enjoyed a moment or two of silence before I was joined by my father, who perched himself on the edge of the garden table.

"Do you remember the year we got the big plastic swing set?" he asked, gesturing towards the overgrown lawn, the ghost of a childhood faded from in front of us. "She loved the slide. You and Danny were always fighting, struggling to take turns on the swing and the monkey bars, but she wasn't bothered about that. She just loved the slide."

Throat thickening, I couldn't find the words to respond. Dad seemed to understand and didn't push me. We fell into a comfortable silence, broken only by me sniffing noisily. Damn hormones.

"Does it feel weird? Being back here?" I asked, suddenly.

He paused for a moment, toying with his answer.

"No," he said, finally. "It felt weird being in the house without Beth being there. She still isn't here. So no, it doesn't feel any weirder than that."

Christmas dinner was a pleasant affair, with the majority of the party having helped themselves to copious amounts of wine. Under the watchful eye of Calvin, I treated myself to a small glass of white wine. I drank it slowly, carefully, like a tonic. And when he wasn't watching, I helped myself to another, casually dismissing the guilty feeling in my stomach with an "it's Christmas" rationale.

As dinner began to wrap up, I found myself volunteering for kitchen duties. Dad had stayed resolutely sober and played the dutiful taxi driver to an inebriated Frank and Danny, leaving Calvin and I washing and drying up.

"And to think, this time next year we'll be celebrating our baby's first Christmas," Calvin smiled, handing me a dish to dry. "Who'd have thought it, eh?"

"Not me," I smiled back, a little sadly. "I just wish my mum had lived long enough to know she was a grandma. I wish…"

It took a moment before I realised I was crying. Sobbing noisy tears into my tea towel. Abandoning the washing up, Calvin pulled me into his arms. He smelled of clean laundry, soap and shampoo. His arms, strong and tight around me, rubbed the middle of my back as I cried into his chest. Before either of us realised what was happening, our mouths had found each other; our lips pressing against each other with a sense of urgency, a sense of belonging.

It felt familiar, recognisable, *safe*.

His mouth worked its way down to my neck, hungrily kissing my skin in a way which made it tingle. His hands pulled the hem of my jumper up over my head, causing my hair to fall around my shoulders in disarray. As he pulled me closer towards him, I could feel his heart racing underneath his shirt.

"Should we go upstairs?" he murmured into my mouth as our lips found their way together again.

Wordlessly, he linked his fingers in mine and we headed up the stairs, him slightly ahead of me, pushing open the door to the nearest bedroom. Without speaking, he flicked the light switch and the room cascaded into a rosy glow, emanating from the pink stripy wallpaper engulfing the room. He hadn't realised. He hadn't noticed. He couldn't see anything other than the there and the now. He went to kiss me once more and I moved my head, forcing him to plant his lips on my cheek.

"What's wrong?" he asked, his eyes desperately searching for mine, his breathing rapid. "Are you okay? Do you want to stop?"

I couldn't speak. My throat was thick with emotion. I gestured around the room, silently. Suddenly, it dawned on him – the single bed, the bookshelves filled with teddy bears, the faded girlish wallpaper.

"We're in Beth's room, aren't we?" he muttered, his cheeks flamed.

I couldn't bring myself to respond. Instead, I lay on my sister's bed, wrapped up in the faded quilt, trying to ignore the light layer of dust present. Calvin had gone into my mother's room to sleep, leaving me lying there awake, until it began to get light outside. As the sun rose, the room was filled with light, bouncing off the numerous photo frames dotted around on my sister's desk and chest of drawers. Photo after photo of her linking arms with friends on school trips, smiling cheesily at the camera. A treasured photo of her, me and Danny one Christmas. A photo of her with Mum on Mum's birthday.

"We'll get him, Beth," I promised the smiling girl in the photographs. "It's nearly time."

Chapter Fifteen

It was the first week in January when we learned that Uncle Tony's DNA didn't match the DNA of Beth's killer. To describe the feeling was difficult. In a sense, we were all relieved that she hadn't been killed by a family member, by someone we knew and cared for. In another sense, it felt as though we were slipping further and further from the truth. It felt impossible, overwhelming almost, to gain the truth. Like we were trying to count the grains of a sand on a very large beach.

The investigation still hadn't been opened officially. Frank had asked an old police colleague to put in a favour for him by sending Uncle Tony's hairs off to a lab for examination. The police officer had ummed and ahhed about it for a while before making Frank promise that it was a one off. Frank said he felt his ex-colleague had sounded relieved when he'd called Frank with the results from the lab. I think we all understood the enormity of what would happen if it had been a positive match. Frank's ex-colleague would have had some explaining to do.

"We just need to regroup," Dad insisted one evening that week. "Maybe we're going about this the wrong way. I've been thinking. Maybe we should set targets for us all to follow on a weekly basis."

"Targets?" Danny rolled his eyes.

"At the moment, we're working very much as a group," Dad went on. "While that makes sense, it might be more beneficial to break off into smaller groups or work independently. That way, when we come together, we'll have regular updates."

"How is that ever going to work, Dad?" Danny asked. "Think about it. Two of us have jobs. Sophie's getting ready to have a baby. We don't all have the time to work on the case independently."

"I know that," Dad assured him. "Frank thinks it makes more sense for each of us to focus on a different area of the investigation as and when we can."

"So, who gets which area? And what are the areas?" I asked.

Frank cleared his throat. "I think there are four key areas of interest. Number one. The list of men who didn't present themselves for a voluntary DNA sample still needs looking at more closely. Recently, we've put all of our consideration into the possible involvement of Tony. We know he isn't responsible for Beth's death, but he wasn't the only person missing off the list. Someone needs to locate the missing people and contact them. Ask them what they were doing that night and why they didn't come forward to give a DNA sample. Make a list of anyone who seems a bit shifty. Anyone whose reasons feel more like excuses. Mike, I'm going to delegate that area to you. It'll take the most time to complete and it will require someone who can drive," Frank explained, methodically.

Dad nodded, his brows furrowed.

"Secondly, I think we need to take a closer look at the CCTV images from the school and the surrounding area. We now know that Beth didn't leave the school wearing her mustard coat. That makes things slightly more complicated visually but it's not impossible to try to track her down on those images. Danny, can I hand that task over to you?" Frank asked. "You could also speak to the council. See if they have access to any footage from 2005, including the days leading up to her disappearance. If she's been abducted, there's every chance that this was a targeted attack. She might have been watched, followed even. Speak to your tech savvy friend from work. See if he can get clearer images."

Danny nodded, immediately whipping his phone out of his jeans pocket to text his friend.

"The third area of interest is speaking to Beth's friends again. People in and out of school. Kate mentioned an after school netball club. Who else went to that club? Did they ever play games against other schools? Who did Beth sit with on the school bus? Did they notice anything unusual on the morning of 31st October 2005? All of these questions have been asked time and time again but not by us. Sophie, I'm going to delegate this task to you. I think people might open up to you more than they did to a stuffy old policeman thirteen years ago," Frank smiled. "Speak to the school. See if you can get hold of any teachers still working there who knew Beth. And see if you can get hold of any teachers who knew her who have left. Ask the school for a phone number. Call them. Write to them."

"Okay," I smiled back.

"And the final area of the investigation – I'm going to tackle this one. It's a biggie. Any odds and ends. I'm going to start by investigating similar previous crimes. Work out if there's any sort of pattern. There was a suspicious death in 1999, about a fifteen minute drive away from Hawleybrook. A teenage girl who'd taken an overdose in a park. According to her friends and family, it was very out of character for her. We know she'd been speaking to someone at a bus stop two days before her death that we were never able to trace. A man in a long dark coat with a distinctive walk. I'm going to try to get my hands on those case notes. See if there are any similarities. I'm also going to take another look at Beth's internet history records," Frank went on. "We knew she had a MySpace account which she hardly used so our attention was never really on that. But I now think it's possible that she had another account, a secret account, that she used to chat to girls. One that couldn't be traced back to her. I'm going to do a bit of digging around that. Then I want to get my hands on her chat records from this MSN Messenger," Frank said, gesturing towards Danny.

"Was that not done at the time?" I asked.

"It was but I looked through the boxes and I can't find much. There were a couple of conversations but none with anyone called Kate which struck me as odd because Kate specifically said they'd spoken on MSN Messenger quite a bit," Frank explained, calmly. "So I'll try to dig a bit further there too. Then I'm going to pick up on a dead end from 2006. We knew that Sue was very passionate about the fox hunting ban. It came into force not long before Beth died. She'd been out on a protest a few months earlier, hadn't she?" Frank directed his question towards my father.

"Yes: Beth went with her. There were always lots of families protesting there. Do you think that has something to do with it?" Dad gasped.

"No idea," Frank said, simply. "But we know that the hunting group she was protesting against are known for being violent towards sabs."

"Sabs?" Dad frowned in confusion.

"Saboteurs. Protestors. Those defending the innocent," Frank explained. "Nigel Graham – the head of the Hawleybrook Hunt - was charged with assault on a minor in 2009. The child in question was the son of a known sab. Nigel beat him to a pulp after sinking pint after pint in the pub one night. I checked the list of men who voluntarily gave a DNA sample. He wasn't on the list. He was on our no-show list."

The room was completely silent. A familiar lump found its way to my throat. It felt ridiculous to suggest that my sister had been murdered because our mother had protested against foxes being hunted but I also knew it was wrong to assume anything. As Frank often said, stranger things had happened.

"And someone needs to contact Tony's wife to tell her that the DNA sample wasn't a match," said Frank, softly.

"I'll do it," offered Dad. "I'll go round tomorrow evening. I probably owe my brother an apology while I'm at it."

My task began the next morning as I was sat behind my desk at work, clutching a predictably disappointing decaf coffee in my left hand and navigating my way through people's Facebook profiles with my right hand. Some faces were recognisable. Most weren't. Between baby brain and the many years spent with my head stuffed down a bottle of vodka, I could barely remember who any of Beth's friends were.

The obvious people – Beth's immediate friends – had been questioned to death at the time and the years that followed. They were so young at the time that Frank had probably been right – it most likely was frightening. If anyone had known anything, there was a good chance that they'd been too intimidated from being quizzed by a burly policeman to give any honest answers.

By lunchtime, I couldn't ignore my growling stomach any longer or dismiss the pangs of guilt I felt for not feeding the baby anything other than a tube of Smarties and a packet of Skips earlier that morning. I fired off a quick email to Erica, proposing a lunchtime jaunt to the pub for a sandwich and fries, then dashed off to the toilet for what felt like the hundredth time that morning.

As I came back out of the ladies toilets, I heard an unmistakeable kissing and giggling sound coming from inside the disabled toilet. Knowing exactly what – or, rather, who – I would find inside the cubicle, I decided to wait outside. Low and behold, sixty seconds later, I was standing face to face with Erica and Chris Sheridan. The expressions on their faces was priceless and I had to steel myself so as not to burst out laughing.

"Sophie," Chris said, instantly straightening the knot of his tie. "You're looking well."

"Thank you. You're looking rather flushed if you don't

mind me saying, Chris."

"Ah, yes," Chris said, his cheeks slowly turning from salmon pink to puce. "Yes, there's a – a nasty bug going around at the moment, isn't there?"

And with that, he turned and left, leaving me alone with my best friend who until moments earlier had probably had a penis in her mouth. She couldn't quite meet my eyes as she struggled to find the right words to say. Taking pity on her, I decided to help her out.

"Pub?" I suggested.

"Definitely," she gasped, gratefully.

Half an hour later, we had each devoured a chicken salad baguette and fries and helped ourselves to a small glass of wine. Erica was the only person I felt I could drink alcohol in front of. Panicked, I had initially wondered if the waitress would think ill of me as she brought over a tray containing our food and glasses of wine. However, in a long woolly cardigan draped over me, it was impossible to detect even the slightest hint of a bump.

"Why do I feel like you're about to give me the third degree?" Erica scowled, draining the last of her glass.

"I'm not," I promised her. "I just think you're being silly. What would Will say if he found out?"

Will was always incredibly polite whenever we met, usually with him driving me and Erica home after a drunken night out. I'd once puked in the passenger footwell of his car. He hadn't complained and I'd tactfully handed him a ten pound note the next time I saw him as recompense for the car having to be cleaned professionally. He wasn't what I would call good looking but he was fine. Safe. Nice. And he and Erica had been together for a long time. And regardless of whether or not I thought Will was nice looking, I couldn't stomach the idea of having sex with Chris Sheridan.

"I don't think he'd be particularly bothered considering he moved out the week before Christmas," she said, quietly, absentmindedly gnawing on a hard chip.

"What?" I whispered.

"You heard. He's moved out. Gone. Left me," she muttered.

"Why?" I pressed.

"He wanted kids. I didn't. He wanted marriage. I didn't.

We were two very different people wanting very different things, Soph," she said, simply.

"Bloody hell," I breathed. A moment passed between us. "And so, you and Chris are... together?"

"No," she said, quickly. "Chris is just – well, Chris. He's a welcome distraction from the otherwise shit show that is my life."

"So, sleeping with Chris Sheridan makes you feel better about your life?" I laughed and once I started, I couldn't stop. I was howling. All the tension in my body began to ooze out of my pores. After a while, Erica joined in the laughter until we were both squawking into our hands. It felt good to laugh. With a jolt, I realised I hadn't laughed so hard in weeks.

"Fancy another?" Erica asked, tilting her head towards her empty wine glass.

"I shouldn't," I murmured.

"Go on," she grinned. "I won't tell if you won't."

Erica went up to the bar to order two more glasses of wine and then went off to the toilet. I took the opportunity to check my phone. Nothing from anyone, other than an email from a receptionist at Hawleybrook High School informing me that they were unable to provide the names or contact details for any of their staff, past or present.

"Sophie?" came a voice to my left, distracting me from my thoughts. "It is Sophie, isn't it?"

A woman with wavy honey blonde hair and a carefully made up face stood in front of me, squinting at me in disbelief.

"I'm so sorry. I've drawn a blank and have no idea who you are," I laughed, guiltily.

"My name's Lorna Gallimore. I'm Calvin's fiancée. Well, ex-fiancée," she said, bluntly.

The wine went straight through me, hitting the walls of my stomach like a knife as I felt my insides jostling uncomfortably. I stifled a burp. Silently, I prayed I would not throw up.

"I – I don't know what to say," I said, finally.

"It's fine," she shrugged. "I don't really know what I expect you to say. I'm not here to question you. I'm just meeting a friend for lunch."

Silence descended on us, engulfing us with its stifling awkwardness.

"How did you know who I was?" I asked.

"I looked at your Facebook and Instagram profiles," she shrugged, nonchalantly. "They aren't private. Anyone can access them."

"Oh. Right." I had no words. Was this woman about to read me the riot act? I thought, panicked, desperately scanning the room for Erica.

"I presume the two of you are an item now?"

"No," I said. Then I paused. Were we? We hadn't really spoken about our Christmas Day tryst and it hadn't happened again or even come close to it but there had been similar moments of electricity between us when we were alone. "Well, I'm not really sure." I thought it was as honest as I could be.

"How far gone are you?" she demanded. No niceties were to be exchanged, I noticed. She wanted information, not to make a friend.

"I'm seventeen weeks."

Right on cue, the waitress arrived, shortly followed by Erica who was wiping her presumably damp hands down her black pencil skirt. Erica sat down, silently, glancing in confusion at the sudden unexpected arrival of Lorna and accepted the glass of wine being handed to her by the smiling waitress before sliding the other glass over to me. Lorna's eyes dropped to my glass, then to my stomach, then back to my face. She was disgusted.

"You know, he did say you were a wino," she smirked, tossing her hair over her shoulder.

"Did he?"

"He said you liked a drink and a bit of weed. Evidently, you still do. Pass on my congratulations to him, will you? It looks like he's done really well for himself," she said, the sarcasm not even barely contained in her voice, before stomping out of the bar in her heels, her tiny waist emphasised by her even tinier leather jacket.

"Wow. What a bitch. No prizes for guessing who that was," Erica snorted, tipping a generous helping of wine down her throat. Suddenly, the very last thing I wanted to do was to drink alcohol. I felt as small as a Borrower, as slimy as seaweed. "Hey," Erica said, softly, reaching out to squeeze my hand. "Don't take any notice of her. She hates you because her fiancé got you pregnant. It's not your fault but it sure as hell isn't her fault either. She's entitled to hate your guts. Don't take it personally."

"Calvin called me a wino," I cringed.

Erica nodded. "He probably did. But, in his defence, you probably did come across that way at times. Don't get me wrong – I loved it. You made the very best drinking partner. I'm dreading these next couple of months drinking on my own. But from a potential boyfriend's perspective? Yeah. Total piss head."

"Do I ask him about it?"

"And say what? 'Oh, Calvin. The woman you loved for years and asked to be your wife told me you called me a wino today when I was sat in the pub drinking wine at midday at seventeen weeks pregnant'? Come off it, Soph," she laughed, taking another almighty sip. "If it makes you feel better, I'll drink it for you."

"You'll be going back into the office sozzled at this rate."

"Might make the afternoon go a bit quicker," she winked. "Anyway, enough about me and enough about old stroppy knickers and her wino comment. How are you getting on with your sister's investigation?"

I launched into an explanation of the tasks Frank had set each of us. She was a captive audience, raising her eyebrows and oohing at just the right parts.

"But now I've just received an email back from my old high school telling me that they can't give me any information due to data protection," I sighed.

"Well, you should have seen that coming a mile off," snorted Erica. "Everyone hides behind the Data Protection Act. You know that. And your idea about going into the school and questioning people who worked there in 2005? You need to knock that on the head. For a start, they wouldn't let you through the school doors. You have to prove you're not on the sex offender's register. Then you have to have a legitimate appointment. You can't just waltz up whilst they're teaching a class and interrupt it with questions about things that happened thirteen years ago. You'd have to do it outside of school hours in order to have a proper conversation with these people. And is it really reasonable to expect people to stay behind after their shift at work has finished to answer questions that in all likelihood, they've probably already answered before?"

"What do I do?" I sighed.

"What you need is a sort of open evening. A night in a

church hall or a community centre. Advertise that you're going to be there. Make posters. Make a Facebook event page. Explain to people what you're doing. Invite anyone and everyone who lived locally at the time Beth was killed. Remind them of her movements. Tell them that she didn't leave the school wearing that bloody coat. Get people talking about her again."

"I don't want a fuss. I don't want the press finding out," I said, hurriedly.

"And I totally get your reasons why. It can't have been nice having the media poking their noses in to your life when you were a spotty teenager grieving the loss of your little sister," she agreed. "But don't you think it'll be different now? For starters, you aren't the police. This isn't anything official. The press are less likely to want to be involved in something that's being ran under the radar. Secondly, so what if you get some attention from the press? The more awareness you get, the more people get talking. And the more people get talking, the more questions start to get asked. Like – 'Oh, darling, where were you on the night Beth Maguire was murdered? You weren't at home with me'. If you make a topic too hot to handle, people start to sweat. They panic. And when people panic, they start to trip up."

Chapter Sixteen

"I can't believe I let you talk me into doing this," I muttered under my breath.

I was stood on the stage in the community centre in Arlington Heath, a black microphone swinging from my hand. There was real danger that I would drop the microphone due to my ever-increasingly sweaty palms. Without realising, I was instantly transported back to my early childhood years when I was stood in the exact same community centre, dressed in a pale pink tutu, as I thudded around in a ballet class. I had the same level of elegance and sophistication as a potato. My ballet career had been short lived, with my mother persuading me to spend my Saturday mornings at swimming lessons after my ballet teacher – kind faced Mrs Robinson – had explained that not all little girls were meant to be ballet dancers.

There were approximately two hundred people sat on red plastic chairs in front of me, all eyes on me. It was doing nothing for my fear of public speaking. Actually, I realised with a thud that appeared to originate from my stomach, it wasn't so much a fear of speaking in public. It was a fear of doing anything in public. After years of being photographed, written about and followed by the press, I liked nothing more than to blend in and be forgotten about.

I hadn't anticipated so many people turning up. Initially, I'd made a few posters on my work computer and printed them off when Chris wasn't looking. Together with Calvin, we'd stuck the posters up around Arlington Heath and Hawleybrook. Then on Erica's orders, I'd created a Facebook event page and invited as many people who were local to Arlington Heath as I could. Word soon got out and before long, there were over five hundred people who'd said they were attending the event. Whilst it was clear that less than half of these people had actually turned up, it still felt a little overwhelming. It was also evident that a reporter was sat at the end of the first row of seats, a recording device in his hand.

It was enough to make me shudder.

"What?" hissed Erica, incredulously. "This is a brilliant idea. Look at all these people. They've turned up tonight of their own accord because they want to help."

"Or because they fancy a gawp at the dead girl's family?"

I muttered.

"Erica's right," Danny said, softly, squeezing my hand in his. "We needed this. People need to know that we're taking this seriously. Whoever did this is out there. We want him to be afraid."

"Well, the only person who is afraid right now is me," I whispered, my stomach churning. "How did I end up being the one doing the introductions?"

"I've told you – I'll do it," offered Frank. "I don't want you putting any pressure on yourself. Not in your condition."

"Are you sure?" I whispered to Frank.

Frank nodded and winked at me, kindly, before taking the microphone out of my hand and clearing his throat into it. It had the desired effect. Everyone sat in front of us settled themselves, stopping their conversations and focusing their attention at the five figures stood before them on stage. My palms moistened horribly.

"Good evening, ladies and gentlemen," Frank began. His voice was calm, warm and collected. I wondered fleetingly how many times he had briefed the police officers working on my sister's investigation. With a thud to my heart, I wondered how defeated they felt when he announced that the case had been closed. "For those of you who don't know me, my name is Frank Perry. I'm a retired sergeant in the police force. In 2005, I was the lead investigating officer in the disappearance and murder of Beth Maguire."

A silence descended upon the room, filling every avenue with its emptiness.

"There isn't a single person sitting inside this room who doesn't recognise that name. Beth Maguire was just thirteen years old when she disappeared from Hawleybrook High School on 31st October 2005. Her body was found two days later in Griffin Woods. She had been raped and strangled. To this day, her killer has never been found."

Frank's words were chilling. I watched as people reacted to the all too familiar story of my sister's early demise. Some people sat, frozen to their seat, scared to move. Others had lifted a hand to their mouths, utterly repulsed by the retelling of the tale. One lady, dressed entirely in black from head to toe except for a scuffed pair of greyish white trainers had began to silently weep.

Glancing next to her, I realised who she was sat near to. Uncle Tony and Magda were both sat in the hall. I wondered if Dad had realised.

At the very back of the room, smiling warmly and encouragingly up at me from her several layers of clothing was a familiar face. It took a moment for me to process where I recognised the smiling face from. Then it hit me. It was Patsy, the old lady who shared a hospital ward with my mother before she died. Somehow, and for reasons I couldn't quite fathom, it comforted me.

"I stand here today with Beth's father and her brother and her sister. We cannot accept what has happened. Her family in particular cannot accept that her murderer is still at large. As a town, you should not be able to accept that the person responsible for the abduction, sexual assault and murder of a child is still walking your streets. He must be found. He must be brought to justice," Frank said, slowly, giving his audience enough time to digest his words.

"It's now been over thirteen years since Beth was murdered. She has been gone longer than she was here. Yet the heartache continues for her loved ones, who spend day after day, night after night, wondering what happened to their daughter, their sister, their friend. A few months ago, I approached Beth's father – Mike Maguire – after reading a newspaper article about Beth. Mike explained that he was unable to rest until he had answers. Together with Beth's siblings and their friends, we've pieced together bits from the day in question. We now have further questions. And we need your help."

For one wild moment, I wondered if I was going to pass out. I'd been stood in the same uncomfortable position for well over twenty minutes. Slowly, I shook my head to rid myself of the thought. As I did so, the door leading into the hall of the community centre opened, creaking noisily. The two hundred heads which, until that moment, had been fixated on Frank suddenly turned to face the source of the sound. It was Calvin, who held his hands up apologetically as he took a seat towards the back.

"The official investigation has not been reopened," Frank continued. "Unfortunately, the police deem Beth's murder to be a cold case. Unless we get our hands on any solid evidence which could potentially lead to a conviction, they do not deem it necessary to reopen the case. It's just us. It's a lot for us to take on. We don't have the appropriate channels or bodies required for such a case. But we're determined to find him. It's difficult to know where to start with something like this, so I propose we refresh everyone's memories with the details of what happened."

With Danny's help, Frank managed to project images onto the wall of the community centre which were visual aids to accompany the sorrowful story Frank was retelling. At first, there was a heart achingly lovely photograph of Beth. It was her last official school photo, taken in the September as she'd began Year Nine. Then it changed to the last official known photograph of her, grinning away in her mustard coat as she walked through the school grounds. I knew there wasn't a person in that room who hadn't seen that haunting image. Next there was a map of Hawleybrook High School displayed, with possible CCTV blind spots highlighted.

Frank launched into an explanation of the work we'd carried out more recently. He described the initials written in the condensation on the bathroom mirror and explained our recent discovery on what they stood for. He explained that Beth hadn't been wearing her mustard coloured coat, causing the audience to turn and mutter to each other at this latest piece of information.

"Yes?" Frank asked, gesturing at the woman on the second row of seats whose hand had shot in the air.

"So, if Beth wasn't wearing the mustard coat when she went missing, where is it?" she asked.

"That's a very good question," Frank smiled. "Right now, we have no idea."

Frank continued to describe the more recent turn of events, emphasising the list of men who hadn't presented themselves for a voluntary DNA sample at the time that Beth went missing. I couldn't help but notice a few of the men shifting uncomfortably in their seats. Immediately, my mind flitted to the list of men as I tried desperately to remind myself of their names.

He entered into a question and answer session. At first, the number of arms waggling in the air in front of us was limited. However, once one person began to query something, it was like a chain reaction with people's questions prompting further questions.

"I don't think that went too badly at all," Frank smiled, walking towards us from the stage. I hadn't realised that the speech had come to an end. Danny and my father had jumped down from the stage and were handing out flyers containing bullet points of information and a contact phone number for anyone whose memory we had jogged. We'd hesitated when deciding whose phone number to put down, then eventually decided on Danny's. He usually used his work phone on a day to day basis so we had deduced that this wouldn't impact his work life. We'd also set up an email address, which we all vowed to monitor as often as we could in a rota. I'd suggested Frank was to go through the four key areas of the investigation, but he'd advised that it may be a bit too much for people to take in.

"You give them the information, then give them the resources to contact us, let them mull it all over and get back in touch," he'd said at the time.

The hall began to empty, a slow release of people still goggling us up on the stage. Uncle Tony and Magda had lingered, waiting awkwardly to speak to Dad. Tony caught my eye at one point and smiled at me, nervously. I smiled back. I watched as they spoke to Dad briefly before taking a flyer and leaving. Danny watched them both rather sullenly.

"You were brilliant," I smiled at Frank. "Really brilliant. I wouldn't have had a clue where to begin."

"Years of experience," Frank smiled back.

I looked up and realised I was looking straight into the kind, smiling face of Patsy.

"Patsy," I smiled, warmly and I found myself pulling the old lady towards me into an embrace. "I didn't realise you'd be coming."

"I don't know why," she clucked. "I've lived in Hawleybrook all my adult life. I remember that day as clear as anything. It was a terrible shame what happened to your sister."

"How are you feeling?" I asked her.

"Much better, although I've been put on a whole host of medication. If I walk too quickly, you'll hear me rattle," she chuckled. "Anyway, enough about me. How are you getting on? You're absolutely blooming now." Her eyes and hands met my prominent bump. "How far along are you now?"

"Twenty one weeks."

"Excuse me," came a rather timid voice behind us. The weeping lady dressed all in black except for her well worn trainers had climbed the small amount of stairs to the stage. Her eyes were bloodshot. She looked tired.

"Can I help you?" Frank asked.

"I'm not sure. I think you might be able to help me," she said, quietly, her eyes darting nervously from Frank to me to Erica. "Actually, on second thoughts, I'd better be going."

She turned and headed back down the stairs of the stage.

"Wait," I called out, following her. I touched her arm gently. "You look really troubled. Is there something on your mind?"

"It's probably nothing," she murmured, not quite able to meet my eyes. "I don't want to bother you."

"Whatever it is that you want to tell us certainly isn't you bothering us," Frank insisted, as he made his way down the stairs of the stage.

"I've been telling myself to come to this meeting all day. I almost chickened out at the last minute. Almost made an excuse. I still can't believe I'm here."

"Thank you for coming," I said softly.

Her eyes, a pale green colour awash with tears, softened.

"Do you have some information you think might be useful to us?" I continued.

Slowly, she nodded.

"My son – Aaron – he went to the same school as Beth," she said, finally. "They weren't friends or anything, but you know what small towns are like. He knew her."

Her voice had gone weak. I wanted to push her, to encourage her, to urge her to continue but I didn't want to frighten her off. I remained completely silent before realising I was holding my breath.

"On the night she went missing, he – my son, Aaron - came home from school very late. I'd seen the posters up around Hawleybrook town centre, advertising the school Halloween party. I assumed he'd gone to the party and forgotten to tell me."

Her voice trailed off. She closed her eyes.

"When he got home, his school blazer was covered in mud, and his school shirt had ripped. There was – there was a bit of blood on his shirt sleeve. I asked him outright what he'd been up to but he told me he'd had a fight with another lad from school. He never gave me any names which was odd because I knew all the boys from his school year. He put his school uniform straight into the washing machine. I was too pleased at the time to think it was strange," she rattled off, her eyes still closed. It felt as though she was reciting a well rehearsed speech. "I'm not saying he was – I don't know if he had anything – I don't think he's capable of hurting someone, not like that. But..."

"Do you think your son had something to do with the murder of Beth Maguire?" Frank asked, quietly, watching as the door of the community centre hall swung shut – the last of the people exiting.

"I don't know," she whispered, her eyes brimming with tears. "I know that's a terrible thing to say about your own child. My instincts tell me that he had nothing to do with it. I just think, as a mother, I'd know if my own child was a – a murderer."

"What's your son's full name?" I asked.

"Aaron Montgomery."

"Yeah, I think I remember him," I said. "He was in the year below me at school. The year above Beth. Tall, dark hair, used to be captain of the school football team?"

She nodded. "That's him. I'm not saying I think he had anything to do with this. Deep down, I know he isn't capable. But I never did get a proper explanation of what happened that evening or why he was late. It just didn't feel like the story about the fight with his school friend was plausible. And I guess – well, I guess it's always played on my mind."

"What sort of person is Aaron?" I asked. "What's he like now?"

"Don't you remember what he was like at school?" she asked me.

"Vaguely. But people change a lot once they leave school. I know I'm not the same person I was back then."

"He's a good lad. He went away to university to train to be a teacher. He dropped out after the first year. He spent a couple of years working in a few dead end jobs – call centre work and the like. Then he got a job working for an accountancy firm in the city."

Something in Mrs Montgomery's body language indicated that there was more to her story than she was giving out.

"What are you not telling us, Mrs Montgomery?" I murmured.

She shook her head over and over, her bottom lip beginning to wobble and her hands shaking.

"He got into some trouble last year. Nothing like this. He had a car crash on the motorway. Wrote his car off. They breathalysed him. He was drunk. They swabbed him and the swabs revealed he'd taken cocaine too. Then they found a stash of cocaine in his glovebox. He said it was for personal use but there was – there was just too much. The driver of the other car was badly hurt. It was touch and go for a while. He lived – just about. He still uses a wheelchair now. Aaron got six years. He could be out after three. That's what his solicitor says," she sniffed. "Me and his dad were gob smacked. We couldn't believe our son could be so stupid, taking such a bloody great risk. And it was clear that he'd been selling drugs or at least passing them on to someone else. We couldn't believe it. His sister has never so much as smoked a cigarette. We've brought them up exactly the same, yet we've had no trouble from our Natasha. After that, I suppose I've always wondered... do I really know my son at all? Do I really know what he's capable of?"

"So, just to clarify matters, Mrs Montgomery," Frank continued, clearing his throat. My father and brother gathered around us. "Your son Aaron was in the year above Beth at school. On the night she went missing, he came home from school late. You weren't expecting him to be so late. His school shirt was ripped and his clothes were caked in mud. He got in and immediately began to wash his clothes, which was out of character for him. He provided an explanation for why he was so late but you weren't sure you believed him. And now he's in prison because he was driving under the influence of drink and drugs and put someone in a wheelchair for the rest of their lives?"

Mrs Montgomery began to weep again.

"I know how this all sounds," she whispered. "I don't think I'm painting him in a very good light. He's a good person deep down. We brought him up well."

No one said anything. There were so many thoughts whizzing around my head that I was surprised nobody could hear a literal buzzing sound.

"What's going to happen now?" she sniffed, wiping the

tears from her eyes. "Is he going to get into trouble? He's a good lad really."

"I think we may need to speak to your son, Mrs Montgomery," Frank said, quietly. "I think we may have a few questions for young Aaron."

Chapter Seventeen

Having never known anyone who'd spent a spell in prison, I was completely unfamiliar with the visiting process. In my mind, I pictured us all squashing into one car the very next day and driving down to the prison where Aaron Montgomery was based before meeting him in a canteen style room and questioning him until he finally admitted that he was the person responsible for my sister's death. As it turned out, that couldn't be further from the truth.

Firstly, we had to apply to become official visitors to Aaron. Whilst this sounded simple enough, it wasn't. It involved filling in a lot of forms – some of which required details that we didn't know, such as Aaron's unique prison identity number. Frank put a call in to an old police friend who advised how he could apply to become a visitor without needing to fill in such a form. Once Frank had completed that, we then had to wait to hear back from Aaron as to whether or not he accepted our request to visit him.

"What if he doesn't?" I asked Frank at the time, worriedly biting my bottom lip.

"Then there's not a lot we can do," he admitted. "If he doesn't consent to us visiting him, then that's that. If we had genuine suspicions that this person was somehow involved in Beth's murder, we could pass this information on to the police. If they thought he was a potential suspect, they could interview him inside the prison itself. They'd have more rights, of course."

"Why don't we just do that then?" Danny pushed. "Why not just tell the police that we think we've got the little shit?"

"Because we don't have the foggiest whether or not this lad is actually involved yet, do we?" Frank reasoned. "Imagine their reaction if we led them on a wild goose chase. They'd never take anything else we told them seriously, and we need them."

"No, we don't," muttered Danny, sulking in his seat on the couch like a child.

"You'll be singing a different tune when we get the bastard. We aren't the ones who'll be arresting him," Frank explained, calmly.

As it turned out, we needn't have worried about Aaron not accepting our visitation request. It was a few weeks after the meeting at the community centre when we received two security passes in the post. They were only valid for one specific date, which neither Danny nor my dad could make – much to my father's annoyance. It was a Tuesday, meaning I should have been in work so I tried not to feel too guilty as I rang in sick that morning, feigning a rather nasty bout of morning sickness. Almost as punishment for my pretend illness, I felt a lurking headache growing behind my left eye.

The prison was based in Durham, which was around a two and a half hour's drive away. I stopped at Frank's block of flats at just gone eight o'clock in the morning and, to my surprise, he was already ready and downstairs waiting in the car park for me. He'd brought a file of notes and a flask of coffee along with him, which he insisted on pouring into a cup and passing to me whilst I drove. I didn't have the heart to tell him I shouldn't have drank anything with caffeine in and besides, the sudden burst of energy was welcome.

The journey to Durham was a relatively quiet one. We were both anxious but I felt more than just anxiety about meeting Aaron Montgomery. I was beginning to feel inexplicably light headed and woozy, as though I had a terrible hangover without the wine. We hit traffic as soon as we got onto the motorway. I wasn't in the mood for small talk so I fiddled with the knobs on my radio and let the sound of Take That fill the car.

As soon as we pulled into the visitor car park, I took two paracetamol to ease my headache. Swallowing them with a generous mouthful from my bottle of water, I briefly wondered if I was going to throw up.

"Are you feeling okay?" Frank asked me, as he stood up outside next to the car to stretch his legs.

"Mmhmm," I murmured, still unsure if I was about to see my breakfast cereal in reverse.

"It's a hard day," Frank soothed, patting me on the arm gently. "If at any point you want to stop, just let me know. You don't even need to see him if you don't feel up to it. I can speak to him while you wait here in the car."

Like hell, I thought as I got out of the car and locked it, heading in the direction of the foreboding dirty white building in front of me.

The Aaron Montgomery I remembered from school was

cheeky. He was good looking but he knew it and he used his looks and his charm to play the teaching staff, most of whom fell for it hook, line and sinker. He was naturally good at athletics and hung around with the loud, outgoing and sporty crowd. He wore perhaps a little too much gel in his hair, as was the trend in the early noughties, and bore an almost permanent tan from all the outdoor sports he participated in.

The Aaron Montgomery that approached us from the line of identically dressed men couldn't have been any more different. Everything about him was grey. He was wearing a grey coloured tracksuit, as were the other prisoners. The tracksuit was baggy, particularly the jumper, but it didn't look faded. It gave the impression that Aaron had lost a lot of weight in a short space of time. His skin was no longer golden, reflecting long summers spent playing football on the school field. It had taken on a grey sheen, leaving him looking unwell and greasy. His hair was mottled with flecks of grey. His once bright green eyes had faded into a murky grey, with only the blacks of his pupils really visible. Even his *walk* was grey; a sad shadow of a schoolboy swagger, no longer existing in the empty shell of a man.

"Thank you for agreeing to meet with us," Frank began, his manners intact as usual.

"Who are you? What do you want?" Aaron asked, squinting directly at me. He had a nervous tic which affected his neck. Every few seconds, he inadvertently glanced to his right. He didn't even seem to notice. Perhaps he was used to it.

"My name is Frank Perry. I'm a retired detective chief inspector. I was the lead investigating officer in the Beth Maguire case," Frank explained.

There it was. The moment I'd been waiting four weeks for. It was why I was so certain I would be the one to visit Aaron. I wanted to see the look on his face when he realised why we were there. In the nanosecond it took for him to process Frank's words, I realised that he wasn't the person we were looking for. I knew it in my heart but would have been unable to explain it to anyone if they'd asked me to.

"And this is..." Frank's words were cut short by Aaron speaking.

"I know who you are," Aaron said, looking directly at me again. "You're her sister, aren't you? Beth's sister? Your name's

Sophie, isn't it?"

I nodded, suddenly unable to speak. My head was pounding and I had become increasingly aware of the smell of poorly cooked food orbiting around us. Ever since becoming pregnant, my sense of smell had been heightened enormously, yet I was unable to determine the meal which was the source of this smell. Perhaps that was testament to the calibre of cuisine on offer in HMP Durham, I thought with a grim realisation.

"So, what do you want from me?" he asked. Straight to the point. I liked it.

"We're investigating the disappearance and murder of Beth Maguire. We've recently obtained intelligence which we'd like to clarify with you," explained Frank.

Aaron's forehead creased with confusion. It was genuine. He had no idea what we were going to ask him.

"O-kay," he said, slowly, still frowning.

"As you will already know, Beth Maguire was abducted from Hawleybrook High School on 31st October 2005. Her body was found two days later, raped and strangled, in Griffin Woods. On the night she went missing, you were late home from school. When you eventually got home, your school uniform was ripped and muddy," Frank explained. "Can you tell us anything about that, Aaron?"

Perplexed, Aaron said, "Yeah. I got into a bit of a fight with my mate if I remember rightly."

"Where did this fight take place?"

"On the school field."

"The police spent hours trawling through CCTV footage from Hawleybrook High School taken on the day in question and no fistfight was ever detected," Frank said, sharply.

"Course it wasn't," Aaron snorted. "We weren't stupid. We weren't going to have a fight right in front of the teachers' noses, were we?"

"You mean, you were aware that there were areas that the CCTV cameras didn't cover?"

Aaron laughed, shaking his head in disbelief. "It was common knowledge that there were blind spots. It's where we'd all go to buy and sell stuff."

"What sort of stuff?" Frank persisted.

"Cigarettes. Alcohol. Porn," he laughed. "Surely you

remember that?" His question was aimed directly at me.

"I knew people bought cigarettes on the school grounds. But I didn't smoke, so I didn't know where any of it took place," I admitted.

"Bit of a goodie goodie, were you?" Aaron grinned, leaning back in his chair. For a split second, I recognised the old Aaron Montgomery. The cocky, smug arsehole.

"Who were you fighting?" Frank asked him.

"God, I don't know. It was years ago," Aaron sighed.

"Did you get into a lot of fights when you were in school?" pushed Frank.

"Not particularly."

"Then it can't be too difficult to remember," insisted Frank. "Come on. Think. Presumably, you'd had some sort of problem with this person, if you felt it could only be resolved by physical violence."

Aaron hesitated. Then -

"It wasn't like that."

"Well, what was it like then?" I asked.

Seemingly surprised at my input in the questioning, Aaron raised his eyebrows. "I was fourteen. Some bloke stopped me on my way home from school one night. A black man. Kind of scruffy looking with dreadlocks. Always smoking. He said he was running a bare knuckle fighting club and was recruiting members. He said he'd seen me playing football and rugby and thought I was the right sort of lad. I went along to the club but it wasn't my thing. It felt a bit – seedy, you know? A bit unofficial. Like this fella could have been anyone. I didn't know him from Adam. Anyway, I told him I wasn't interested and I got off. It was a few days later when he stopped me on my way home from school again. I was with my mate Tom. He offered us money if we agreed to fight. He placed bets on us. He made money from us fighting. He made sure the fights were filmed. He gave us a really good mobile phone to film them on."

"Who was this man?" Frank frowned.

"His name was Andy. That's all I know. He never gave us his second name," Aaron replied.

"Where was this bare knuckle fight club based?"

"In a big empty warehouse in Hawleybrook. I think it used to be a gym."

"Can you remember roughly where it was in Hawleybrook?" asked Frank.

"Just outside of the high street. Next door to a closed down chip shop."

"How much money did he give you?"

"Not much. About twenty quid each, I think," he said.

"And who was he placing bets with? Who were the other people involved in this?" Frank persisted.

"I don't know. I mean, I only got involved twice. I had that fight with Tom and then a fight with a lad in the year above me. I didn't know him. Couldn't tell you his name. Anyway, it got a bit out of hand. Tom and me fell out. It's hard to stay mates with someone when you've punched them in the head several times," he grinned, still maintaining eye contact with me. "That Andy fella kept following me after school, asking why I didn't want to have any more fights. He told me there were loads of people who kept placing bets on me. They thought I was good. I kept telling him I wasn't interested and handed the phone back to him. You know – the one he gave me to film the fights on. After a while, he gave up. I never heard from him again."

"And why did he want you to have the fights in school when he had a warehouse you could use? Seems a bit risky to me," I frowned.

"I guess he thought he was less involved if it happened on the school grounds. It could be passed off as an innocent school boy fight," suggested Aaron.

"And he made sure you filmed the fights so he could put the videos on the internet?" Frank asked.

Shrugging, Aaron said, "I guess so. I never really asked. To be honest, it all happened around the same time Beth Maguire was murdered so there were more interesting things going on."

Interesting. The word made me shake with anger. My sister's murder was not *interesting.* It was abhorrent. It was despicable. It was not *interesting.* My already pounding head gave a vibrating thump. I swallowed, dimly aware that the paracetamol I'd taken weren't cutting the mustard.

"Would you recognise this Andy again if I showed you a photograph of him?" Frank asked Aaron. Aaron simply shrugged. "Did you see anyone else inside that old warehouse?"

"Yeah, there were other blokes there. They sat at the side,

watching us."

"Did you recognise any of them? Were there people that you knew there?"

"Only one man, and that was only because his picture was sometimes banded around the Hawleybrook Gazette. I can't remember his name off the top of my head but he was a short fella. Ginger hair. Bucked teeth. Bit of a posh bloke really," Aaron described.

"Nigel Graham?" suggested Frank.

Shrugging, Aaron appeared totally disinterested. "No idea. Could be. That name does ring a bell. But I couldn't say for sure."

"Nigel Graham?" I asked Frank, quietly. "Who's that?"

"He's the one I mentioned a few weeks back. He was head of the Hawleybrook Hunt. Got charged for assaulting a minor in 2009," Frank explained, his mind whirring away.

"Yeah, that's the guy," Aaron nodded. "The ginger guy who was always in trouble for fox hunting after the ban."

"Do you think he's had anything to do with Beth's murder?" I asked him.

"I'm not sure. But an angry man who enjoys watching animals rip each other apart and who potentially also likes to place bets on children beating each other senseless? Someone who, a few years after your sister's death, physically assaulted a child? He didn't present himself for a voluntary DNA sample either. It stinks of a bad egg to me," muttered Frank. "I tried the phone number which was listed as his on the Hawleybrook Hunt's website, but it didn't work. Said the number wasn't recognised. In all honesty, I'm not sure how up to date the website actually is. The last time anything was posted was almost two years ago. I sent Nigel a few emails a couple of weeks ago, asking a few questions. He never got back to me. I think it's about time we found out where he lives and paid him a visit."

Standing up and shrugging his coat onto his shoulders, Frank nodded curtly at Aaron.

"Thank you for your time. You've been most helpful," he said, warmly and gestured for me to stand up.

As we turned to leave, Aaron's voice called out: "When you two came here today, what were you thinking? What was the point in you coming to see me?"

Without turning around, Frank replied, "We thought you

were the person who had raped and strangled Beth Maguire."

And with that, we were gone.

Chapter Eighteen

"I think you have preeclampsia, Sophie," said the midwife as she rolled the sleeve of my jumper down with just a little too much force. "I can hardly say I'm surprised given what you've been up to recently."

It was the following day and I was sat in the doctors' surgery attending an emergency appointment. The surgery was beginning to feel like my second home. No one ever mentions how many medical appointments you have to go to when you're pregnant. My arms were prodded and poked so many times by needles that I resembled a pin cushion.

Since driving home from Durham, I'd taken some time out for myself. I got home in the early afternoon and ran myself a bath, generously pouring thick blue bubble bath into the swirling steam of water. Allowing myself to soak in the bath for well over an hour didn't do the trick so I put a pan of soup on the stove and began buttering some crusty bread when I was overcome with dizziness. Reaching out and grabbing the kitchen worktop to steady myself, I vomited onto the recently mopped kitchen tiles.

Calvin had arrived home within half an hour of me ringing him. He insisted I went straight back to bed and kept popping upstairs to bring me food or endless cups of tea, all the time speaking in uncharacteristically hushed tones. It was sweet at first but quickly grew annoying. He told me I needed to book an appointment with the midwife. I didn't have the energy to do it there and then so waited until the following morning when they managed to squeeze me in.

I'd then spent the majority of my medical appointment being questioned on my movements over the last couple of weeks. At first, the midwife had appeared genuinely interested in my sister's investigation. Then, as if reality had set in, she scolded me for doing what she deemed to be too much.

"You want to be taking it easy," the midwife continued, turning to her computer screen and tapping away at the keyboard, occasionally shaking her head in disbelief. "You're about to go into your third trimester. You should be thinking about winding down, putting your feet up, resting before the baby comes. Certainly not stampeding up and down the country, trying to put the world to rights."

"It was hardly stampeding," I sighed. "I drove two and a half hours to Durham."

"And sat chatting with a potential murderer? Your *sister's* potential murderer?" the midwife clucked, still shaking her head.

"He's not though, is he? That's what we found out. He had nothing to do with my sister's death," I explained.

"Sophie, I know what happened to your younger sister was terrible. Absolutely bloody awful. I remember it when it happened all those years ago. We were all shocked, none more than me. I've got a daughter about your age. I remember it well. But you can't be getting yourself all worked up over it, not in your condition. Now, your blood pressure is high and there's a lot of protein in your urine sample. That indicates preeclampsia," she sniffed.

I didn't have the energy to challenge her. I'd heard of preeclampsia but wasn't entirely sure what it actually was. Rather than risk another lecture, I figured I'd Google it once I got home.

"What happens now then?"

"I'm going to sign you off sick from work for the next two weeks and you're going to take it easy. Plenty of rest and relaxation. In the meantime, I'll send your blood sample off to the lab to be looked at. If it is preeclampsia, you'll get a phone call from the hospital's maternity ward. They'll want you to come in. So make sure you're about. Don't go swanning off to Doncaster again."

"It was Durham," I muttered as I clutched my sick note in my hand and walked out of the surgery.

The conversation with Chris Sheridan was surprisingly easy. It was clear that Erica had told him that I knew about their workplace romance and he was keen to do anything he could to avoid talking about it with me. He ushered me into his office, offering me a tea or a coffee, and spoke ten to the dozen about anything to fill the silence until a kind faced lady from HR came to join us.

Bemused, I simply handed Chris the sick note from my midwife and explained I was going to be taking a bit of time off. Chris, understandably from the circumstances, looked slightly relieved.

"Do let me know if there's anything I can do for you whilst you're off sick," he smiled at me as I stood up to leave his office.

"Don't worry. I'll tell Erica if anything's wrong and I'm sure she can pass a message on to you if needs be," I grinned as the glass door of his office swung shut behind me, leaving Chris red faced and silent.

I had been at home, wrapped in a fleecy blanket on the couch watching daytime television, for less than an hour when my phone rang. My father's name popped up on my screen.

"Hi, Dad."

"Sophie? It's your dad," came my father's booming voice.

"Yes, Dad. I know. That's why I said 'hi, Dad'," I laughed to myself. "Is everything okay?"

"I see. Yes, everything's fine. I've just had a phone call from Frank. He's managed to get hold of Nigel Graham's home address. He suggested we nip round there later today," he explained.

"Why hasn't he phoned me?" I demanded.

"Calvin rang us all last night. He told us you were tucked up in bed after being sick and nearly fainting. You're clearly doing too much."

"Am I heck," I scoffed. "I'm fine. I've just not been eating as well as I should be. That's all."

"Well, Frank seems to think it's best we carry on without you for the time being. We don't wish to be unkind but you're obviously not very well," Dad stuttered, clearly nervous about broaching the topic with me. "Perhaps it's best if you sit this one out."

"Dad," I whined, rolling my eyes with great force. "Don't be so ridiculous. I'll drive us. Where does this Nigel live anyway?"

"According to Frank, he's still living in the same house he's been in for years. It's in Hawleybrook," he explained.

After negotiating with my father around the particulars, I arrived to pick him, Frank and my brother up that evening. We drove over to the house a little quieter than we would have normally. We were all nervous. Danny kept inadvertently shaking his leg. Dad kept sighing. It was a big moment, a potential movement in the right direction, and the atmosphere was so thick that it could have choked us.

"Here it is," Frank murmured, gesturing unnecessarily at the small row of cottages to our left as my sat nav called out that we had reached our destination.

After an awkward moment whilst I attempted to parallel park between two other cars, we walked towards number one seven five. It was small but pleasant, with a wooden heart shaped ornament on the windowsill and the curtains almost fully shut. Light could be seen from inside the window, with the images from a television screen flickering. Collectively, we held our breath as Frank tapped the silver knocker on the front door.

A small woman came to the door, already dressed in her pyjamas and fluffy pink dressing gown. She appeared to visibly shrink in front of us as she stared, looking from one to the other, her face creased with confusion.

"Can I help you?" she asked, finally, her voice trembling. My heart went out to her. I realised we looked rather intimidating; an unfamiliar foursome stood solemnly on her doorstep.

"Is it possible to speak to Mr Nigel Graham?" Frank asked, his manners ever present.

"I'm afraid that won't be possible at all," she said, her eyes wide and unblinking. "Considering that he's dead."

Her words hit my stomach like a firework on a cold night – slow, then unmistakeably clear.

"I'm so sorry to hear that. I had no idea," Frank explained, his fingers twitching over his snowy white facial hair.

"Is there something I can help with?" she suggested, peering at us all slowly.

No one responded. The situation was unexpected. No one had anticipated that the person we wanted to speak to had died. In my peripheral vision, I saw my father nervously glance at Frank for answers.

"Do you want to come in?" the woman asked, kindly.

We trudged into the brightly lit house, gawkily pulling off our shoes and foisting them into a small pile by the front door, before following the woman into the living room. She stood by an armchair which had an obscenely large cat lay, seemingly asleep, on the arm and gestured for us to sit on the remaining armchair and sofa. We did so wordlessly.

"Can I get anyone a cup of tea?" she offered, smiling.

As we exchanged pleasantries – "Do you take milk? Sugar?" – I got the distinct impression that this woman was lonely. The photographs in the house were of her and the same horse faced man. He, I assumed, was her husband. Once she had returned to the living room, expertly balancing a pink and white gingham tray in one hand and a biscuit tin in the other, the mood in the room settled slightly. The atmosphere felt easier to breathe in.

"Now, what did you want with poor Nigel?" she asked, pouring a generous helping of milk into each cup. My stomach churned with the thought of such a milky tea.

"Was Nigel your husband?" asked Frank.

She nodded, gesturing to the framed photograph on top of the television. A man and a woman dressed in a long white dress, drowning in confetti with smiles to rival the Cheshire cat's.

"When did he pass away?" Frank asked, accepting his cup and saucer with apparent ease.

"It'll be a year in May," she said, scooping the large cat into her arms and burying her face in his fur. "Cancer. Pancreatic. It was quick." Her words were sharp, fixed, well rehearsed. They reminded me of my own way of explaining my sister's death and then, more recently, my mother's. It was almost as though if you said it fast, no one would question you further. The first of many barriers to go up. Brief protection from the pain.

"I'm so sorry for your loss, Mrs Graham," I muttered from behind my teacup. She made eye contact with me and smiled.

"We were unaware that he had passed away. We were hoping to speak to him about – about the murder of Beth Maguire," Frank explained, slowly.

Mrs Graham's hand, halfway up to her mouth with a teacup in tow, paused dramatically in the air. Her kind face drained of blood. Any compassion I felt for her evaporated. For reasons I could not explain, I felt that Mrs Graham had expected a meeting of this sort to occur. I felt she didn't know when or where or how, but she knew that at some point, someone would be asking her questions about my sister.

"You look worried," I blurted out.

The occupants of the room turned to stare at me. Danny shook his head.

"I don't mean to be rude," I continued, quickly. "But when Frank explained what we were hoping to talk to your husband about, you looked very worried. But not surprised."

"I don't – I don't know what you're – I think you should

all leave," she said, suddenly, placing her teacup back on its saucer and onto the mantelpiece above the fire with icy precision.

"We're not going anywhere," I muttered, resolutely still in my seat. "We have a few questions for you, Mrs Graham. We'll go once we have satisfactory answers to our questions."

"Satisfactory answers," she sniffed, staring at me. "You lot aren't the police. Are you?"

"No, Mrs Graham," answered Frank, his eyes still on me. "But I was in the police. In fact, I was the lead investigating officer in Beth Maguire's murder. And this is Beth's family. We're investigating the events that led up to her disappearance and death."

"What's that got to do with my husband?"

"Nigel was head of the Hawleybrook Hunt. He was charged in 2009 with assaulting a child. Recent intelligence suggests that he was also involved with an illegal bare knuckle fighting club. A club which paid children to fight. A club which placed bets on which child would win. A club which supported aggressive behaviour of children who went to Beth's school," Frank explained, calmly, his eyes fixed on Mrs Graham.

"I honestly don't know what you're talking about," she repeated. "Yes, Nigel was involved with the fox hunting group. But I don't see what that has to do with little Beth Maguire. And as for that mishap in 2009, it wasn't a *child*. He got into a fight with someone in the pub. He thought they were in their twenties. It was only when he was arrested that he learned they were only fifteen. They shouldn't have been drinking in a pub really. And I don't have a clue what you're on about with this fight club."

"Was your husband an angry man, Mrs Graham?" I asked, feeling the eyes of the three people to the left of me boring into the side of my head.

"I beg your pardon?" she hissed. "What sort of question is that?"

"You see, I think he was an angry man. He enjoyed watching hounds tearing foxes to shreds. He encouraged it. He was in charge of it. And now someone's told us he used to enjoy watching kids beating each other black and blue. Was he ever violent with you?"

"Sophie," muttered my father, worriedly.

"I think you should leave," Mrs Graham repeated. "I'm not

going to sit here in my own home and be accused of being married to a – a violent man. Nigel may have had his faults but he was a good person and I won't allow his name or reputation to be tarnished. What exactly are you getting at? What does any of this have to do with Beth Maguire?"

"A few months after Beth died, there was an appeal for local men to present themselves to give a voluntary DNA sample in order to eliminate themselves from the investigation. The majority of men in the area came forward. Your husband didn't. Do you know why that was?" I continued, feeling my heart racing under my skin.

Mrs Graham's mouth opened and closed but no sound came out.

"Where was your husband on the night Beth went missing?" I persisted. "She was abducted from school on the afternoon of 31st October 2005. It was a long time ago so allow me to jog your memory. It was Halloween. It was a grey, overcast day. Beth's body was found in Griffin Woods two days after she went missing. She'd been raped and strangled. Did your husband ever go to Griffin Woods, Mrs Graham? Was it a place he felt familiar with? Did your husband get home from work late that evening? Were his clothes muddy? Did you ever ask him what he was doing that night?"

Mrs Graham was staring at me, then at Frank. She was silent. Lost for words. Her silence pushed me into an anger like I'd never felt before.

"Maybe you knew all along that he had something to do with my sister's death. Maybe you always knew that the weak excuse he gave you as to why he was late home that evening didn't make sense. Perhaps you felt you couldn't question him any further. After all, he had a temper, didn't he? He was an angry man. Maybe you kept quiet to protect him, to protect yourself, your children!"

I was shouting. My voice was loud but steady, although my heart was anything but. It was racing, little jolts of electricity rushing through my veins. I was gasping for breath. My head was spinning but I continued, standing up in front of this shrinking violet of a woman.

"Women like you disgust me," I sneered. "You'd stand by your man for anything, wouldn't you? Even child murder?"

"Get out!" she screeched, her voice high pitched and squeaky.

I heard the slap before I felt it, like a rumble of thunder in a stormy evening. Then my cheek was hot and stinging.

"I think we'd better leave it there for now," Frank said, quickly, bundling me into his arms and half dragging me out of the living room and into the hall. Danny was ahead of us, stuffing his feet into his trainers and dragging my boots over to me.

Then two things happened.

Firstly, Mrs Graham followed us into the hall of her house, her head cocked to one side to support the mobile phone pressed against her ear. She was ringing the police. In one movement, I bent down and stuffed my feet inside my ankle boots, throwing my coat around my shoulders without stopping to put my arms in the sleeves. We all rushed for the door, Danny in the front and me fumbling with my car keys in my coat pocket.

And secondly, I fainted.

Chapter Nineteen

"I remember the last time you were staying overnight in hospital. You were about twelve and you had suspected appendicitis. I had to bring your pyjamas and toothbrush and I got in trouble with your mother for bringing the wrong ones. I'd just reached into the laundry basket and pulled out girls pyjamas, not realising that they were your sister's and were three sizes too small for you. You spent the night in pyjama trousers that looked like pink long johns and what looked like a crop top. Do you remember?" my father asked me.

Shaking my head whilst laughing, I winced as the drip in my hand pulled.

"Are you okay? Are you in any pain? Shall I get the nurse?" Calvin began, jumping up and scanning the room for any available medical professional.

Sighing, I said, "Calvin, I'm fine. I just tugged the drip in my hand. If you want to do something to help me, you can bring in my laptop."

"I'm not bringing anything which means you can log on and start doing work. You've been signed off sick for a reason," he sniffed.

"I'm not bothered about catching up on work," I laughed. "I want to crack on with some work for the investigation."

I had been living in hospital for three miserable days. Three days of having to piss in a plastic container and have someone inspect the contents of it. Three days of terrible plastic looking food. Three days of feeling helpless and cooped up. At first, the thought of being an inpatient excited me. I pictured meeting lots of new people on my ward and perhaps even getting to ogle an attractive young doctor. As it turned out, I was bitterly disappointed. My ward was only full of pregnant women, the majority of whom had their husbands with them all day and therefore, had the curtains around their bed closed. And any doctors I had seen were all female.

"You need to be taking it easy, young lady," Dad said, unnecessarily smoothing my stiff hospital blanket in his hands. "We'll take things from here. Don't you worry about a thing."

"But I want to worry about things!" I cried. "I'm bored. I'm fed up."

"Didn't you say Erica was coming to see you later?" Calvin pointed out. "That'll cheer you up."

He made a very valid point. Neither my father nor my not-quite-my-boyfriend would smuggle my laptop into the hospital but my irresponsible and reckless work companion definitely wouldn't mind. As soon as my dad and Calvin left, I fired off a quick text message to Erica begging her to nip round to my house to pick up my laptop before coming to see me. I also asked her to check on Mr Darcy and Clive. As well as both being fed, Clive was being let in and out of the house by my neighbour for his necessary trips to the toilet, which coincidentally took place in the very same neighbour's back garden.

She didn't let me down. Clutching a polystyrene drinks tray with two Starbucks coffee cups in one perfectly manicured hand with a holdall bag balancing off the other one, she stormed into the hospital ward, quietly locating me with a quick scan over the rim of her sunglasses. Taking one look at me, Erica gasped.

"Bloody hell, Soph. You look absolutely terrible," she said, scanning me up and down.

"Thanks a lot," I said, sourly and she burst out laughing. Her booming chuckle forced a smile out of me.

"I'm just saying – I've definitely seen you looking better," she grinned, thrusting the navy blue holdall bag at me. One handed, I rifled through the contents of the bag. Erica had come up trumps. She'd brought dry shampoo, face wipes, my make up bag, some nice instant coffee sachets, my laptop and charger, a few pairs of knickers – none of which would fit me anymore but I didn't have the heart to tell her – my headphones, my book and the most basic of essentials – a large box of Maltesers.

"So, tell me about that crazy woman and the police," she instructed me as she sat in a yellow plastic hospital chair and immediately – and predictably – complained about how uncomfortable it was.

"We went round to see her husband initially but it turned out he'd died almost a year ago. We thought perhaps he had something to do with Beth's death," I explained, taking an almighty sip out of my Starbucks cup. Proper coffee with caffeine! Heaven, I thought, smugly, only wincing slightly as a guilty afterthought of the baby popped into my head.

"And why did you think that?"

"We went to see that Aaron Montgomery in prison after his mum approached us at the community centre. He had nothing to do with Beth's death but he did tell us something quite interesting. He said he was approached by a stranger, a black man, after school a couple of times and he tried to recruit him for this illegal bareknuckle fighting club. Aaron went along with it for a while, probably because this bloke paid him to do it. They would organise fights – all on the school grounds – which were filmed and then uploaded onto the internet for men to place bets on. One of the men who regularly betted on the fights was a guy called Nigel Graham. He's well known for being a bit of a dickhead. He ran the fox hunting group based in Hawleybrook and apparently got charged a few years after Beth died for assaulting a minor," I described.

"Charming. What a lovely bloke," Erica said, rolling her eyes into oblivion.

"Exactly," I replied, swallowing another huge mouthful of coffee. "Anyway, Frank got hold of his address so we drove round there a few days ago but his wife told us he'd died of cancer last year. When we told her what we'd gone round to talk to him about, she lost it. She asked us to leave over and over again, which of course we refused to do, but then she slapped me."

"What?"

Erica's mouth formed the perfect O shape.

"Yep. She hit me in the face and then rang the police on us. We scarpered and I passed out next to my car," I laughed.

According to my brother, I'd landed on the ground with quite a considerable thump. When I'd come round in the back of the car, my stomach and back were hurting and my knickers felt unpleasantly damp. I quickly realised I was bleeding but in a car full of men, I felt uncomfortable mentioning it, so I'd taken the opportunity to whisper in the nurse's ear when we first arrived at the hospital. She'd arranged a scan for me, so I was whizzed down to the maternity unit and lay, nervously, on the hospital bed.

Calvin still hadn't arrived. The thirty second pause between the cool gel being squirted on my raised lower abdomen and the images flickering on the screen felt stifling. A moment later and I saw a chubby fist being waved around inside me; my stomach rippling with movement from the unexpected prodding and poking.

"Your baby is absolutely fine," soothed the ultrasound technician, tapping away at her keyboard. "Has anyone told you the baby's sex?"

Fervently, I shook my head. "We want it to be a surprise. Apparently, it's meant to make you push harder." The sonographer laughed. Technically, *Calvin* wanted it to be a surprise. I was itching to know what colour to fill my basket with in Mothercare but I'd agreed not to find out as, in Calvin's own words, I "couldn't hold my own water".

"I'll switch this off then. The baby has their legs wide open," she grinned, tilting the screen towards her.

The following day, Calvin by my side, we had another scan as I had continued to bleed. Again, the baby was grumpily woken from its slumber but quickly became quite active, tossing and turning and displaying its nether regions in all its glory. Smiling to myself, I was almost certain I had seen a tiny little willy – or perhaps a distinctive umbilical cord.

"So, what happened then?" Erica asked, gripped, dragging me from my thoughts.

"Not that I remember very much of it but Danny said he scooped me up, stuffed me in the car and drove us all straight to the hospital. My dad went to my house to pack a few things up for me and brought it back here. Then when he got home, he had two police officers waiting on his doorstep. He had to answer a few questions and they told him never to contact Mrs Graham or any of her family again in future."

"I can't say I'm surprised," soothed Erica.

"Neither were we. So you can imagine my dad's surprise when he had a knock on the door the following day from Mrs Graham," I said slowly. Erica's eyebrows all but disappeared into her hairline.

"What did she want?"

"She'd dug out some old travel documents which showed that Nigel Graham was in Berlin with her from 30th October to 2nd November 2005. It was their silver wedding anniversary the week before. She said the trip was memorable, hence why she'd kept hold of the documents in some sort of memory box. It couldn't have been him. He wasn't in the country. He wasn't my sister's murderer."

Erica nodded, slowly, processing the information. "And so

you guys have hounded a grieving woman in her own home about a child murder which had nothing to do with her or her late husband?"

I sheepishly nodded. "I know. It sounds terrible, doesn't it? Thinking about it, Dad was lucky to get off with just a word of warning from the police. Anyway, now I'm stuck in here, bored out of my brains, whilst they're all carrying on working on the investigation. It's not fair. Hence why I asked you to bring my laptop."

Erica frowned. "What are you planning to do on your laptop?"

"A couple of things," I replied, pulling my computer out of the bag and firing it up on my lap. The familiar buzzing sound as it booted up was soothing. "I've sent a few messages to people on Facebook. Just a couple of people in the same school year as Beth. I've contacted Aaron Montgomery's friends – or at least, the people he was friends with in school – to see if they remember this Andy bloke who ran the bareknuckle fight club."

"Do you really think they're linked?" Erica asked, draining the last of her coffee in one quick motion. "I mean, it's one thing to operate an illicit fighting club which makes you a bit of money on the side. It's a whole other kettle of fish to abduct a young girl, rape her and then strangle her, isn't it?"

"I just think it's worth looking into. Hawleybrook and Arlington Heath aren't exactly the Bronx, are they? One's a sleepy little village and the other is a small town. To have something so seedy being run from there, using children from the village, is sick. Whoever was involved with it is sick. Whoever was involved with it might know something," I rationalised. I tried not to notice Erica's look of disdain as I logged onto the hospital Wi-Fi and booted up the internet. "Look, I know it sounds mad but I want to at least explore…"

My voice trailed off. Erica's words were barely audible over the sound of blood rushing round my head.

"What? What is it? What's wrong?" she said.

"We've had an email," I breathed, my hand shaking as I turned the laptop screen towards her. "Remember after the meeting at the community centre when we agreed to set up an email address for people to use as a point of contact?"

"Yeah?"

"We've had an email. Actually, we've had a few emails but they've mostly gone unread. But yesterday, we got this," I said, gesturing my hand towards the screen.

Squinting, she got off the plastic chair and moved closer to the screen, her mouth moving as she read the words in her head. An odd look came over her face.

"*I know what happened to Beth. Someone confessed his involvement to me six years ago. He still has possession of her mustard coat,*" she breathed. Then she read it aloud again. "What the hell?"

Without saying anything to Erica, I hit *reply* to the email and began formulating my response.

"Wait. What are you going to say?"

"I'm going to ask who the hell they are. I'm going to ask to meet up with them," I said, my eyes unblinking as my hands raced up and down the keyboard. "I've put my phone number at the end of the message."

"Do you think they're telling the truth?" Erica asked, softly.

"I don't know. It's worth a try though, surely?" I pointed out as I fiddled around my bedside table for my phone, clumsily punching the screen with my shaking fingers as I first dialled my father's number. When he didn't answer, I tried my brother. When he didn't answer, I tried Frank. "What is going on? Where is everyone? Why is no one answering?" Frustrated, I tossed my phone down the bed, watching it becoming buried by a hospital blanket.

"Send them all a text message," Erica suggested, calmly. "They'll get back to you later. It'll be interesting to see what Frank makes of it all."

Her words were insignificant to me; birdsong in the midst of morning traffic. My inbox flashed – *one new message.*

"They've replied!" I exclaimed, inching the laptop screen closer to my face. The woman in the bed next to me had looked up from her iPad to stare at the commotion. Without speaking, Erica understood that I needed privacy and tugged the cheap pink curtains around my bed.

"What have they said?" she asked.

"*Meet me at St George's park on Richmond Avenue in an hour. I need five thousand pounds to talk. Bring it in cash. Involve the police and I'll never speak. The truth will die with me,*" I read out, my head starting to spin. Without a moment's hesitation, I looked around for my shoes. "Where are my shoes? Where's my coat?"

"Sophie, hang on a minute. Aren't you forgetting something? You're in *hospital.* You're not well. You can't be charging off to the park with five grand over something you don't even know is legit," she reasoned with me. "And where are you going to get five grand from anyway?"

Scoffing, I said, "My mum's will. I got the cheque last week as executor of her will. I cashed it on Monday."

"Sophie, please. Just stop. Think about this for a second. You don't know if this person is telling the truth. If they were any sort of decent person, they'd have told you anything they know years ago. Why would they wait until now? It's a bit convenient, don't you think? Over thirteen years since Beth was killed and you've just held a very public forum appealing for information – the first time since she died. People know you're interested. They know you're looking for answers. They know you're *desperate.* And there are some sick bastards out there who will try to cash in on that."

Glancing at her, not taking in anything she was saying, I tried to work out the best route from the hospital to the park. I wondered if Erica would drop me off or whether I'd be forced to take a taxi. Clearly mistaking my staring at her as being me having second thoughts, Erica persisted.

"Think about it," she continued. "This is blackmail. They're offering you potentially incorrect information in exchange for five thousand pounds. They've contacted you anonymously. Do you really think this person knows anything at all? Because I think it's more likely they'd ask you to leave the money in a bin and they'd help themselves without even speaking to you. It could even be kids messing around. Sophie. Soph? Please tell me you're not seriously considering meeting this person?"

Her words were meaningless. Empty. I winced with pain as I tried to whip the cannula out of my hand.

"How do I pull this out without it hurting like a bitch?" I said, aware of blood starting to drip down my hand.

"You don't. You'd have to get a nurse to take it out and no

one will because you're not ready to go home yet."

"I'll discharge myself," I dismissed. "I don't have to stay here."

"Sophie, I think this is a really bad idea," Erica warned, her face looking more and more concerned. "Even if they think that they're volunteering accurate information, they could have been told a pack of lies themselves. I don't think you should be spending this sort of money on something like this, Soph. Your mum wouldn't have wanted you wasting five thousand pounds on someone who's at best, exploiting you and at worst, exploiting your dead sister."

Her last sentence hit my chest like a bullet. Shaking my head, I dismissed her words. She didn't understand. No one did. Except perhaps my father.

"Look, you can stand here and try to warn me off all you like but the bottom line is, I'm going to St George's park and I'm going there today. I just need to stop at my bank to withdraw the cash. Even if I didn't have it, I'd take out a bloody payday loan if I had to. Now, you can either take me or you can hang around here huffing and puffing all day," I explained. "But either way, I'm going."

Erica paused, torn. She sighed. She shook her head, helplessly. Then –

"Right. Fine. I'll get the nurse."

Chapter Twenty

"I told you it was a bad idea," Erica grumbled from the driver's seat. "Oh and you're dripping blood on to my upholstery."

We waited for over an hour in the car park at St George's. Each minute that passed made me realise how silly I had been. Of course no one was going to turn up. I'd been fooled, duped, hoodwinked.

With a start, I remembered a similar scenario in the weeks that followed Beth's murder. We began to receive prank phone calls. Some started off with silence, followed by giggles and cackles of laughter. Some had a muffled voice offering up false information. Even though my mother had known deep down that the latter carried no real evidence, she reported each one to our family liaison officer until finally, with great encouragement from the police, we changed our landline number. The phone calls stopped but as social media grew, our online presences were tainted with strangers seeking validation. Messages were sent from local people offering their condolences; their curiosity starved as my sister's death became widely unreported. Poorly constructed online articles were linked to our profiles from friends seeking confirmation on its contents.

In the years leading up to university, I deactivated all my social media channels, wishing to remain anonymous as opposed to going through young adulthood in the eye of the British media. It was only after graduation that I took the plunge and started new accounts, all under the name of Sophie Grace with no mention of Maguire anywhere. Despite confining my friends list to people I actually knew and trusted, and maintaining highly restrictive privacy settings, photographs still somehow made their way into the tabloids. *"SISTER OF THE GIRL IN THE MUSTARD COAT GRADUATES FROM UNIVERSITY – A happy day tainted with the memory of the sister that should have been watching in the audience"*. That was a genuine newspaper article posted about me in the days that followed my graduation ceremony. After a few years, I stopped caring and allowed myself the luxury of a non-private account.

I found that if you don't try to hide yourself, people don't go looking for you.

"Shall I drive you back to the hospital now?" Erica suggested, turning the key in the ignition.

I shook my head, a painful lump forming in my throat and a burning sensation welling behind my eyes.

"Hey, Soph. I'm sorry. I wanted this to be the ending we're all hoping for," she murmured.

"It isn't fair," I sniffed, hot tears making their way down my cheeks. I looked up at Erica through spiky eyelashes. "Why would someone do something like this?"

"Because they're a prick," she said, simply, pulling out of the car park. "A low life with no girlfriend and a tiny penis."

At that, we both burst out laughing. I was immediately cheered up.

"So – hospital?" she suggested again.

I shook my head. "Can you drop me off at my dad's house? He's rang me about ten times since I called him from the hospital. I'll stay for something to eat and he can take me back later."

Within fifteen minutes, I was approaching my father's house, walking rather tentatively down the garden path. The first thing I noticed was that the front door was open, just a tiny crack of outdoor light protruding through.

"Dad?" I called out, pushing the door open and making my way inside.

My father was sat on the middle seat of the sofa, a bag of frozen peas – badly wrapped in a soggy tea towel - being held to his eye. He looked up, squinting.

"Why are you here?" he asked.

"What happened?"

"You're meant to be in hospital," he continued.

"You're one to talk," I pointed out, gesturing at the large bruise beginning to form over his left eye. "What on earth has happened? Who hit you?"

My father paused, biding his time by wounding the tea towel around the bag of peas, slowly. He sighed, wincing slightly, as he lifted the frozen peas back to his face.

"It's nothing," was his eventual response. "It probably looks a lot worse than it is."

"What happened?" I repeated.

"I went to see a bloke who hadn't presented themselves for

the voluntary DNA sample," he began. "I've been trying to do one person a day. So far, I've had doors shut in my face, I've had dogs jumping up me and barking, and I've been sworn at more times than I care to admit. But today was the first time that someone has actually hit me."

"I don't understand. Who hit you?"

"His name is Colin Needham. I don't know if you remember him. He used to live in the street next to your primary school. He was a bus driver. Tall fella. Dark skinned. A bit scruffy looking in all honesty. He has a stammer," my father described, kneading his face into the bag of peas.

Vague, patchy memories of a black bus driver with prominent stains under his armpits came to mind.

"Why did he hit you?" I persisted.

"I managed to track him down using his Linked In profile. He works for a mental health charity now. He had listed his place of work on his Linked In page so I went on the charity's website and found the head office address. It was about a forty five minute drive away but when I got there, I saw him straight away. Looked like he was headed for the smoking shelter. He stood and spoke to me for a while but he didn't like it."

"Didn't like what?"

"My questions. He was sketchy with some of his details too, like he was glazing over a lot of information. He got agitated. He told me to leave. I didn't. He punched me in the face."

"On his work grounds?" I asked, incredulously.

Dad nodded.

"What happened then?"

"A couple of people ran over. I was lying on the floor of the car park by this point. Someone helped me up and offered to call for an ambulance. I got back into my car and watched Colin go back inside the main building," he explained.

Without realising, my father's words from thirty seconds before echoed through my mind. *A bit scruffy looking in all honesty.* Where else had I heard someone describe a person as being scruffy looking? Then it hit me.

"Are we being thick?" I gasped.

"Eh?"

"Remember what Aaron Montgomery told me and Frank when we went to the prison? He was approached by a black man who was scruffy looking who got him into the bare knuckle fight club!"

"Yes but didn't Aaron say that that bloke's name was Andy?" pointed out Dad.

"Would you give your real name to a child you're trying to recruit for an illegal fight club?"

"Good grief," whispered Dad, shaking his head at nothing in particular. "You're right. You're absolutely right."

"Bloody hell," I breathed. "He sounds like an angry man. If he's the sort of person to lose his cool and knock someone out in their own place of work in broad daylight in front of witnesses..." My voice trailed off. I couldn't quite bring myself to finish my sentence.

"I know," Dad agreed, quietly. "He could be our man."

"What sort of vibe did you get from him?" I pushed.

Dad shrugged, sighing, as he held the bag of frozen peas in one hand and gingerly rubbed his eye with the other. "I don't know anymore. I've met so many unsavoury characters in the last few weeks. But my instincts tell me he's someone to watch out for. Someone to question again."

"It can't be too hard to find out his home address. Let's go round there tonight. I'll pick Frank up," I offered.

"Don't be daft. You've already had a slap from a potential suspect's wife. I'm not having you going anywhere near Colin Needham, do you hear?" Dad warned. "Not in your condition. Speaking of which, why aren't you in the hospital?"

My stomach dropped. My heart began to pound. Staring at a specific flower on the rug on the living room floor to steady myself, the room began to spin less.

"We received an email from someone claiming to have information about Beth's killer," I explained, calmly, not quite able to meet my father's gaze. "The email was anonymous. The person who sent the email was asking for money in exchange for information. I discharged myself from hospital to go and meet this person."

"Oh, for God's sake," my father cried.

I took a long intake of breath, predicting the next few moments of conversation.

"Are you stupid, Sophie? Why on earth would you agree to meet someone who's blackmailing you?"

"They didn't turn up."

"That doesn't make this any better. You could have died," he sniffed.

"I know."

"How could you be so careless? I've already lost one daughter to a madman. I don't know what I'd do if I lost you too. Please be more vigilant in future. Anything of that nature – dodgy emails, prank phone calls, weird messages – anything. Ignore it all. Some people are sick and quite frankly, they get off on this sort of thing," he said, his words an echo of Erica's earlier speech.

"I know. I know it was stupid. I know I was daft. I just wanted..." The lump in my throat prevented me from speaking any further. I sat in silence, simply staring at the floral rug until my eyes burned with tears.

"Shall I make us both a cup of tea?" Dad suggested.

Blinking away the tears, I stood up. "I'll make it. And then we're ringing Frank to tell him about this Colin bloke."

The kitchen was in disarray, with a pile of unwashed dishes mounting up next to the sink. Silently, I gagged as the smell of stale food hit my already heightened nostrils. To distract myself, I filled the kettle up and rooted around in the fridge for milk when something caught my eye. A half empty bottle of whisky lay on the bottom shelf of the fridge. It was only then that I noticed the empty beer cans lined up next to the dirty dishes and the empty wine bottle balanced on top of the kitchen bin.

I walked back into my father's living room empty handed.

"What happened to you making me a cup of tea?" he laughed, then stopped as he caught a glimpse of my face.

"You're drinking again." It wasn't a question.

He couldn't deny it, his crestfallen face crumpling with shame.

"Dad," I breathed, my voice catching. "Why have you let this happen again? You've come so far."

He remained unresponsive, the room filled with the sound of his heavy breathing.

"I'm struggling, Soph," he said, finally. "I'm finding this all very hard."

"Is it because of the investigation?" I pushed. "Because you don't need to be involved, Dad. We can manage without you if you need some time to yourself. You mustn't let yourself fall back into old habits. It's a slippery slope."

"It isn't the investigation. Not really," he said, simply.

"Then what is it?" I choked.

My father fell silent, his mouth opening and closing like a goldfish swimming around its tank. After a moment or two, he cleared his throat. His bottom lip was wobbling.

"For over thirteen years, I've wanted to know what happened to her. It's been the very core of my existence. I've lived and breathed the last few days of her life every day, questioning how it happened, why it happened. It's ruined me. I had nothing else to give. It was all consuming, taking over my thoughts and my mind, eating away at me until I was nothing. That's why I drank. I did it to numb myself, to get some protection from the pain I carried around with me. It killed me. It still *kills* me, not knowing what happened to her, not knowing which bastard did this to her," he whispered. "But now we're so close to discovering the truth. I can feel it. I know we're close. And I used to think not knowing was the worst thing that could have ever happened to us. But now? Now I think knowing everything – knowing how she felt in her last moments... I'm frightened that that might be the thing that destroys me."

Chapter Twenty One

It was a few weeks later when I received an email from Chris Sheridan, suggesting I popped into the office to speak to him and someone from HR. I'd been signed off work sick for longer than any of us initially anticipated, so I knew exactly how the conversation in the office would go. They would ask if I was feeling better. I would lie and tell them that I was. And so it would continue, day after day, week after week, until I birthed an infant.

As it turned out, the conversation went a little differently to how I'd expected it would.

"Maternity leave?" I repeated, beadily eyeing the lady from HR to see if I'd misheard her. "Isn't it a bit soon to be thinking about going off on maternity leave?"

"Not necessarily," she replied, breathing in deeply as if she was ready to launch into a well rehearsed speech. "Pregnant women can take maternity leave from their twenty ninth week of pregnancy."

"Is this something you'd consider doing, Sophie?" asked Chris, looking thoroughly relieved that he wasn't doing the majority of the talking. "Calling it a day a little earlier than thought? Getting some much needed rest before the broken sleep and the dirty nappies?"

His rueful smirk didn't go unnoticed.

In another life, I'd expected the weeks leading up to giving birth would be relaxing and idyllic, wrapping up my work projects and setting my out of office response with a jaunty, yet informative, message about how I would be back in a year's time. I pictured coming into the office on my last day to find my desk adorned with sickeningly blue balloons and banners claiming that everyone was going to miss me alongside baskets of neatly organised presents and hastily written cards. I didn't expect to be rushed out of the building weeks before the baby was due to be born, as though I'd been caught misbehaving. In essence, I felt like I was being punished. Like I was being denied of a proper send off.

"It just seems a bit soon, that's all," I said, finally.

"You don't have to. You can leave on the date we initially agreed on," pointed out the lady from HR, although I detected a hint of impatience in her voice, as though she'd already filled out the necessary forms and scanned them over to the powers that be.

Glancing down at my slightly swollen feet stuffed into the only flat shoes I felt comfortable in that weren't my slippers, I thought about their not so generous offer. Perhaps it wasn't the worst idea in the world, I thought. It gave me time to get everything ready for the baby. It gave me time to finalise the sale of my mother's house. And, I realised with a jolt, it gave me more time to focus on my sister's investigation.

And so it was decided. My maternity leave would officially start once my sick note came to an end. I wasn't quite escorted out of the building but Chris did make a point of standing awkwardly next to reception as he gripped my forearm and did his best to smile at me kindly.

"Do keep in touch, Sophie," he said finally and off he went, disappearing into the lift. I tried not to mind that he exhaled air in a relieved and reassured manner when the lift doors were closing.

As a treat to celebrate the start of my maternity leave, I drove to a nearby teashop. Erica and I had been there for afternoon tea for her birthday and their scones were to die for. The teashop was empty apart from a woman in her thirties who was nose deep in a book with a snoozing toddler in a pushchair to the side of her. As I sat down on a squashy armchair after placing my order, I caught her glancing wistfully at my bump. The bump itself was getting difficult to ignore, and I had even found myself adopting a bizarre form of waddling like some sort of constipated penguin.

It wasn't quite eleven o'clock in the morning but I closed my eyes and enjoyed my mid-morning treat when my peace and serenity was interrupted by two things. Firstly, the aforementioned sleeping child suddenly woke and, starved of attention from her mother, threw her head back and began to unceremoniously roar. Secondly, my phone vibrated noisily on the table in front of me.

"Hello?"

"Soph? Soph, are you there?" came my brother's voice.

"Yes, I'm here," I answered. "Can you hear me?"

"Hardly. It sounds like you're in a zoo or something. What's that god awful screaming noise?" Danny asked.

I watched as the child's mother attempted to soothe her toddler's screams with a handful of cake being passed to her. Not only did the child take the cake and instantly drop it onto the floor, she began thrashing around inside her buggy like an animal of prey trying to free itself from the jaws of a lion.

"I'm just out having some tea and cake."

"Where are you? I'll come and join you. I've got an hour to kill in between clients," he explained.

It was quite comfortable, sitting in a teashop whilst it poured down with rain outside, having my brother refill my mug with tea every few minutes. Once we'd eaten as much as we could muster, we sat back and tried to let our food settle.

"Good grief. Look at the size of your stomach!" Danny exclaimed with a grin.

Not for the first time, I realised that pregnant women very rarely received compliments. Instead, people simply stated facts to them such as they look big, they look tired or they'll know the meaning of tired in a few months time.

"What are you going to do with your time off then?" he asked, absentmindedly nibbling at the last slice of a Victorian sponge cake.

"Other than birth a child, I was thinking about ramping up my involvement with the investigation. It feels like it's stagnated a little in the last couple of weeks," I admitted, ruefully.

"It only feels that way because we had so much happen in such a short space of time a few weeks ago," Danny reasoned.

"I still don't like it."

"Well, Dad doesn't like it that you're getting yourself into bother when you're ready to drop," Danny laughed.

I stayed resolutely silent. The audacity of my father saying he didn't think I was capable of handling the investigation was despicable, particularly considering it was driving him back to alcoholism.

"Look. Dad told us not to tell you anything. But if you're going to sit there and sulk..." Danny teased.

"I'm not sulking!"

Danny grinned. "We've found where this Colin Needham lives – or lived, anyway. I remember Dad saying he used to live in the street next to the school. Last week, I dug out an old copy of The Yellow Pages from one of the drawers at Mum's house and there was a C and a J Needham living in St Roscoe's Street in 2010. We knocked on the door last week but no one answered and to be honest, the house looked like it was empty. The living room was bare. No furniture and no TV," my brother explained.

"What? Why didn't you tell me any of this?" I hissed. "I would have come with you."

"Dad doesn't think you should be doing any of this anymore."

"Dad can piss off," I said, simply and my brother roared with laughter. "I feel like I'm behind with the investigation now. What happened next?"

"We went back again the following day but there was still no answer and a woman who was collecting her washing off the line in the garden from the next house told us that no one's lived there for months. We asked her who used to live there. She didn't know his name but her description of him was definitely Colin Needham."

"Let's go back there again tonight," I suggested, my eyes glittering with excitement.

"Absolutely not."

"Why not?"

"You've just been told to take early maternity leave because you're experiencing a number of health problems," Danny pointed out. "I'm not adding to your worries by taking you to see a potential murderer, sis."

Rolling my eyes, I said, "Taking me? I could go on my own. I don't need a babysitter, Danny."

"I know you don't. I know you can handle yourself. But there's not just you to think about now, is there?" he said, gesturing his hand to my prominently round stomach. "If you're itching to get involved, I'm meeting up with my mate James from work tonight in the pub. He's blown up the images from the CCTV cameras at the school and he's worked his magic on them to make them clearer too. And I got a phone call from Frank two weeks ago to say he'd finally heard back from his mate in the force about the images we didn't have. You know, the ones caught on the CCTV cameras on the corner of Folly Lane and the ones at the traffic lights on Victoria Street. He met up with Frank last week and gave him a copy of the files on a memory stick, which I also passed on to James. He said he'd see what he could do with it but he's pretty confident he'll be able to blow up some nice, clear images for us."

"He sounds like a bit of a whizz kid," I smiled, picturing a computer nerd living in his mother's basement.

I couldn't have been further from the truth. James was tall, well built and tanned with olive skin and very white teeth. He was dressed in a simple t-shirt and jeans but they were designer brands and obviously very expensive. When he leant across Danny to shake my hand, I got a whiff of a delightful aftershave.

Danny had got him a pint of beer in already, which he sipped from, gratefully, as he pulled out a folder and pushed it across the table towards us.

"Here you go," he said after swallowing a huge mouthful of beer. The folder contained two plastic wallets, both full of documents. "Some of the images – particularly the ones from the school – were a little trickier to make clearer. I don't think the CCTV cameras themselves were very good quality, but the images captured by the council were actually pretty good considering how long ago it was."

"Are these the images from the council?" I asked, pulling out several photographs of A4 sizing. James nodded. Without speaking, Danny and I took ownership of a plastic wallet each. I was examining the images taken at the school while Danny pored over the images from the council. The images were second nature to me. I'd seen them so many times before but there was a new twist to them as I could see people's faces a little clearer and could even identify the different bricks in the building.

With a sad pang to my heart, I realised I couldn't recognise my sister.

I flicked over to the third and fourth images, which were taken from the camera positioned at the entrance of the school. Right next to the school's driveway, as though it was parked just outside of the school boundaries, I could see a white vehicle. Only half of the vehicle was captured in the shot but from the width, it was clearly a van. Rifling through the rest of the images, I couldn't see it anywhere else.

From the positioning of the vehicle, it appeared as though it was parked at the house immediately next door to the school. Racking my brains, I tried desperately to think of the family who lived next door but I couldn't. I remembered there was a woman who lived there who frequently complained about the noise from the playground or the lack of space for parking during school pick-up and drop-off time. I could picture her face, remembering her unfortunate facial hair, but couldn't for the life of me remember her name.

"What is it?" came my brother's voice, luring me from my thoughts. "You look like you've just stumbled upon something interesting."

"I'm not sure if it's interesting but in this image, I can see part of a vehicle parked next to the school's driveway," I explained as both men gathered around me to examine the photograph in front of me. "I've never noticed it before. I think the poor quality of the images previously has restricted anything in view here, here and here. Like they were too blurry to pick up on anything on the outer layer of the CCTV image."

"There's a white van at the traffic lights on Victoria Street too," Danny said, flicking through the bulk of paper and plucking one out to lie on the table in front of us. "I don't know if it's the same one though. Look at the times."

"The one just outside the school was taken at nine minutes past three on 31st October 2005," I read out.

"And the one by the traffic lights was taken at thirty eight minutes past three on the same date," Danny read out.

"Is it the same van?" I asked, holding the two photographs next to each other. It was impossible to tell. The first image only contained a fraction of the van in the photograph. The second one included a lot more of the van but had a pedestrian crossing the road in front of it, narrowly covering the number plate.

"I don't know," my brother answered as he rifled through further photographs in an attempt to locate the van in any other image. "It could be. But then again, how many white vans are there in Hawleybrook?"

"No one ever came forward though, did they?"

"Why would they if they weren't guilty of anything?" Danny pointed out. "It'd be very unusual practise if someone contacted the police to declare that they'd driven a van in the vicinity of the area where Beth went missing but they were – I don't know – delivering a pizza or something. You wouldn't do that unless you saw something that you thought would be of interest to the police, would you?"

"But none of the neighbours ever reported seeing a van parked up next to the school, did they?"

"Again, why would they? It was probably someone parked there waiting for their kid to finish school."

"It's a van hanging around a school, Dan," I sighed, rolling my eyes at my brother for the second time that day. "It's suspicious. Do you think it's worth us knocking on the house next door to the school and asking a few questions?"

"Hasn't Dad already done that? It could be classed as harassment if we go back and do the same thing. We don't want another episode like the one with Mrs Graham, do we?"

"But did Dad actually speak to the occupants of that property? Is it the same people who lived there in 2005?" I questioned as I continued to flick through the images in front of me.

"I don't know but I'm sure he can – Sophie, what are you doing?"

Without realising, I had jumped up from my seat and was stood almost blocking the gap between the fruit machine and the bar, a different photograph clutched in my hand. Catching a glimpse of my reflection in the glassy front of the fruit machine, I realised I looked like a candidate in a game of musical statues; a caricature of fun and games in the midst of terror and uncertainty.

"Oh my god," I breathed, handing my brother the piece of paper in my hand. "Look at this photo."

"It's a white van," Danny said, quietly. It was parked in the small area designated to teachers' cars. It was partially hidden by a car parked quite closely next to it but it was there, shining out to me like a beacon, almost tantalisingly obvious. We hadn't noticed it before. Again, it was almost on the outskirts of the image which - until James had edited the footage – had always been blurry and unclear.

"It's parked up at the back of the school in the teachers' car park. But look at the date!"

James sat quietly, sipping his pint, looking from one to the other. My brother's face crumpled as he recognised the significance of what I had seen.

"October 27th 2005."

"Exactly. So, a white van is parked outside the school around the time that Beth went missing. It isn't normally parked there, otherwise it would be present in all the images taken from that particular camera. A white van was seen driving locally a short while later. And a white van was parked inside the school grounds just days before she was taken."

I looked down at my brother to see him with tears spilling down his cheeks.

Chapter Twenty Two

"Oh, come off it!" I cried, exasperated, banging my fists on the pub table in sheer frustration. "A van is seen in close proximity to the school, the last known place that Beth was alive at, and a van of the same description is seen near some traffic lights a stone's throw away from the school. A van. A big vehicle that could easily contain a person if someone was abducting them. And a matter of days before she was abducted, a white van was actually inside the school grounds."

"We don't even know if it's the same van," Frank pointed out, calmly.

"No but surely it's worth a try?" my brother begged. "You said this Bill was a mate of yours. You said you could call him up and put in a favour."

"And I already have if you recall. Time and time again. Who do you think sent off Tony's DNA to the lab to be examined? Who do you think got his hands on the files sent over from the council and passed them over to me?" Frank reminded us, calmly. "I can't keep asking him to do these sorts of favours for me. He could lose his job. It's gross misconduct to PNC a vehicle with no valid reason to."

"But this is a valid reason," I said.

"Not to the police it isn't. The case hasn't been re-opened. To them, we're just random civilians trying to access information that we shouldn't have access to. And anyway, like I said, we don't actually know that it's the same van on any of these images."

"Surely you agree it's a bit of a coincidence?" I persisted.

Frank nodded.

"And surely you agree that if these images had been made clearer all those years ago, then the police would have known about this white van then?"

"We had no reason to question the driver of the white van seen at the traffic lights. We had no reason to suspect that this van was a part of your sister's disappearance. We still don't," Frank pointed out. "The van photographed at the traffic lights could just be an ordinary person on his way home from work. If we were to question that driver, we'd have had to question every driver of every vehicle seen in every image from the council CCTV."

"Why would a van be at the school in the first place?"

"A teacher's vehicle perhaps?" Danny suggested.

I snorted. "How many teachers do you know who rock up in a white transit van to school every day?"

"All the teaching staff had their vehicles forensically examined at the time. None of their vehicles were vans," Frank reminded us. "They were all cars."

"Didn't the school provide a time sheet of every visitor in and out of the school building?" I asked Frank.

"Yes, they did. But if the van belonged to – for example – the husband of one of the teachers, then they wouldn't actually be signed into the school building, would they? If they just stayed sat in the van parked on the school car park?" Frank pointed out.

"Why else might a van be on school grounds?" Danny continued.

"Workmen, perhaps?" I suggested. "There wasn't any work being carried out on school premises at the time though. Unless there was some sort of on-site consultation being carried out regarding the work on the canteen that took place the following year."

"Pest control maybe? Or a plumber? Or perhaps one of the students was taken ill and their parent came to pick them up in their work van?" Danny suggested. "I mean, the image taken on 27th October 2005 was taken at quarter past one in the afternoon."

"I think the latter is the most likely scenario," Frank said.

"What do you think we should do then?" I asked him.

Frank paused for a moment, choosing his words carefully.

"I think we need to think about this logically. There are two different angles being presented to us at the moment. There's the possible involvement of the white van and the possible involvement of Colin Needham. I believe the aggressive behaviour from Colin Needham would certainly indicate his involvement. If we combine his physical reaction to Mike's questioning with the potential involvement of the bare knuckle fight club, I think it's more important than ever that we make contact with him again," Frank said, finally.

"Do you think it's him?" Danny asked.

"I don't know," Frank admitted. "But I think his name and his face are cropping up in too many places for him to be completely uninvolved. And let's not forget that he didn't provide a voluntary DNA sample either."

"Do you think we ought to forget about the van?" Danny asked. His question forced an internal groan from me.

"No, I don't think so," Frank replied. "We need to explore all avenues. But I think Mr Needham is our biggest threat at the moment. If he is involved, he knows we've whittled down the list of men who didn't provide a DNA sample, and he'll know that we've got his card marked after he was violent. The last thing we want is for him to make a run for it."

"Maybe we should try and get the police to reconsider opening the investigation again," suggested Danny, frantically pacing back and forth. "We've come so far. We've got these two leads. Surely they'll realise the significance now. And besides, it seems ludicrous that we're doing all the hard work only for them to swoop in at the last second and take all the credit and arrest the bad guy."

"We aren't doing this for credit," I sighed.

"No but surely you understand where I'm coming from?" Danny continued. "They haven't bothered to listen to us so far but once we've got a name, they'll be all over it like a fly round shit."

"Danny," I cringed, as I saw people in the pub turning to stare at us. My brother wasn't troubling to keep his voice at a low volume.

"I agree with Danny," Frank said, suddenly, his words prompting us all to turn and stare at him. "We've got more than enough evidence and intelligence now for the police to re-open the case. I suggest we go down to the police station first thing tomorrow morning. When it's been re-opened, they'll be able to track down other CCTV cameras in the vicinity or alternative angles of the shots we've already got so that we can get the van's full registration. Then it can be PNC'd for genuine purposes. They could have a name and a home address for the registered keeper of the vehicle within minutes."

His words had presented a nervous jitter in the pit of my stomach, like the adrenaline filled moments when you're strapped into your seat on a rollercoaster and you're simply waiting for it to plummet.

"I'll go with you," I offered Frank and he winked and smiled at me, kindly.

It had been almost two hours since we had reviewed the

images. My stomach was starting to growl. The baby was lazily kicking me, booting me in the bladder as if to remind me that it was still there. I realised I hadn't eaten since my tea and cake before lunchtime. Just as I was about to suggest we reconvened the following day, my brother spoke.

"You're being very quiet," he said, his comment directed towards our father. "Is everything okay?"

"Everything's fine, son," he said, finally looking up at us all. His eyes were bloodshot and his skin was clammy and red. It was obvious he'd been drinking again. Despite me already being aware of his lapse, the deterioration in his physical appearance still took me by surprise. "It's just a lot to take in, that's all."

"It is," Frank agreed, clapping my father on the back. "We're so close. We're days away from getting the bastard now. I can feel it in my waters."

Chapter Twenty Three

"Would anyone like a cup of tea or a coffee?"

Detective Chief Inspector Peter Hennessey was surprisingly handsome for a man in his early fifties. Whilst his hair was flecked with grey, it was still exceedingly thick and long, as were his eyelashes. The skin around his eyes crinkled every time he smiled, which he did so frequently as if to put us at ease.

In comparison, Detective Sergeant Christina Taylor gave off an unpleasantly cool vibe; her strong eye makeup seemingly as dark as her soul. She stared at me, hard, with one fiercely shaped eyebrow raised and the beginnings of a smirk cleverly disguised behind bold red lipstick. Her icy demeanour could be misconstrued for professionalism but I knew better. Detective Sergeant Christina Taylor was everything I didn't like in a female and it was a cruel act of fate which brought her not only into my life but also sat opposite me as I talked about the part of my life which hurt the most.

"No, thank you," Frank smiled.

"Miss Maguire?" Detective Inspector Peter Hennessey asked me.

"I'm fine thanks," I replied, although I was gasping for a proper cup of coffee. Somehow it felt rude to take him up on what I presumed was an empty offer when we had so much we needed to talk about and such a short space of time.

We'd arrived at the police station before it had opened. The pair of us waited in my car across the road, somewhat nervously, until we saw the main double doors being opened from the inside. We were the only ones stood waiting behind the glass counter, yet no one came to speak to us for over ten minutes. Frank had been far more patient than I had, as I found myself wracking my knuckles on the glass to draw attention to us.

A butch looking person with short hair had taken the initial details. Until this person spoke further, I couldn't identify whether it was a man or a woman, but I quickly realised it was a woman. She was kind, patient and understanding – everything I knew Detective Sergeant Christina Taylor wouldn't be. However, she explained that everyone was very busy and offered to take a phone number from us with the promise that someone would be in touch.

Frank had introduced himself and asked to speak to a specific detective. We were told to wait. It was another forty minutes before anyone came to see us, but I felt as though we wouldn't be listened to. It was clear that Detective Chief Inspector Peter Hennessey, as nice as he was, was a very busy man.

"How about a nice cold glass of water? It's going to be another unseasonably warm Spring day today or so it says on the news," Detective Chief Inspector Peter Hennessey smiled at us.

I shook my head as politely as I could manage without seeming rude turning down his hospitality.

"Okay. How about we start at the very beginning?" he suggested, flipping over his notepad to start writing on a fresh page. "How did all of this come about?"

Naturally, I didn't speak as I assumed that Frank would take over the summary of events, as he so often did. However, Frank didn't say a word and I realised it was because both detectives were glancing at me, wanting me to explain.

"As you know, my sister was abducted from school in 2005 and her body was found two days later in Griffin Woods," I began, the words feeling almost like a script to me, but I was abruptly interrupted by Detective Sergeant Taylor sighing. "He asked me to start at the beginning," I pointed out, not troubling to keep my annoyance from my voice.

"I think DCI Hennessey was referring to your own personal investigation," she said, smiling just a little too sweetly, with extra cautious emphasis placed on the word *investigation*. "I think we're all familiar with your sister's story."

"My father inadvertently gave some information to an undercover journalist. It was published in a newspaper a few months back. It had been a long time since anything regarding my sister was spoken about in the media. To all intents and purposes, she'd been forgotten about. People had moved on. But the interview with my father brought it all back to the surface. As a result, Frank got in contact with him and the two of them got talking and eventually decided to take another look at my sister's case," I explained.

"Okay," smiled DCI Hennessey, patiently. "And how does Mr Needham become involved?"

I hesitated, unsure where to begin. Thankfully, Frank came to my rescue and began to explain the initial starting point of the investigation. Throughout the time Frank was speaking, I felt DS Taylor's gaze firmly fixed on my face. I made a point of not reacting.

"So, you believe that Miss Beth Maguire was a lesbian?" asked DS Taylor, a faint note of disbelief present in her voice.

"We don't know if she was a lesbian but we think there's a possibility she was attracted to other females, therefore the theories that my sister had planned to run away with a boy, for example, are wildly inaccurate," I explained. "However, when we met up with Kate Marshall, she told us that Beth hadn't been wearing her mustard coloured coat when she left school on the day she went missing. She said she had been wearing it that day but when she came to leave school before the Halloween party started, she wasn't wearing her coat."

"Which means all of our earlier efforts to locate Beth Maguire on CCTV images were fruitless," Frank calmly explained. "We were looking for an incorrect description of her."

"How do we know that this Kate Marshall is a reliable source?" asked DS Taylor.

"We have no reason to doubt the credibility of her statement," Frank replied.

"And what happened after that? Where are you up to with regards to your, erm, own investigation?" asked DS Taylor, her smug grin not moving from her face.

Frank launched into a brief but detailed description of our findings over the months. Smugly, I sat back and fixed my own gaze on DS Taylor's face, which had gone from bored to mildly amused to downright riveted. Once Frank had stopped speaking, the room plummeted into silence.

DCI Hennessey stood up from behind his desk and made his way to the back of the room where there was a whiteboard affixed to the wall. Without another word, he produced a whiteboard marker out of his trouser pocket and began scrawling on the surface in front of us. Not for the first time, I wished my eyesight was a little better.

"As you can see, I've put five bullet points on the board," described DCI Hennessey, not taking his eyes off his work. "Each bullet point reflects an important piece of information discovered in your investigation. Firstly, we have the fact that Beth Maguire didn't leave Hawleybrook High School wearing the coat we initially believed she had. This means she potentially left the school earlier or even later than we originally suspected, meaning the window of opportunity for her abductor was much wider. Secondly, there's the presence of this white van. It may not necessarily be the same van in each of the images but it's coincidental. Thirdly, the fact that we suspect Beth wasn't in a secret relationship with an older man means she was less likely to go off with someone willingly. This may mean that if the van is the same van in all of the CCTV images, she was potentially targeted a few days before she went missing. Next, I find the involvement of this bare knuckle fighting club very interesting indeed. In all honesty, it may have no relevance to Beth Maguire's death whatsoever but – and this ties in with the last bullet point – if the black man from the bare knuckle fighting club is in fact Mr Needham, and Mr Needham responded to your questions with physical violence, I would say that he is potentially a person of interest."

"So," I continued, struggling to contain the smugness in my voice. "What happens next?"

"We re-open the investigation. Officially. We ask you both – and your brother and father – to make formal statements. We pass the information to the relevant department and then we take it from here," DCI Hennessey explained.

"And what do we do?" I persisted.

"You do nothing. You leave us to do our job," smiled DS Taylor.

Horrified, I said, "You can't expect us not to do anything at all. We've lived and breathed this investigation for months now. We can't just go back to our day to day lives and wait for you lot to pick up the pieces. It's been over thirteen years since she died. No offence but you haven't exactly impressed me with your speedy investigative skills."

"Nobody's expecting you to stop all involvement," soothed DCI Hennessey. "We'll keep in touch with you all and keep you in the loop as much as we can with regards to any updates. But until then, you put your feet up. Rest. Goodness knows, you must need it." His gaze dropped from my eyes to my stomach. Why did everyone think I was at death's door? I thought, angrily.

After filling in what felt like hundreds of forms and

signing the forms over and over, I drove Frank home and called in at the supermarket on my way back. As I was pushing the half filled trolley round the latter end of the store, my stomach pulsated with pain. It had been happening on and off for days and I knew it was just Braxton Hicks but paracetamol hadn't taken the edge off. With this in mind, my gaze lingered just a little too long at the wine cabinet by the tills. Several chilled bottles of white wine looked back at me, calling out to me for me to take them home. Without a moment's hesitation, I scooped two bottles into my arms and placed them into the trolley, as tenderly as one might place a baby down in its cot.

Once I got home, I felt restless. Despite lying on the couch with Clive sprawled comfortably across my bump, I wasn't able to concentrate on watching anything on TV. I couldn't get into my book and found myself reading and re-reading the same page over and over again. Eventually, I decided to cook myself a brunch. The bacon was sizzling in the frying pan when I was distracted by my mobile phone ringing in the living room. Abandoning the bacon, I quickly pounced on my phone and realised the call was coming from an unknown number.

"Hello?" I said into the receiver.

"Hello. Is that Sophie Maguire?" came a familiar voice that I was unable to immediately place.

"Yes."

"Hi, Sophie. This is DCI Peter Hennessey here. We spoke earlier on this morning," he reminded me. Ah, of course, I thought to myself. His kind voice was instantly recognisable.

"Hi, DCI Hennessey. What can I do for you?" I asked.

"As promised, I'm calling with an update regarding your sister's investigation."

"Wow. I didn't expect to hear back from you so soon."

"Well, once you'd left the station this morning, we had the go ahead to re-open the case officially. Once we'd done that, we were able to have a team delegated to the case. So far, we've managed to unearth half a registration plate for the white van seen at the traffic lights. There was another camera further down the street which has captured some of it – although part of the reg was missing due to the positioning of another vehicle. We've got the team running through the national databases now to try to get more information surrounding the number plate. Once we've secured that, we'll be able to run the number plate through the Police National Computer – or PNC as it's known – to see who owned the van in 2005," he explained, slowly.

My heart thudding painfully quickly, I could barely hear his words over the rushing of blood in my ears. I made what I hoped was a reassuring and appropriate sound. Perhaps DCI Hennessey felt sorry for me, as he continued with, "I know it's a lot to take in right now. Once I've heard more, I'll let you know."

"Okay. That's great. Thanks so much," I managed to choke out, before terminating the call with a shaking hand.

It was a good few minutes before I was able to construct a well-composed text message to my father, Danny and Frank. I received text messages back from both Danny and Frank in quite quick succession, but it was only as I smelled burning – and subsequently dashed back into the kitchen to rescue my chargrilled bacon – that I wondered if I ought to drop in to see how my father was getting on.

After my phone call with the police, I was too wired to want to eat anything but I forced down a few mouthfuls of eggs and bacon for the baby's sake. I fired off another quick text message to my brother to explain that I'd been worrying about our dad and thought we should drop round to his house to see how he was. I hesitated before adding *"And perhaps we should stay for tea – what do you think?"* Danny responded in a timely manner saying he would pick up fish and chips on his way over.

As the hours ticked by, I tried desperately to forget about the two bottles of wine, now both at room temperature as they lay forgotten about in a plastic carrier bag on the kitchen table. In the end, it was difficult not to give into temptation so I drove round to my father's house at five o'clock. The house was tidier than the last time I'd visited but it was desperately in need of a good clean, so while he pottered around upstairs – unsuccessfully attempting to put up a cot which he intended to keep in the spare bedroom – I gave the house a once over with the hoover and washed and dried his dishes.

"Will you get that, love?" Dad called out to me from upstairs as a knock on the front door was heard. "And if it's our Danny, tell him to use his spare bloody key for once, will you?"

It wasn't Danny. It was DCI Hennessey and two unfamiliar people.

"Oh," I said in surprise as I opened the front door. "Hello. How did you know I was here?"

"We didn't. We're actually looking for your dad, Sophie," explained DCI Hennessey. There was something too urgent in his tone of voice. Too business-like. Too serious. Something flickered in the pit of my stomach and I didn't know if it was Braxton Hicks or a sick foreboding feeling. At the sound of voices, my father made his way downstairs, still clutching pieces of wood from the cot.

"Can I help you?" he asked, glancing from one person to another.

"May we come in?" asked one of the unfamiliar people, gesturing his hand towards the living room behind me. I stepped aside, allowing all three people into the house, and followed behind them somewhat uncomfortably before perching on the arm of the sofa. None of the three new arrivals took a seat. Instead, they all hovered awkwardly in the hall.

"My name is Detective Chief Inspector Peter Hennessey. I spoke with your daughter and Frank Perry earlier on today about re-opening the investigation into your daughter's murder. This is Detective Inspector Rachel Fisher and Detective Inspector Adam Ricci," said DCI Hennessey, his words directed specifically at my father. "Michael Maguire, I'm arresting you on suspicion of the murder of Bethany Maguire. You do not have to say anything but it may harm your defence if you do not mention when questioned something which you later rely on in court. Anything you do say may be given in evidence."

Chapter Twenty Four

"Sophie? Sophie, do you understand what I'm telling you?"

My right leg was shaking uncontrollably. It had always done that when I was nervous. On my driving test, it shook so much that I was inadvertently revving the car's engine as my foot tapped up and down on the accelerator. Suddenly, the shaking stopped and I realised it was due to my brother's hand which had been placed firmly over my knee. It was only then that I realised someone had been speaking to me. Up until that point, I'd simply heard a ringing sound in my ears.

"I'm so sorry. I didn't catch that. Could you say it again?" I uttered, my teeth chattering as if I was cold. I wasn't. The back of my neck was starting to sweat.

Fiona, the ginger freckly family liaison officer smiled at me and started again. "We discovered some further images of a white van taken on CCTV cameras in the area near to Hawleybrook High School on 31st October 2005. We were also able to locate an alternative angle to the image taken inside the school grounds on 27th October 2005. The end of the van's number plate on both images was Kilo Golf Papa. It was the same van. Using the make and model of the van plus the partial registration, we ran some checks on the national database. It brought up two vans registered in Great Britain. One was written off in 2002 and the other was written off in 2007. The one written off in 2007 had belonged to a Mr Stanley Maguire."

At the mere mention of his name, my mind was filled with the taste of Worther's Original sweets and the smell of Old Spice and soap. My heart panged wistfully.

"Our grandad," I managed to choke out.

"Our grandad died in 1999," my brother explained. "He wasn't alive when Beth was killed."

"I understand that," soothed Fiona. "Your grandfather was listed as the van's registered keeper. The details were never updated. However, an insurance claim was made for damage in 2003. The insurance records show that the person who made the claim was your father. He'd been listed as a named driver on the original insurance policy and it was your father's bank details which were set up for the direct debit. Ultimately, we were satisfied that this confirmed that he continued to drive the van after your grandfather passed away."

"This is ridiculous," Danny muttered. "Absolutely ridiculous. What a waste of everybody's time."

"I know this must be really hard for you," Fiona smiled. "Can I make anyone a cup of tea?"

"A cup of tea?" he scoffed, dismissively. "Do you really think that that's going to make everything okay?"

"Danny," I scolded him.

"Do you know how many cups of tea we've had made for us by total strangers?" Danny continued, breathless and unblinking. "I bet there's been enough to sink the Titanic."

"I understand that this has come as a shock," Fiona continued. "My role is to support you as a family. To answer any questions you may have. To keep you updated as much as I can."

"We know what a family liaison officer is," Danny sighed. "We've had a lot of involvement from FLOs over the years."

"Is there anything you'd like me to do? Would you like me to call anyone and ask them to be here with you? Or I could -"

"This is a complete waste of time," Danny interrupted her, immediately jumping up to nervously pace back and forth across the room. "We've been through all of this before, years ago. For months, the police had it in for Dad. He was arrested at the time. But they let him go because he had nothing to do with it. He did a voluntary DNA sample which proved he hadn't – that it wasn't his – he hadn't raped his own daughter or killed her or had anything to do with what happened to her. He had an alibi, for Christ's sake. He was off shagging that good for nothing Cassie. Why is no one paying any attention to that? Meanwhile, my sister's killer is roaming the streets, potentially slaughtering more innocent lives."

His words rang out, seemingly bouncing off the walls. It felt empty, unusual even, to be in our father's home without him, like celebrating someone's birthday when they aren't with you. Like we'd done all those years for Beth.

"What happens next?" I asked Fiona but before she could respond, my brother cut in.

"We hire a solicitor for Dad. The best in the country. We can use the money from Mum. She wouldn't have minded. She'd have thought this was a disgrace as well."

"Your father is entitled to legal representation and he will have someone with him now if that's what he chooses," explained Fiona.

"Has anyone stopped to think about the fact that our dad eliminated himself from the investigation by providing a DNA sample?" Danny said, aiming his question at Fiona who hesitated like a deer in headlights.

"I'm sure my colleagues have done everything in their power to -" her voice trailed off to nothing but a whisper, paling in comparison to the deafening roar of Danny.

"This is ridiculous," he repeated. "We need to get down there." He was looking directly at me, his eyes wide and still unblinking. "I'll drive us."

"I don't think that's a good idea," Fiona began. Danny dismissed her comment with a snort. "Your father's being questioned and it could go on for quite a while. It might be best to wait here for an update before going anywhere."

"We need to speak to him," Danny continued, as though he wasn't listening to a word Fiona was saying. "He's not been too great lately, what with the drinking. He'll be all over the place. He needs us."

Out of nowhere, my father's words rang out to me: *"I think knowing everything – knowing how she felt in her last moments... I'm frightened that that might be the thing that destroys me"*.

"Soph?" came my brother's voice, dragging me from my thoughts. "Are you coming?"

"Maybe Fiona's right," I said finally, clearing my throat. "Maybe it's best just to wait here until we know what's what."

"What are you talking about? We know what's what already. Our dad's been incorrectly arrested for the second time in his life for a crime he didn't commit. *That's* what," he sniffed, shrugging his jacket on and zipping it up. "Come on. I'll drive."

I didn't move. My stomach twinged with pain. Danny stared at me, rooted to the spot. From an outsider's perspective, we looked like oversized pawns in a chess game.

"You think he did it, don't you?" he asked, simply.

"Well..."

"I don't believe this," he exclaimed. "This is our dad we're talking about, Soph. Or are you forgetting that? He's the one who started all of this. He's the one who began digging in the first place. He was desperate to find out what happened to Beth. Why would he do that if he was the one who killed her?"

"Deep down, I don't think he's capable of it," I began but couldn't bring myself to finish the sentence.

"But?" my brother prompted.

"You've got to admit there's a lot of questionable factors," I finished, a lump forming in my throat.

"Such as?"

"Such as Dad coming home from work late that night, reeking to high heavens of alcohol. Cassie vouched for him and provided a somewhat seedy alibi but what if she was lying for him? She was young, she loved him, she was *impressionable.* Very easy to manipulate. And it's more than just that. He appears to be struggling recently, unravelling almost. He's back to his old ways, polishing off a bottle of whisky per night. And now we find out that Grandad's old work van was seen inside the school a couple of days before Beth was taken and outside the school grounds on the day she was taken. He's never told us any of that before. Why would he have been anywhere near the school on either of those days?"

"To pick one of us up early? To drop one of us off after the orthodontist? To drop off a forgotten packed lunch or a form for a school trip? I've no idea, Soph, but I know it won't have been to ogle his own child or case the joint."

"I'm not saying I think he meant to do it. I don't think it was – if he did it, it wouldn't have been... planned. Perhaps he just had a lot to drink. Perhaps he was drunk and they argued and he – he lost his temper," I suggested, tears streaming down my face.

"You can't seriously believe this."

"He's an alcoholic, Danny! God knows when he started drinking. Was it when we were little? Was it earlier? Was it before he met Mum? He's a different person when he's drunk. You wouldn't know. You haven't seen him like I have. I picked him up from the hospital once. He'd been throwing up in Tesco. He'd been trying to buy more alcohol but they wouldn't serve him and he started vomiting everywhere. Someone called an ambulance for him and the hospital rang me. I went to pick him up and I was – it was – he was stood, pissing up against the curtain around his bed. Some poor nurse, barely older than I was, was horrified. He was laughing – he thought it was hilarious, spinning his penis around like a bloody windmill. I dragged him out of there before they could shop him to the police. He'd have been on the sex offender's register for life. Of course, he had no recollection of it whatsoever the next day. It was just another story in a very long list of stories of Dad's toxic relationship with alcohol," I spat, ferociously wiping my eyes.

No one spoke. The silence in the room was stifling.

"Do I honestly think that it was our dad who murdered our sister? No, I don't. Do I honestly think he's capable of it? No, I don't. But do I think that it *could* have happened during a drunken stupor? Absolutely," I whimpered.

"He didn't do it," Danny murmured.

"I just don't understand why he wouldn't have told us that he was at the school a couple of days before Beth was taken. It's such a huge piece of information."

"Maybe it isn't that huge. Or maybe he forgot."

"And he also forgot that he was parked outside the school on the same day she went missing?" I continued. My brother's face fell. "I know what you're thinking. It doesn't seem plausible. It isn't plausible. It doesn't make any sense. But it isn't adding up, is it? Something isn't right."

Danny looked utterly crestfallen, his shoulders heaving up and down with every sharp intake of breath.

"All the more reason to get down to the police station then. We need to speak to him. Hear his side," Danny croaked.

I hesitated, unsure of how to respond. My knowledge of the British judicial system was patchy at best but I knew there would be virtually no opportunity to speak to our father. A yelping noise came from nowhere. I realised my little brother was crying. Then –

"Okay. Fine. But we pick Frank up on the way," I agreed.

As Danny drove, I filled Frank in on what had happened. His skin took on a new level of redness, as the veins in his neck stood out more prominently than I had seen before. After the initial discussion regarding Dad's arrest, none of us spoke until we had parked up in the pay and display car park opposite the police station. As I stood up outside the car, my breath was taken from me as another sharp pain shot through my abdomen. Not now, I thought to myself, slamming the car door behind me. I simply didn't have the time.

A few hours passed with no information. We endured tepid machine-made coffee in little plastic cups, more to have something to do than anything else. No one was prepared to tell us what was happening and everyone that crossed us in the waiting area simply told us to go home and speak to our family liaison officer.

"Maybe we should," I suggested to Danny as I wriggled around in my seat, my back aching from the uncomfortable stiff position I'd been in for hours.

"I'm not going anywhere," he said resolutely and folded his arms as if to signify that the matter was closed.

The sound coming from the television on the wall in the waiting area was out of sync with the movement on the screen, meaning that actors were speaking but their mouths didn't quite match up with the words we heard. Once I noticed it, I couldn't see anything else. It was irritating. To distract myself from it, I began picking at a hangnail. When it had bled down my hand, I got up and walked about, stretching my back out as best I could. As if to scold me for sitting in such an uncomfortable position for a long period of time, the baby dropkicked me right in the bladder.

"I need the toilet," I muttered, making my way out of the waiting area and down the corridor to locate the toilets. Just as I was pushing open the toilet door and simultaneously holding my breath for what I suspected would be an unpleasant aroma greeting my nostrils, I saw my father.

"Sophie!" he called out as he was being led down the corridor and into a room on the right hand side. We were no more than forty yards apart but it felt like different planets. My initial instinct was to rush over to him, despite the fact he was behind a fenced off area. My second reaction was to punch him in the face.

"Dad!" I heard myself calling out to him. "Dad, are you okay?"

The police officer stood next to my father was unlocking the door adjacent to him, looking over his shoulder at me nervously. It was clear he was desperate to usher my father into the room.

"It wasn't me, Soph. You know that, don't you?" he called

back, desperately. The police officer had unlocked the door with a loud definite clunk of metal on metal. His hands were on my father's shoulders, not so gently pushing him into what I presumed to be a cell. Before I had chance to reply, my father yelled: "Jack Connolly! My old boss. Jack Connolly. Speak to him about the van!"

And with that, he was gone.

Chapter Twenty Five

"I don't remember anything about Jack Connolly. Do you?" my brother asked me five minutes later after I'd relieved myself in the toilets and rushed back to the waiting area with my news.

"I have a vague picture of him in my mind. He owned the garage that Dad worked at. He was old. Well, older than Dad anyway. He was overweight but small. Dumpy. Always wore overalls. That's all I can remember," I described, my eyes tightly closed.

"Do you know if he still lives in Arlington Heath?" Frank asked me.

"I've no idea," I admitted, biting my lip. "I guess not. The Arlington Heath curse had probably taken effect on him like it did everyone else in the village."

Whilst I'd been speaking, Danny had whipped out his mobile phone despite the sign displayed on the wall immediately above him stating that the use of mobile phones was strictly prohibited. He was scouring the internet, starting first with social media.

"There's a Facebook page set up called J Connolly's Motor Repairs. It's based just outside Hawleybrook. There's even an address. It's got to be him, surely?" Danny murmured, his fingers fervently scrolling down his phone screen. I fished my own phone out of the back pocket of my jeans. Three missed calls. All off Calvin. A text message from him sent two hours previously, which read: *Where are you? Do you fancy fajitas for tea? Ring me x*

Hurriedly, I fired off a brief text message to him to explain that I wouldn't be home and wasn't sure what time I would get back but that he had nothing to worry about and that I was fine. I hesitated before firing off a second text message to remind him to feed Mr Darcy and Clive. He replied instantly but I didn't look at his message as I was performing a quick Google search for J Connolly's Motor Repairs. There were a few customer reviews of the garage, most of them rather positive, but no official website. I went back to the original Google search, methodically working my way through the list of hits.

There was nothing of real substance until I reached the

seventh listed hit. It was an online newspaper article for the Thurlow Gazette. Thurlow was a fifteen minute drive from Hawleybrook, and it appeared as though that's where J Connolly's Motor Repairs was based. The article was talking about plans to introduce a new train line running through Thurlow into the city.

"I think this is him," I murmured, my voice catching in my throat as Frank and Danny crowded behind me, both of them squinting to see what was shown on the screen of my phone. "It's an article in the Thurlow Gazette from November 2017 about plans to introduce a new train line running through Thurlow and they interviewed a Mr Jack Connolly."

Taking my phone from my hand, my brother read out loud: *"Although the plans have been met with enthusiasm from residents, there has been some criticism from local businesses. Mr Jack Connolly of J Connolly's Motor Repairs on Tobago Avenue expressed his dissatisfaction with the plans, as he feels the work being carried out will negatively impact on trade. 'The idea of having a main line running through the town is wonderful. However, my concerns lie with the work being carried out beforehand. There will be roadworks all through the town centre, making it very difficult for customers to access the shops and cafes on Tobago Avenue and Forsythe Street'. Mr Iman Begum of National Rail has declined to comment on the timescale of work being carried out'.* There's a photo of him too."

Danny twisted the phone around to reveal the photograph to the pair of us. It was him. He'd been in his early to mid fifties around the time Dad was working with him, which made him well into his sixties by the time the photograph was taken. Despite the obvious aging – a few more wrinkles, less hair and more grey – he hadn't changed from the vague memory of him in my head.

Danny handed the phone back to me. I immediately brought up an online map, typed in "Tobago Avenue – Thurlow", located the postcode and read it out to Danny and Frank.

"A thirty one minute drive away, according to the map," I added and realised both Danny and Frank were already making their way out of the room. I quickly followed, dismissing the dull ache present in my stomach and breathing deeply to try to rid myself of the pain. I had bigger fish to fry than Braxton Hicks.

The drive over to Thurlow was quiet but electric. Danny

exceeded all speed limits but I didn't comment, although I pulled my seatbelt around me just a little tighter as we reached the motorway. The three of us barely spoke. It wasn't as if we didn't know what to say. It felt as though we were reflecting internally on what was about to happen.

"Do you remember anything about Jack Connolly during the initial investigation?" I asked Frank, suddenly.

He thought about my question for a second before responding. "Other than the fact he gave a voluntary DNA sample, no."

"There it is," Danny announced, pulling into a poorly lit street. Thurlow town centre had seen better days. It was tired looking with run down shops and littered pavements. J Connolly's Motor Repairs was easily identifiable, sandwiched between a café and a school uniform shop. Danny parked the car on double yellow lines opposite the garage, sticking his hazard warning lights on as a precaution.

"It's almost nine o'clock. I don't think it's going to be open," Frank calmly pointed out, as we got out of the car and silently headed for the garage. He was right, of course, and I think we'd all anticipated that it would be closed but in collective agreement, none of us had wanted to simply sit on the information given to me by my father.

"What do we do now?" I asked no one in particular.

"We go into the café and order something to eat whilst we regroup. You look absolutely dead on your feet. Nothing that a nice cup of tea won't fix, I'm sure," Frank smiled at me, gesturing his hand towards the yellowy glow of the café. A bell above the door tinkled as we pushed our way through. We weren't the only customers. There was a table of four youths, probably in their early teens, nursing frothy mugs of hot chocolate whilst poring over something on a mobile phone and giving the occasional shriek of laughter. In the background, the radio blared as a woman in her forties with a perm and a weather beaten face wiped down tables with a J cloth whilst humming along to the song absentmindedly.

"What can I get you?" she asked us after we slid into seats closest to the window. It was clear to her that we hadn't given much thought to what we would order – and as both me and Danny were sat staring out of the steamed up windows at the street ahead of us, Frank took the opportunity to order three cups of tea.

"You know," the woman began, jotting down our order on a notepad in her hand, "it's cheaper to order two pots of tea, which will give you around five cups worth."

Her words had fallen on deaf ears. I couldn't bring myself to respond and Danny didn't appear to have heard her speaking. He was totally absorbed in the comings and goings of the street, watching each car and each passer-by with great earnest.

"Yes. Two pots of tea would be wonderful, thank you," smiled Frank, his manners ever present. "And I wonder if you could kindly recommend something to eat for my friend here?" The waitress glanced down at me, first making eye contact before her gaze predictably reaching my protruding stomach. As if aware that it was being eyeballed, the baby decided to somersault inside me, causing a bizarre rippling effect under my t-shirt. I tried not to mind too much that the waitress appeared to recoil in mild horror.

"It all depends on how hungry you are, love," she said, finally reaching my eyeline again. "We do a lovely jacket spud with cheese and beans but it's quite filling. If it's more of a light bite you're after, perhaps just a couple of slices of toast? You'll have to order quite quickly, mind you. We close at nine."

General chit chat about food seemed so trivial and felt almost like we were in a pantomime, trapped by a wall of manners and polite humdrum. Perplexed, I simply nodded and went back to staring out of the window.

"Yes, two slices of toast would be lovely. In fact, if we could each have two slices of toast, we'd be most grateful," Frank chimed in. The waitress, not trying too hard to disguise her curiosity, looked at me as if I was a character in a badly written soap opera.

"Okay," she said eventually. "So that's two pots of tea and six rounds of toast coming right up. Is there anything else I can do for you?"

"Actually, yes there is," Frank carried on. "The garage next door. You don't happen to know the owner by any chance?"

"Oh, Jack?" she beamed, looking thoroughly relieved to have reached safe conversation. "Course I do. Everyone knows Jack. He's in here most mornings for an egg and bacon sarnie or a full English if it's a Friday."

"Do you have a phone number for him perhaps?" continued Frank, carefully keeping his voice chatty and conversational. His efforts were thwarted by me and my brother who must have looked a picture as we stared, almost open mouthed, up at the waitress, waiting on her response whilst holding our breath.

She frowned, her heavily pencilled eyebrows creasing. "I'm not sure he'd like me giving out his details to all and sundry. Who *are* you?"

"My name is Frank Perry. I live just down the road in Hawleybrook. And this is Sophie and Danny Maguire. Sophie and Danny's father used to work with Jack. We were hoping to get in contact with him, that's all," Frank smiled. "But unfortunately, we arrived here just a little too late and the garage is closed."

"It's closed to the public but knowing Jack, he'll still be in there tinkering on a car," she smiled back and watched in utter confusion as we all leapt out of our seats and scrambled for the café door. "Oi! What about your tea and toast?" The door tinkled loudly as it opened and closed, the three of us jostling to get outside.

Calmly, Frank knocked on the metal shutter hanging over the door of J Connolly's Motor Repairs. We hesitated, each holding our breath, until Danny – no longer able to maintain any efforts of patience - beat the shutter repeatedly with his fists. The unmistakeable clanging sound of skin on metal rang out, echoing against the walls of the high street. My heart sank as I realised no one was inside. Wildly, I began to formulate a plan of action which involved sleeping in Danny's car overnight when Frank spoke.

"Let's call it a day for now. We'll come back first thing in the morning," he said, patting my brother on his back.

"We can't go back now," Danny cried, exasperated. "Dad asked us to speak to Jack Connolly, so that's what we'll do even if it means camping out on the bloody pavement all night."

"I know you're disappointed – we all are, Danny - but we mustn't let our feelings get in the way of logic. You can't expect Sophie to lie on the pavement, can you? Not to mention my bad knee. I wouldn't be able to walk for a week," Frank chortled, trying desperately to make us smile. "Come on. We'll be back in twelve hours. I think a hot bath and a good night's sleep for us all will -"

His voice was interrupted by the sound of a person whistling and walking up the cobbled path that led to the garage. In sync, we all turned to face them. In front of us stood a short, portly looking man carrying a polystyrene tray overloaded with fish and chips. He was wearing baggy faded jeans complete with splashes of oil and paint and a white t-shirt. He stopped when he saw us stood there and smiled at us whilst pushing another chip into his already full mouth.

It was Jack Connolly.

Chapter Twenty Six

"Can I help you?" Jack asked us, revealing his half eaten chips in his mouth as he spoke.

"Yes. I wonder if you can," Frank began, instantly taking control of the conversation. "We were just passing and we've been having some difficulties with our car. It started to cut out as soon as we joined the A road. We popped into the café next door to use the facilities and call a breakdown recovery service but the waitress told us you might be able to help. It *is* Mr Connolly, isn't it?"

"Aye, that's me," he announced as he fiddled with a small silver lock on the metal shutters, which sprang open and began to retreat upwards. "Is that your car?" He was pointing towards Danny's Vauxhall Astra which sat there, the yellow hazard lights blinking away as if perfectly in character.

"Yes. That's the one. Can you help us?" Frank continued. My heart inexplicably filled with affection for him as he donned the persona of a stranded passenger.

"Course I can," replied Jack, gesturing with his hand for us to follow him inside the garage. With one hand, he tossed the keys to the shutter on a small table inside and with the other hand, shoved more chips into his mouth. We all stepped inside the garage, nervously glancing around us at our surroundings. "I just need to finish up this MOT, then I'll help you push the car inside. Do you think it's the -"

He was cut off by the sound of the metal shutter slamming shut. I looked up to find my brother locking the shutter from the inside with the keys which had been tossed to one side by Jack just moments earlier.

"What the bloody hell do you think you're doing?" Jack shouted and he made his way towards Danny. Danny was too quick for him as he reached inside a toolbox and pulled out a large hammer, holding it in the air in front of him defensively.

"Right. This is what's going to happen and you better listen up because I'll kill you if you don't," he hissed, spit flying out of his mouth. "You're going to sit in that chair. We're going to ask you some questions. You're going to answer our questions and you're going to be honest. Understand?"

In the nanosecond between my brother speaking and Jack's

brain registering his words, I recognised a slight shift in facial expressions. The movement was tiny, too small for most people to detect. But I was waiting for it. It wasn't fear. It wasn't confusion. It was *guilt*. A slight sense of panic as he realised what was happening. He hadn't recognised us when he first saw us but as he was being pushed into a swivel chair pushed up against a desk in the far corner of the garage, it was clear that he knew exactly who we were and exactly why we were there.

Danny reached into the toolbox to the side of him and pulled out a red cable tie, securing it firmly over Jack's wrists, binding them together. Jack looked helpless. Dark stains began forming under the armpits of his t-shirt. "Do you know who I am?" Danny asked him, stepping back from the swivel chair which Jack was sat in, his stomach spilling over his jeans.

Jack muttered something inaudible.

"What did you say? You're going to have to speak up!" Danny roared, his voice echoing throughout the garage. I was rooted to the spot, unable to move. With a slight turn of my head, I glanced at Frank and for the first time since I'd known him, I saw his face unsmiling. Instead, it was curled up in loathing.

"I said yes. I know who you are. You're Mike's boy," Jack replied.

"And do you know why we're here?" Danny continued.

"I have a fair idea, yes."

"Go on then," Danny whispered. "You can be the one to say it."

"You're here to ask me some questions. You've just told me that," Jack said, curtly.

"Don't get clever with me."

"I'm not doing anything of the sort, lad. You said you came here to ask me a few questions."

"Do you know what I find unusual, Jack?" Frank took over, walking slowly towards him. "We've turned up here unannounced, locked you inside your own workplace, thrown you into a chair and demanded to ask you some questions about a topic you are allegedly unaware of. Yet you don't seem confused or worried or frightened at all. In fact, you seem quite the opposite. Forgive me if I'm wrong but it feels like you've been expecting us. Not necessarily tonight, but it seems like you've been waiting for a visit of this nature for a long time."

"I don't know what you're talking about," Jack sniffed.

"Bullshit," sneered Danny. "I'll repeat what I just said. We're going to ask you some questions, which you will answer with absolute honesty. If you lie to us, you're not walking out of here alive. I need to know that you understand just how serious I am about that."

Jack said nothing but nodded; a tiny fraction of movement with his head.

"Frank?" Danny asked with a nod of his head, wordlessly asking him to take over the questioning. As if this was a role he'd been preparing for his entire working life, Frank cleared his throat and crouched down in front of where Jack was sitting on the swivel chair.

"On the afternoon of 27th October 2005, a white van was seen inside the grounds of Hawleybrook High School. The same van was seen just outside of the grounds of Hawleybrook High School a few days later on 31st October 2005. On this day, a thirteen year old girl went missing from that school. She was raped and strangled, and her body was left to rot in Griffin Woods. That girl was Beth Maguire. She was Sophie and Danny's sister. We'd like to understand your involvement with this heinous crime, Jack," Frank calmly explained.

"I don't know what you're talking about."

"I don't believe you," Frank murmured, his watery blue eyes wide and fixed directly on Jack's face. Despite his pretences, he was beginning to look worried. "I think you know exactly what we're talking about. Tell me everything you know about Beth Maguire."

Shrugging, Jack said, "She was Mike's daughter. His middle child. She was killed a few years back."

"That's all you know about her?" Frank pushed.

"Pretty much."

"It's crazy how little you know about her considering how closely you lived and worked to where she lived, where she went to school. Not to mention the fact that you employed her father and worked with him every day. I think you could approach anyone – man, woman or child – in any part of the country and ask them what they know about Beth Maguire and they'd know a lot more than you," Frank reasoned.

Jack sighed, shifting uncomfortably in the seat.

Occasionally, his eyes would flicker behind us to the metal shutters, as if he was plotting his escape.

"You can knock that on the head for a start," was Danny's input as he clocked Jack's little glance. "No one's coming in here to rescue you. If that dozy cow from the cafe hears you screaming, Sophie will pop out and reassure her that everything's fine. And besides, the café closes in less than five minutes. She'll be going home. There's no one else around except us. Now speak."

"I don't know what you want me to say," Jack cried.

Wordlessly, Danny let out an impatient sigh, the hammer twiddling in his hands.

"Did you do it?" Frank asked.

"Did I shite," he sneered, spit forming in the corner of his mouth.

Frank persisted. "Do you know who did do it?"

"No," Jack said firmly. "But I assume you think it was me otherwise you wouldn't have barged your way in here with some cock and bull story about a broken down car just so you could speak to me. I don't know how else to say it to you. It wasn't me."

Unable to keep a lid on his frustration, Danny launched the hammer in the air, smashing it against the wall. A lump of brick scattered to the floor. He did it again, clawing at the bricks until a hole in the wall appeared. Jack's eyes widened, as though he was finally realising that my brother meant business. Sensing his fear, Danny launched the hammer into the air again, directly above Jack's head –

"Alright!"

The word rang out around the garage.

Sixty seconds passed with no sound whatsoever other than the heavy breathing coming from my brother. For once, he wasn't nervously pacing back and forth to work off his frustration. He was stood as still as a statue, his eyes wide and unblinking.

"You were right," Jack said, finally, directing his comment to Frank. "What you said before. Thirteen and a half years I've been waiting for this conversation to take place. And here we are. I have a feeling that whatever I say to you tonight will not result in my life being spared. I am therefore prepared to answer your questions with total honesty on one condition."

Danny sneered. "You don't get to set any conditions."

"You leave my wife and children out of this. You leave them alone. I don't care what you do to me but you don't harm a hair on their heads."

His next words were deafeningly quiet. They rang out into the night, like a foghorn emerging through the mist: "I killed her. There. You have your confession."

Throughout my entire adult life, I'd always expected to feel relieved when I knew who had killed my sister. I expected the final piece of the puzzle to feel momentous, definite, *conclusive*. But as I stood there, looking into the face of the man responsible for my sister's death, I felt none of those things. I simply felt lost. Vulnerable.

"We're going to need more detail than that, Jack," Frank pushed. "And you have my word that we will not approach your family in an intrusive or violent manner."

Jack nodded, slowly. He turned to face Danny and me.

"I worked with your father for years. He was a good bloke. Terrible mechanic. He was scatty, disorganised, forgetful. It was a few years before I realised he was drinking on the job. I confronted him but he denied it. He knew I knew though and that it was a matter of time before I let him go. It was my business, my livelihood at stake. I couldn't afford to take such a risk, having a drunk looking after the cars of the people in the village. Our working relationship became strained. We'd always enjoyed a pint in the pub after work on a Friday. That became a thing of the past. I knew a lot about Mike. I knew he was married, I knew he had kids, I knew he regularly cheated on his wife with whichever bit of skirt he could get his hands on once he was blind drunk," Jack said. "More often than not, he had no knowledge of his infidelities the following Monday."

My chest ached with hurt for my poor lovely mum.

"One day, we got an emergency phone call from the school. One of the teachers had broken down. She'd managed to push the car inside the grounds but it was a goner. The job was meant to be your father's but he was drunk. I knew he shouldn't have been driving. So I took your father's work van and drove it over to the school to pick up the job. And that's when I saw her. Beth."

The mere mention of her name sent goose bumps down my

back. Danny closed his eyes, trying hard not to cry.

"I recognised her, of course. I'd seen photos of you three kids for years. I'd seen you at every village fete, every Christmas carol concert. I'd even been to your house a few times over the years. Eaten your mum's beef casserole. I liked her, Beth. I was – shall we say – *attracted* to her, for want of a better word. I suppose this is the point where I explain that I like young girls. Not usually as young as her. They were normally a bit older. But there was something about her. She was loud and funny and had the most memorable laugh," he grinned.

I leant against the side of a work station, feeling dangerously close to having my legs fall from under me.

"She'd been queuing up to go into some sort of cloakroom after lunchtime. Possibly a changing room. I saw her hang her things, including the coat, up on a peg. After that day, I was unable to shake the thought of her from my mind. I wanted to see her again. I wanted to speak to her. To hold her. I bided my time until I couldn't take it any longer. I drove back up to the school but I didn't go in. I waited outside, waiting for her, for Beth. It wasn't quite time for school to finish but I made my way in to the grounds using the back entrance where I knew there were no functioning cameras. I'd helped my brother-in-law to fit the cameras a year or so earlier," Jack explained.

He swallowed, his teeth chattering. Then he continued, speaking into the night as though he'd forgotten we were there. "He's self-employed. An electrician. A general handyman. He's lived in Thurlow for years but often did call outs to Hawleybrook. He worked on his own most of the time but installing the cameras was a two person job and he'd asked me to help out with the promise of two hundred quid, cash in hand. Not that I needed the money, mind. No. It was more of a day out for me. I was like a kid in a sweet shop, surrounded by all those girls."

My stomach lurched. For one wild moment, I wondered if I was going to be horribly sick.

"I was surprised at the time to learn that the school wanted the cameras as a deterrent, rather than to actually film inside the grounds. Almost half of the cameras weren't functioning."

Another stomach lurch, except more audible than before. Frank's eyes darted across the room to me.

"On the day in question, the bell went as I waited near the

playing fields and I managed to get inside the cloakroom. One of the kids held the door open for me. I guess I looked like a workman in my overalls, or maybe they recognised me from being inside the school grounds a few days earlier. I found her coat. It smelled of her. Sweet, like vanilla. I couldn't just leave it there," he continued, breathless with nostalgia. "I needed to have it with me. It would have felt like she was there with me. So I took it."

Tears were pouring down my cheeks. I glanced across at Danny and Frank. Neither of them were crying but they both bore a sickened expression on their faces.

"I waited just outside the school grounds in the van. I didn't think I was in sight of any genuine cameras. I don't know what I planned to do other than to speak to her. The bell went and I saw a sea of kids pouring out but none of them were her. I drove round to the back entrance of the school and after a while, there she was. I got out of the van and I..." his voice trailed off, his eyes looking down at the ground. "I told her that there'd been an accident. That her father had been hurt and she needed to come with me to the hospital. She was worried. She got in the van but she was insistent that she needed to check if either of her siblings were at home. So we stopped outside her house. I circled the street in the van. I didn't know whether to drive off, in case she returned with her brother or sister. None of the neighbours batted an eyelid at the van. How many times had they seen Mike driving down the street in a van? I saw her rush back out of the house. She was alone. And then..."

"Then you killed her?" spat Danny through gritted teeth.

"I just wanted to hold her. To feel her heart beat next to mine. To be close to her and smell her sweet scent. She struggled. She was a screamer. I just wanted her to stop screaming – screaming out for her mother. And then before I knew it, she was gone."

My heart sank miserably. I'd heard her closing the front door that fateful day. I'd been in the bath. She mustn't have realised I was there. If I'd done something, if I'd called out, she'd have heard me. We'd have rang Mum and discovered that Dad was fine and Jack wouldn't have taken her.

"You monster," Danny breathed, his eyes screwed firmly shut. "You fucking monster." He lifted the hammer into the air once again, this time with his eyes piercing into Jack's as he went to swing it into Jack's head. I squealed but my brother was stopped with a surprisingly firm hand from Frank. Silently, Frank shook his head.

"Where did the act take place?" Frank asked, turning his attention back to Jack quietly, his voice shaking.

"In the back of the van."

"What did you do with her coat?"

"I kept hold of it for a few days before donating it to a charity shop a few miles away. I'd doused it in bleach so it was no longer a mustard colour. It was more of a dirty cream colour. It was buried amongst a ton of other clothes – none of them mine – in a binbag."

"You presented yourself to provide a voluntary DNA sample in order to eliminate yourself from the initial police investigation," Frank began. "But it was traces of your semen found inside Beth Maguire. How did you avoid being caught?"

"My brother-in-law owed me big time. He'd been playing away from home about six months before – before it happened, and he'd got his bit on the side pregnant. She'd been blackmailing him, threatening to tell his wife – my sister - unless he handed over money. A lot of money. More money than he could afford. I gave my brother-in-law the lot in one go and the girl had an abortion. *Relieved* isn't a big enough word to describe my brother-in-law's feelings. He was grateful. He'd promised to repay the favour," Jack explained.

My mouth filled with saliva. Briefly, I thought that the threat of vomit would fulfill its promise.

"When the posters were up asking men from the village to provide a DNA sample, I asked him to go as me. He lives in Thurlow and the police were only asking people from Arlington Heath to provide a sample. He had to take a form of identification to prove he was me so he took a bank statement and my driving licence. The photo was taken years before. It was just a white man with dark hair, virtually nondescript, and my brother-in-law doesn't look too dissimilar from me anyway. No one questioned him on it. The police who were holding the voluntary DNA screenings were the big wigs that had been brought in from the city. They didn't know me. They wouldn't have recognised my name or picked up on the fact that my brother-in-law was pretending to be me. And as far as the police from Arlington

Heath were concerned, Jack Connolly had willingly given a DNA sample and signed a document confirming it. It was easy really."

"Didn't your brother-in-law think it was suspicious that you'd asked him to do that for you?" Frank continued.

"Yes but I told him I'd been involved in some dodgy stuff in the past – robbery, drugs, that sort of thing. I said I didn't want it catching up with me. He believed me or so I think. He's never mentioned it since. Even if he suspected anything, he wouldn't have breathed a word. He was terrified of my sister finding out about his little mistake."

"Does anyone else know? Have you ever told anyone what you did?"

He shook his head. "I've never told a soul until tonight. But someone knows something. One of the volunteers at the charity shop where I took the clothes to managed to find me. I'd purposely not left any clues as to who I was, not even of my details, despite the volunteer asking me for my name and email address to add to their mailing list. I don't know whether it was my manner or the fact that a coat was found in amongst my donation which bore a slight resemblance to the coat that a girl nearby had allegedly been abducted whilst wearing – whatever it was that gave the game away, the volunteer found me. He wanted money in exchange for silence. I pretended I had no idea what he was talking about but he was persistent. Nasty, almost. He followed me one night down by the canal and had me beaten up until I told him I'd give him money or whatever he wanted. He wanted my financial involvement with a sort of back alley fight club he was operating."

"Was this chap's name Colin Needham by any chance?" Frank sighed.

For the first time since he'd opened up, Jack faltered. He looked around at us. "How did you know?"

"We've been interested in Mr Needham for a while. Mike spoke to him a couple of weeks ago about Beth. He asked Mr Needham why he hadn't provided a DNA sample. Mr Needham resorted to physical violence," explained Frank. "Other than Mr Needham, does anyone else know what you did?"

Jack shook his head.

"How could you look our dad in the face afterwards, knowing that you were the one who'd killed his daughter?" Danny cried.

"It was easier than I thought it would be. Your father was hardly ever there in the months that followed and when he was, he was pissed. Before long, people didn't trust him. They'd noticed a shift in his behaviour. He was no longer the cheerful family man often seen helping out at sports day up at the school. He was a drunk who'd left his wife and was being questioned by the police for his daughter's murder. No one wants a drunk fixing their cars. No one wants a murderer fixing their cars. People turned on him. It was easy to turn him away." He hesitated, staring down at his hands which were still clumsily clasped together. "I assume you're going to contact the police."

"Of course we're going to the police, you fucking *animal*," hissed Danny, seething with anger.

"Yes. You'll be arrested and formally charged for the rape and murder of a minor. You'll live out your days behind bars," explained Frank, nodding to my brother who pulled his phone out of his jeans pocket. "Danny here will ring the police now and we will wait for them to arrive before they take you away."

"And don't waste everybody's time by lying or providing sketchy details. Your DNA will match up and you have three witnesses who heard your confession," Danny spat.

"Plus a recording of your confession," I said, dimly aware that I was speaking for the first time since stepping foot inside the garage. In my hand was my mobile phone, which I'd set to record the second Jack had sat down in the swivel chair.

Upon my admission, my brother and Frank simply beamed.

*** *** ***

"Drink your tea," soothed Calvin, rubbing my foot with his hand. After standing on them for so long in the same position, they'd ballooned to twice their normal size. "It's going cold."

"I don't think I can. Sorry, Cal," I muttered, burying my face in Clive's fur. "I still feel a bit shaky."

He smiled, his head on one side. "I'm not surprised. You've had one hell of a day. Should I run you a hot bath? Put some of your scented oils in it?"

I shook my head. My body was aching with fatigue. I'd taken two paracetamol as soon as I'd got home but it hadn't touched my throbbing head. Calvin had been a wonderfully captive audience as I filled him in on what had happened. The police had arrived within ten minutes. Frank calmly explained a summary of events before the police arrested both Jack Connolly and my brother, taking with them my mobile phone. I'd wept as I watched my brother being stuffed into the back of a police car but Frank assured me it was because he'd held someone prisoner and tied them up which would be evident from the recording on my phone.

"He'll be fine. I'll be very surprised if they decide to charge Danny under the circumstances," had been Frank's input.

"Your dad will be out before you know it. Danny too," Calvin said, rubbing the other foot. "You just need to concentrate on you now. You've done all the hard work so try to get some sleep and rest before the baby comes. You've done so well, Sophie. You did it. I'm so proud of you."

His kind words had no effect on me as I tossed and turned in bed that night. Sleep was the last thing on my mind as Jack Connolly's words echoed around my brain: "*I liked her. Beth. I was – shall we say – attracted to her, for want of a better word. I suppose this is the point where I explain that I like young girls. Not usually as young as her. They were normally a bit older. But there was something about her. She was loud and funny and had the most memorable laugh*". More than once, I had to dash to the bathroom to throw up.

I felt lost without my phone and prayed that I'd given my landline number correctly to the police. By the following morning, I still hadn't heard anything from either my brother or my father so I decided to ring the family liaison officer. When she groggily advised me that she'd be in touch once she'd had an update, I realised somewhat sheepishly that it wasn't quite six o'clock so switched the kettle on and sat in the kitchen, simply staring up at the clock. My cup of tea lay forgotten.

Despite being a lovely spring morning with the sun already starting to emerge, there was a definite chill in the kitchen so I switched the central heating on. It warmed up quite quickly and I found myself resting my head on the table in front of me, my fluffy dressing gown pulled right round me.

The unfamiliar sound of my landline phone ringing made me jolt upright in my temporary resting place. It was almost ten thirty. Somehow I'd fallen asleep in the warm haze of my kitchen, my neck aching from leaning across the table for so long.

"Hello?" I croaked into the receiver. I couldn't remember the last time I'd used my landline.

"Hi. Is that Sophie?" came a very familiar voice, not sounding quite as tired as the last time we'd spoken.

"Hi, Fiona. Yes, it's me. Do you have an update for me?"

"Is it okay if I pop round?" she asked. Her dodging my question didn't go unnoticed and my heart sank. Was it really possible that the police had decided not to charge Jack Connolly? I thought, worriedly. Had my phone not recorded the confession correctly?

Half an hour later, freckly Fiona was sat in my kitchen with her colleague, along with me and Calvin, who'd decided to take the day off work to be with me. He'd made himself useful, busying around making us all cups of tea and plating up a selection of posh biscuits which he plonked in the middle of the table. The biscuits remained untouched.

"Okay, Sophie," Fiona began, taking a deep breath as though she was about to deliver a blow. "I can confirm that we have formally charged Jack Connolly with the abduction, rape and murder of your sister."

The breath I didn't know I'd been holding was exhaled, leaving me to feel like a deflated party balloon. I had butterflies in my stomach, fizzing away inside of me with a mixture of nerves and anticipation.

"He admitted what he did and his confession tallies with the confession recorded on your phone," she continued, her fingers clasped tightly around her mug. "We've taken a DNA sample from him which was fast tracked through the lab in the early hours of this morning. It matches the DNA taken from the semen found inside your sister."

Her words, although reassuring, still stung. He knew all this time. He could have put us out of our misery. My mother had died not knowing the truth about her daughter's murder. It was shameful. Despicable.

"Will he be going to prison?" I asked.

"Absolutely."

"It might only be a short stay once his fellow inmates get wind of what he did," Calvin chimed in and Fiona's colleague inadvertently smirked.

Panic set in. "Will everyone find out? The media are bound to find out. I'll be followed down the street again, being photographed and shouted at."

"We'll be releasing a statement later on today. We'll ask the media to respect yours and your family's privacy at this difficult time. You may be required to prepare a short statement too. Matthew here specialises in media prep," answered Fiona, gesturing her thumb towards her colleague. "So he'll be able to help with that."

"I can't speak on TV," I whispered, horrified.

"No. She can't. That's absurd. She's nearly eight months pregnant," Calvin laughed. "Surely someone else can provide a statement on her behalf. Frank Perry, perhaps?"

Fiona nodded but didn't say anything for a minute or so as she finished her cup of tea. "Do you have any other questions? Any concerns or worries at all?"

"My dad and brother. What's going to happen to them?" I asked.

"Your dad is being released as we speak. You're listed as his next of kin so he may have tried to contact you to arrange a lift home. However, the police want to hold on to your mobile phone for a little longer so you might want to drop by the station in a short while to see if he's ready to be collected," she explained.

"I'll go and get him," Calvin offered, immediately grabbing his car keys from the worktop. He stopped before walking out of the kitchen to place a kiss on the top of my head.

"Anything else?" Fiona asked me as we heard the front door slamming shut.

"Not that I can think of," I began but then immediately asked, "Actually – does Jack Connolly's wife and family know what's happened?"

"Yes. They will do by now. They'll have their own family liaison officer with them too."

"They must be devastated," I croaked, my throat inexplicably tightening.

"I imagine they will be. Despite the fact that Jack is a very bad man, he's still a part of their family. They may even struggle to believe he could be capable of such an atrocity. However, he has two young grandchildren," Fiona said, slowly. She hesitated, nervously glancing at her colleague. "We've got a search warrant for his house. When we arrested Jack, we found indecent images of children on his work computer. Very young children."

The uneasy butterfly feeling in my stomach intensified. Again, Jack's words: "*I like young girls*" span around my head.

"He's – he's a monster," I choked out, picturing my sister's frightened face as she realised our father hadn't had an accident and that she'd been lured into a van with a man who would hurt her. Had she felt pain? Or had it been too quick? "He said Beth was calling out for our mum when he – when he..." I couldn't finish my sentence through my tears. Matthew looked uncomfortable being so close to a weeping pregnant woman.

"Jack Connolly won't live to see outside of prison walls, Sophie," Fiona soothed, reaching across the kitchen table to squeeze my hand. "He's going to be in prison for the rest of his life for what he's done."

Matthew and Fiona shared a glance. They had come to a silent agreement. Matthew spoke first: "Jack Connolly's DNA matched with another serious crime on the national database. We can't go into detail about it at the moment as we're still questioning Mr Connolly about it. But we thought you might want to hear it from us first before the media get wind of it."

"We also arrested Colin Needham earlier this morning regarding his involvement with your sister's death," Fiona continued. "He is still currently being questioned."

"What will happen to him?"

"Hopefully he'll be charged with perverting the course of justice. Not to mention assault and demanding money with menaces."

"And what about Jack Connolly's brother in law? The one who gave a DNA sample posing as Connolly?" I persisted.

"I should imagine he'll suffer a similar fate to Colin Needham," Fiona soothed. "He's also perverted the course of justice."

"And – what about – what do you think will happen to..." I couldn't bring myself to finish the sentence as the uncomfortable words lodged firmly in my throat.

"Your brother?" asked Fiona, to which I nodded. "It's anyone's guess but given the circumstances, I'd imagine he'd get away with a slap on the wrist. If that."

The relief that flooded through me as Fiona and Matthew said their goodbyes was immense, even when Fiona turned to me on the doorstep and said, "There's a really good charity that can help with how you must be feeling. It was set up to support the families of murder victims. I think you'd find them really useful. Would you like me to put you in touch with them?"

"No, I'll be fine but thank you for offering," I smiled.

"It might be good to talk to other people who've had similar experiences to you. Might be a nice way to occupy your time," she suggested, smiling at me.

Clutching my seemingly enormous bump in my hands, I grinned and said, "I think I'll have another way to occupy my time soon enough."

Fiona said nothing further as she laughed and climbed into her car alongside Matthew. As I watched them drive to the end of the street, I saw Calvin's car pulling up. My father, looking thoroughly exhausted with the beginnings of an untidy beard forming, leapt out from the passenger seat and ran towards me, pulling me into his arms.

"We did it, Soph," he cried, his tears dampening my cheek. "We only bloody did it for her."

Epilogue

"I took a deep breath and listened to the old brag of my heart.
I am,
I am,
I am."
– Sylvia Plath

The sun rose for the rest of the town, leaving bedrooms drenched in light. People woke for school and work; a clatter of spoons in bowls, feet on stairs, spoons in mugs. Newspapers rustled at kitchen tables, on trains and tubes and buses. Radios blared in cars, through headphones, in work places. Food was shared in kitchens, amongst friends, with family. The world was alive, basking in the sunshine of an Indian summer.

We lay there together, a little longer than we ought to have done; the warmth from the sun soothing my skin. From nowhere, a snuffle turned into a sob, then into a cry. My hands expertly placed my breast into the small of her mouth, masking the cry. No sounds apart from the gentle, rhythmic sounds of a baby feeding could be heard.

"Coffee?" his voice murmured in my ear, his lips finding my neck and nuzzling into me.

He disappeared out of our bed, the unmistakeable sound of feet steadily padding down the stairs. The two of us lay there together, skin touching skin, until our bliss was disturbed with the arrival of coffee and pastries on a tray. The tray was not empty once the coffee and pastries were accounted for. A small box lay before us, shining like a beacon.

"Open it then," he grinned, handing it to me.

A ring, silver and delicate. He placed it on my finger, holding my hand close to his mouth and kissing it. The rhythmic sound stopped. The crying began. I lifted her up, placing her between us. The three of us looked at each other. She was taking it all in, a smile forming on her rosy cheeks, as he took her into his arms and lifted her in the air. The room was filled with laughter and love.

"Eleanor Beth, we love you so much," he said, planting a kiss on her lips. She reached out to him and placed her hand on

his face, leaving a wet mark on his cheek. He laughed, wiping it off, then blew a raspberry on her tummy.

As I watched my family, I couldn't help the tears prick my eyes. My ring caught the sun and reflected a beam of light onto the ceiling. Eleanor was captivated, her blue eyes wide as she watched the light moving from side to side. Calvin reached out and kissed my cheek. I turned my face and met his lips with mine.

"They would have loved this," I murmured. "My mum and sister. They would have loved this."

"They're still around, you know. They're always with you. With Eleanor."

His words were met with laughter from our daughter, who reached out her arms to the ceiling whilst still mesmerised by the mysterious light. His face lit up at the sound of her laughter and he pulled her into us, the three of us lay on the bed in the sunshine together.

Maybe it won't be the same as it should have been, I reasoned. But maybe, just maybe, it's still wonderful.

Emily Rose Chriscoli is a twenty-nine year old writer from Warrington, Cheshire. She has written from a young age and self-published her first book when she was twenty-three.

She is a proud auntie to six nephews, godmother to thirteen and pet owner of two cats and a dog.

Follow Emily on Twitter @emilychriscoli

Printed in Great
Britain
by Amazon

31369215R00123